PETER CH
DON'T GET M

REGINALD Evelyn Peter Southouse Cheyney (1896-1951) was
born in Whitechapel in the East End of London. After serving
as a lieutenant during the First World War, he worked as
a police reporter and freelance investigator until he found
success with his first Lemmy Caution novel. In his lifetime
Cheyney was a prolific and wildly successful author, selling, in
1946 alone, over 1.5 million copies of his books. His work was
also enormously popular in France, and inspired Jean-Luc
Godard's character of the same name in his dystopian sci-fi
film *Alphaville*. The master of British noir, in Lemmy Caution
Peter Cheyney created the blueprint for the tough-talking,
hard-drinking pulp fiction detective.

PETER CHEYNEY

DON'T GET ME WRONG

DEAN STREET PRESS

Published by Dean Street Press 2022

All Rights Reserved

First published in 1939

Cover by DSP

ISBN 978 1 914150 93 7

www.deanstreetpress.co.uk

CHAPTER ONE
MEET PEDRO

DON'T get me wrong!

You can have Mexico. You can have the whole goddam place with my best wishes an' just what you like to do with it when you have got it is your business. Me—I do not want any part of it not even the lump of sandstone that is in my boot or the alkali dust that is jumpin' around the back of my tonsils right now.

Was that sugar at Matehuala right or was she? I'm tellin' you that that babe was talkin' plenty sense when she said that Americanos wasn't doin' themselves any good around here since there's been the trouble over the oil. Anyhow she was only half right.

Nobody has ever done any good for themselves around this dump except Mexicanos an' the only time a Mex ever gives you anything is when he's dyin' an' don't want it. I reckon that some of these guys are so mean they wouldn't even spend a week-end.

Me—I am prejudiced. I would rather stick around with a bad-tempered tiger than get on the wrong bias of one of these knife-throwin' palookas; I would rather four-flush a team of wild alligators outa their lunch-pail than try an' tell a Mexican momma that I was tired of her geography an' did not wish to play any more.

On the other side of the *estancia* some guy in a pair of tight trousers an' a funny hat is handin' out a spiel to some dame about what a first-class bull-fighter he usta be one time. By the look on the dame's face I reckon she has heard this one before an' would not like it even if it was good.

Maybe she's his wife. If she is then all I can say is she is a durn bad picker. Me—I would have married the bull.

I order myself another glass of *tequila* an' when the waiter brings it I open up a little polite conversation. He tells me that I speak the lingo very nicely an' I proceed to tell him how my father was a Mexican on his mother's side of the family an' a lotta other punk on the same line. We flirt around with each other considerably for quite a while. Finally this guy begins to get confidential. He tells me how he is sick of carryin' drinks around this dump an' wants to marry a dame, but that he can't make the grade because he has no jack. I tell him that life can get that way but that maybe if he can do a little quiet thinkin' I might slip him ten dollars—American.

I tell him that I am an Americano who is kickin' around lookin' for a ranch that I wanta buy for some people way back in New York, an' he says that he reckons that any Americanos who wanta buy a ranch in Mexico the way things are breakin' like they are in this dump now, must be nuts. But then he says that he reckons that Americanos are nuts anyhow.

While he is talkin' this guy is lookin' at me with a sorta faraway look in his eye. I put my hand in my pocket an' I take out my roll an' I start peelin' off the bills. He looks sorta interested.

I ask him if he knows some guy called Pedro Dominguez. He says he ain't certain, but he might be able to think around it some time an' let me know. I slip him the money an' he says he does know a guy called Pedro Dominguez an' that this bozo is liable to blow in durin' the evening.

Which is the way I thought it was goin' to be.

It is as hot as hell. Away down the dirt road towards the *mesa* some guy is playin' one of them wailing Mexican fan-dangles that give me that twilight feelin'. Everythin' around here is so damn' depressin' that I reckon it would be a relief if you started dyin'.

There is an old bozo with only one hand sittin' away in the corner tryin' to squeeze salt an' lemon inta his *tequila*. He has taken one or two long looks at me an' I begin gettin' a bit hot under the collar an' wonderin' whether somebody has got wise to me around here.

Such dames as there are in this dump are sundried an' scrawny. When a Mexican dame is good she is good, but when she is bad I would rather look at a movie I have seen seven times before. There is somethin' sorta antagonistic about 'em. If you don't wanta play ball they hate you an' if you do they see you get what is comin' to you an' that is usually a right royal raspberry.

This waiter guy is still standin' there lookin' out through the door. Away on the *adobe* wall on the other side of the room I can see a lizard crawlin'.

I take another look at the waiter an' I reckon that he looks like a lizard too. He has got pale sorta disinterested eyes that wouldn't change for the better even if he was watchin' you being fried on a wood fire. I reckon it might even make him laugh.

I light a cigarette.

I tell him that I reckon that he is a very intelligent guy an' that since he has been able to remember about Dominguez maybe he can remember some dame who I reckon is livin' around this dump some place, a dame called Fernanda Martinas.

He grins. He says it is a very funny thing, but this Señora Martinas comes an' sings in this *estancia* about eleven o'clock, an' when she comes around Dominguez is usually somewhere in the neighbour-hood. He says that Dominguez is a very tough guy when he wants to get that way, an' that he has a certain idea in his head that he is not very partial to other guys hangin' around this Martinas dame. I tell him that I reckon some guys are funny that way, an' he says yes he has always thought that himself.

I wonder about this waiter. I am wonderin' if he is easin' through that side door to go shootin' off his trap to the fat boss I saw when I come in. I was tipped off that the boss wasn't so bad but everybody in this place is a durn liar an' wouldn't even tell himself the truth even if he was paid for it.

I sit there lookin' through the doorway, out across the patio, wonderin' why it is I always have to pull this sorta job. Why the hell don't I get the jobs around New York.

Maybe you've known women in Mexico. They're either good or they're lousy, an' they're usually lousy. Even if their curves are swell they got acid temperaments. Maybe that's through eatin' hot *tamales*. Anyhow a speed cop once told me that it's dangerous to park on a curve.

Guys keep blowin' in, an' occasionally a dame. They sit down an' they order drinks. One or two of 'em look at me, but they don't sorta take much notice. If they do they look as if they don't like me very much, but then Mexicans never like anybody.

After about ten minutes the boss comes over to me. He is a fat guy an' a snappy dresser. He has got a silver shirt cord on an' a big black sombrero. The waistband of his trousers is nearly cuttin' him in half, an' his belly is hangin' over the top of it. I don't like this guy very much.

"Señor," he says, "you ask about Dominguez. Maybe I can help you."

"Maybe you can," I tell him, "an' maybe you can't."

I am gettin' sick of these guys. I learned a long time ago when I first started to play around here that it pays you to be polite to Mexicans, but there are moments when I get sick of bein' polite. This is one of 'em.

"Señor," he says . . .

He sorta spreads his hands. I can see that the palms of 'em are sweatin' an' that his nails are dirty. His fingers are like claws.

"I do not intrude myself into things that do not concern me, Señor," he says, "but I have noticed that when people come here asking about Dominguez there is always a little trouble."

He spreads his hands again.

"I do not want trouble in this place, Señor," he says.

I look at him.

"Why don't you take your weight off your feet an' sit down, Fatty?" I tell him. "I suppose what you're tryin' to tell me is that somebody wants to get Dominguez over the State Line. I reckon he's just another of them goddam bandits you keep around here. Maybe," I go on, blowin' a big smoke ring, "he was the guy who cut the throat of that United States mail carrier over the New Mexico Line three weeks ago. I reckon you Mexicans are doin' pretty good these days. When your Government isn't pinchin' somebody's oil wells you just go in for individual stick-ups."

I signal to the waiter an' tell him to bring me some rye if he's got it.

"If it will ease your mind any," I say to the boss, "I have not come around here to pull any rough stuff with this Dominguez guy. I just wanta talk to him. There ain't a law against that, is there? I believe you can talk to people even in Tampapa."

He smiles sorta polite.

"Of course, Señor," he says. "People can say what they like. I only tell you that the Government people do not like this Dominguez very much. He makes some trouble now and again. He likes to begin small revolutions. Sometimes he is a little successful. That is all."

He sits down. When the waiter comes back with my rye he has brought a drink for him. It looks as if this bozo is keen to talk to me. We sit there lookin' at each other.

"Looky," I tell him, "I'm a curious sorta feller. Maybe I'm a bit interested in these guys who've been tryin' to talk to Dominguez.

Maybe it'd be worth while my slippin' you a little something if you could tell me about them."

"That is very nice of you, Señor," he says, "but I do not know. All I say is that I do not want any trouble in this place."

He takes another long look at me an' then he picks up his drink an' scrams. I watch him walkin' across the floor an' I think I would like to hand him a kick in the seat of those tight pants of his that would make him wonder if it wasn't his birthday.

Then I look away towards the doorway an' just then the Martinas dame comes in. I haven't ever seen this baby before but I heard about her—plenty, an' I sorta sense this is her. It's got to be her anyhow.

She is what the doctor ordered all right. If I wasn't so tired of suckin' in Mexican dust, *frijoles* an' rot-gut *tequila* I would get excited maybe.

She has got a walk on her that only goes with a good Spanish family with just a touch of Indian somewhere along the line to keep the book right. She has everythin'. A smooth, light coffee skin an' hair like black velvet. She knows how to get it dressed too an' she never got that last water wave around this dump. She has that sorta figure that makes you wonder whether you ain't usin' your imagination a trifle too much an' she puts her little feet on the ground in a sorta decided way that tells you she's got that little somethin' called poise one hundred per cent.

She is wearing a silk frock cut low an' a red Mexican shawl pulled tight around her an' a white sombrero. She holds her head right up an' she looks around the place like it was an antheap.

What the hell. Maybe this job is goin' to have some redeemin' features after all. . . .

She walks straight across the room an' she plants herself down at a table on the left of the platform where the band work. When she sits down she just lets the whole world know that she ain't chary about showin' her ankles. I reckon she thinks they're good an' that maybe the male customers will be liable to buy another drink if they see some ankle first. I think they are good too.

After a coupla minutes the band comes in. I look at these three bozos an' I try an' think of some words that will describe 'em. I once heard some guy say that another guy looked like a depraved scarecrow. I reckon that that is what this band looks like. They sit down an' pick up their guitars an' look around with that sorta dead pan look that always comes on to a Mexicano's puss when he's goin' to do a job of work. Then they start playin'. They play a thin reedy tune without any life in it, a tune that makes me sick. I think of Ben Bernie's band, and, boy, do I wish I was back in New York?

O.K. Well, things have started now. Two or three guys get up and start dancin'. It is as hot as hell. They just loop around holdin' the women as if they was goin' to lose 'em. I notice that nobody asks the Martinas dame if she would like to wrestle to music.

I light another cigarette. When I look up I see the waiter lookin' towards the doorway. He looks towards the doorway an' then he looks at me an' then he grins. I reckon he is tellin' me that this is Dominguez. Everybody screws round, sorta uncomfortable. Dominguez comes in an' he stands in the doorway looking around. He sees the Martinas dame. He grins.

He is a tall thin feller, very well dressed in black with silver lacin's down the side of his breeches, a bull-fighter's shirt an' tie, an' a sombrero with silver cords. He has a long thin face an' a nose that juts out. He has a thin mouth an' big white teeth. He has got nothin' on his hip but there is a bulge inside the left-hand breast of his jacket. I reckon this bozo is carryin' the usual mother of pearl handled .32 snub gun with a short barrel that all these punks carry around here.

The band decides to stop playin'. I call the waiter an' buy myself another drink, although I am tellin' myself that I am drinkin' plenty too much especially for a guy who has gotta keep his wits goin'. When he brings the drink over, the band begins playin' again. The Martinas dame gets up an' begins to sing. She has got a funny high voice but not unpleasant an' she hands out the usual wail about her lover in the mountains, the sorta morbid near-hot number that sounds so damn miserable that it makes the Mexicans happy to listen to it. When she finishes everybody claps. They think it is good.

I just sit where I am an' do nothin'. Dominguez is lookin' around the room. He is smilin', sorta appreciatin' the applause that the dame is gettin'. I suppose he thought that some of it was for him. Then he goes over to her table an' he sits down. She looks at him an' grins. Then she looks at the band an' starts talkin' to him, pointin' to the band platform. He grins some more. He looks round. Boy, I knew it, this guy is goin' to sing. He walks up to the band platform an' he grabs a guitar off one of the bozos there an' turns around an' starts singing a song.

Maybe you've heard of it. It is a song called *Sombrero* an' if you're in Mexico you can put your shirt on one thing. It doesn't matter how small a goddam dump is where you are, you can bet your last year's shoe-ties that some dame or guy is goin' to get up an' sing *Sombrero* at any moment. When he finishes this song everybody gives him the big hand.

I reckon that maybe it is time I started somethin'. I walk over across the floor to his table.

"Very nice, Señor," I tell him. "It's a good number but it's sorta old-fashioned. Maybe I can sing for you."

I put out my hand an' I take the guitar off the table. He looks at me. His eyes are cold. Way on the other side of the room I can see the fat boss lookin' worried. Maybe he'll have something else to worry him in a minute.

I give myself a quiet *ad lib* on the guitar, an' I start playin' a hot number. Then I break inta a little Spanish song that some dame taught me one time in Parral. This song is all about how a dame never knows what's waitin' round the corner an' that even if she thinks she's in love with the guy she's got, well, she can still be wrong. You know, it was just one of those.

All the time I am singin' I am givin' this Martinas dame the once over. I sling some hot lingerin' looks at her that woulda burned through a battleship, but she just ain't playin'. She looks at me with a sorta superior little grin. Her eyes are quite steady, they don't flicker or move. While I am singin' I get to thinkin' that this baby would probably spray you with a machine gun with one hand an' pick roses with the other. She is that sorta dame.

I finish the song, an' I hand the guitar back to Dominguez. He is still smilin' but he is only smilin' with his lips. His eyes are like a coupla icebergs. He waves his hand towards a chair on the other side of the table.

"Sit down, Señor," he says. "It is a great pleasure to hear a Spanish song sung with such feeling by an Americano."

"An' how did you know I was an Americano?" I crack at him, in English. "I reckon I speak this lingo well enough to get by without bein' recognised as an American citizen. But maybe somebody told you."

He laughs. I can see that this guy understands what I am sayin' as well as I do myself. But he answers in the best San Luis Potosi.

"The waiter, Señor," he says. "He was waiting outside for me. He told me that an interesting stranger—an Americano was here."

He digs around in his breeches pockets and pulls out a coupla long cigarros. He gives me one an' lights it for me. All the time he is keepin' his eyes on mine.

He signals over to the waiter an' orders some drinks. I reckon that this bozo is comin' out with something in a minute so I don't say anything. I just look around the place as if I was interested in watchin' that dead pan crowd.

An' somehow I get the idea that the whole damn lot of 'em are watchin' Dominguez an' me. Maybe they think that they might see some fun. Well, maybe they are goin' to be right!

When the guy brings the drinks Dominguez sits back an' draws on his cigar. When I look at him I see a grin in his eye.

"I have not the honour of knowing the Señor's name," he says. "My own unworthy name is Pedro Dominguez—possibly you have heard of it? This lady who honours me with her presence is the Señora Fernanda Martinas."

I get up an' make a little bow to the Martinas. While I am doin' it I see a sorta laugh come inta her eye.

I get to thinkin' that this Martinas dame has got a mouth that is pretty swell. Her lips are nice and not thick like most of the women around these parts, an' she uses a good lipstick. I haveta pull myself back to the job in hand because I am lookin' at her too hard thinkin' that I could put in some overtime on a mouth like that one.

"My name's Hellup," I tell Dominguez. "Wyle T. Hellup. I'm down from Las Lunas, New Mexico, an' I'm lookin' for a ranch around here some place for some New York friends of mine."

She laughs. He joins in.

"Your friends must be very foolish, Señor Hellup," she says. "To buy a ranch in this district is madness. Perhaps you saw some of the cattle as you came over the country."

I nod.

"I reckon they're mad, too," I say. "But when people make up their minds I just don't argue with 'em."

Dominguez nods his head.

"Señor," he says. "Heaven forbid that I should suggest that you are a prevaricator of the truth, but you must think that we are very foolish if you really think that we believe that fable about the ranch. The little fairy story that you have already told the waiter!"

I start thinkin' quick.

For a minute I get the jitters. I wonder if I have made a mistake, but then I reckon I can't have made one. There can't be two Pedro Dominguez an' maybe this palooka has got some reason for doin' it this way. I think I'll play it along his way an' see what happens.

"I don't understand you, Señor," I tell him.

He spreads his hands.

"Two or three times," he says very softly, "people come here to Tampapa. They tell all sorts of amusing stories about why they are here, what they are going to do."

He looks like a rattlesnake an' I can see one side of his thin mouth twitchin'.

"Usually these people are interested in one of two things," he says. "One thing is oil and the other is silver. They do not tell us that . . . oh no . . . it is always that they are seeking to buy a ranch or some such fable.

"Only last week," he goes on, "there was a foolish young man who said that his name was Lariat. He got himself into a little trouble here with the police—I am afraid that I had something to do with that. It was perhaps unfortunate that he was shot whilst attempting to escape from the jail in Tampapa. We have a jail—a remote and somewhat hot place, and he would have been better advised to stay there and commune with himself in peace and solitude. But no, he must attempt to escape instead of securing the services of our esteemed and clever lawyer Estorado who, I have no doubt, would have got him out and away—for a consideration."

I get it. I give him a grin that is half a sneer.

"You don't say," I tell him. "An' what am I supposed to do? Am I supposed to get down an' kiss your lily white hand because you ain't tryin' to frame me inta your lousy jail?"

I lean across the table.

"Listen, Dominguez," I tell him. "I heard plenty about you. You're the local bad man with bells on, ain't you? You think you're a god on wheels, but to me you're just another Mexican punk!"

This guy is good. He don't lose his temper. He just sits there playin' with the stem of his glass.

"I am not going to quarrel with you, Señor," he says. "The Rurales patrol will be here at any moment and if I were to lose my temper and deal with you as I would do, I might find myself sharing the same cell for the night, and that would not please me. I have no doubt that I shall find other opportunities for meeting you under more favourable circumstances."

He looks over to the doorway. I screw around an' I see standin' over there, a Rurales police lieutenant an' three troopers.

O.K. Here we go!

I lean across the table.

"Listen, Dominguez," I tell him. "I'm wise to you. Maybe you'll try an' get me ironed out, but you won't get away with it. It'd take more than a lousy guy like you an' that cheap skirt you got stickin' around with you—" I throw a sneer in the direction of Fernanda. "Me—I think that you are just another love-child. . . ."

He slams me. He busts me a straight one in the puss that knocks me sideways. I jump up, grab the *tequila* bottle an' try a quick shot with it. I miss him an' the liquor goes all over Fernanda who is sittin' there with a dead white pan shriekin' for somebody or somethin' to strike me dead for the honour of the Martinas family.

As Dominguez sticks his hand inside his shirt for the gun I bust him a mean one an' go over the table on top of him.

Around me I can hear a hell of a lot of noise an' yellin', an' the next thing I know is that two of the Rurales have got hold of me an' the lieutenant an' the other one are grabbin' Dominguez. Everybody is bawlin' an' shoutin' at once. I can hear the waiter an' the fat boss an' the rest of 'em all tellin' forty-nine different versions of what really broke, an' away above it all I can hear Fernanda shriekin' that I called her a cheap so-an'-so.

The lieutenant—a dirty little palooko with a three days' growth of beard—puts up his hand an' the noise stops.

"Señors," he says, "you will both go to the jail. It is quite some way away. You will have a long walk and ample time to consider your position."

They take Dominguez an' me outside an' tie our hands behind us with a trooper holdin' a length of rope to lead us on. They then get on their horses an' start off down the road, with the horses' hoofs kickin' up the dust in our mouths.

Dominguez has still got the end of his cigarro hanging out of his mouth an' he is bleedin' from a cut over the eye that he won when I hit him.

I look over my shoulder. Standin' in the doorway watchin' us is Fernanda. Her white sombrero shows up in the crowd of dead pans.

"Adios, Americano," she calls out. "I hope you die of jail fever!"

It is midnight when they chuck us in the can at Tampapa. When the guy closes the door of the stone cell Dominguez goes an' sits on the wooden bench against the rear wall.

I stand at the door looking between the bars of the iron gratin' as the jailer moves away.

When he has gone I turn around and look at Dominguez. He has put his feet up on the bench an' he has got another cigarro out of his pocket. He is smokin' nice and quiet as if he hasn't got a care in the world.

I go over to him.

"So what?" I says.

He looks up at me an' laughs. When you look at him this Dominguez has not got such a bad sorta pan after all. It looks like the kinda face that meant to be kind but sorta got deflected in youth if you get me.

"It was the only way, Señor Hellup," he says. "Here we can talk. Outside if we talk everybody looks, everybody suspects. Besides I am not at all popular in this district at the moment. I am glad that you realised what I was about, but I think it was unnecessary to call my poor Fernanda that very rude name."

He shrugs his shoulders sorta sad.

"Forget it," I tell him. "It just sorta came inta my head an' I said it."

I go over to the door an' take another look. Everything is quiet. I go back to him.

"O.K.," I tell him. "Supposin' you talk first. An' talk plenty, Dominguez. Because the more you talk the more you get."

He knocks the ash off his cigar. The moonlight is comin' through the bars of the window way up on the other side of the cell, fallin' on his face. Is this guy goin' to give the truth or is he?

CHAPTER TWO
DUET FOR FOUR-FLUSHERS

IT IS three o'clock an' Pedro is still not talkin'.

I have got the hire of a guitar, a half bottle of *tequila* an' a pack of cigarettes off the guard for three *pesos* an' I am all set to stick around until this bozo decides that he will talk turkey.

I have found that you don't haveta hurry Mexicans. If they wanta talk they'll talk. If they don't, just hang around until they start thinkin' in terms of American dollars—which is what they always finally do. They are sweet guys—sorta polite an' they will always commend your soul to the *Madre de Dios* while they are cuttin' your throat, an' although it don't make any difference to your throat still the thought is very nice if you get me.

I am sittin' with my back against the wall underneath the window with the gratin' over it. This way the moonlight is fallin' on Pedro. I can watch this bozo while he is lyin' on the bench an' I can keep my eye on his face an' see when he is gettin' ideas about comin' across.

I strike a coupla soft chords on the guitar an' I start doin' a little croonin' just to keep myself awake. I am vampin' to a little number that I usta sing to a dame one time when I was doin' a job up in the Ozark mountains. She was a honey that dame. She had everything. She was sorta petite an' clingin' but she was a very forceful character like the time when she tried to stick a meat skewer in my eye for slingin' a hot look at the local school marm. Love can be hell. But maybe you heard about that.

Pedro turns over on his side an' listens as I start croonin'.

> *"Stick around, sweet baby,*
> *An' maybe I'll stick too,*
> *You ain't nobody's business,*
> *But I'll say you'll do.*
> *We'll chew some gum together.*
> *An' croon a little song.*
> *We've lots of time for workin' out,*
> *Who was it done who wrong.*
> *So stick around, sweet baby,*
> *An' maybe you'll see,*

There ain't a guy in Mexico
Can neck a dame like me."

Pedro says that he reckons that this is a swell song. Then he puts his hand out an' I sling the guitar over an' he busts into a cucaracha that woulda made you tingle if you'd heard it. That guy can sing plenty when he wants to.

After he has finished he puts the guitar down an' swings around. He looks serious.

"Señor Hellup," he says, "you must realise that the important thing is the money. You say nothing about the money. As one *caballero* to another. . . ."

I pick up the guitar an' start strikin' chords. The money thing is beginnin' to get this guy down.

"Looky, Pedro," I tell him. "I reckon you an' me talk the same language. I also reckon that you are a brainy guy. The way you fixed gettin' us stuck in this jail so's we could talk things over in peace was very clever an' personally speakin' I would trust you with everythin' I got. But the guys I got behind me are not like that. They are not trustful guys. They do not know what a helluva swell boy you are, Pedro. These guys say that you gotta spill the beans before you collect, an' you can take it from me that as soon as you do spill 'em you'll collect *pronto*. You get me?"

He looks sad.

"Is the money in Mexico?" he says.

I nod.

"Yeah," I tell him. "I could have it in a day, but I gotta have the dope first."

He turns over on his back an' starts lookin' up in the air again. He is thinkin' about that dough. He lights a cigarette an' thinks hard. After a while he turns his head over towards me an' starts in.

"I shall trust you, Señor Hellup," he says, "because I see that you are a *caballero*. Directly I set my eyes upon you I said to myself this Señor Hellup is a *caballero*. I shall tell you what I know. Then we must arrange that you get out of this jail. Then you must have an opportunity to collect the money, after which you will give me 5,000 dollars and I will take you to the place. I will show you everything, Señor."

"Yeah?" I tell him.

I am still watchin' this guy's pan, but it don't tell me much.

"That will be swell," I go on. "Listen, Pedro. How'd you come inta this business?"

He swings his legs down off the bench an' turns round an' looks at me. His face is sorta whimsical. He is sittin' there with his hands on his knees an' his head stickin' forward lookin' straight inta my face with that sorta nice honest smilin', trustin' look that a Mexican always puts on when he's goin' to tell you a bunch of goddam lies.

"Señor Hellup," he says, "you will realise that I am a brave man—very brave. You will also realise that I am a man who is fatally attractive to women. With the greatest diffidence I tell you, Señor Hellup, that women have killed themselves about me before now."

I nod but I am thinkin' to myself that I bet they have. I am also thinkin' that I have never met a guy within one hundred miles of the San Luis Potosi district who didn't think that every dame who took a look at him was all steamed up just in case he wouldn't give her a tumble.

He goes on.

"The fact that there is a little trouble with a woman, and that a small revolution with which I was unfortunately connected went wrong in the Coahuila district, necessitated my rusticating for a little while in the desolate foothills near the Sierra Mojada.

"It is while I am there, Señor, that I first meet the Señor Pepper. Immediately I am attracted to him. He also is a *caballero*. He is living in a shack in the foothills and he also, like you, is looking around for a ranch for some friends in New York."

My ears start flappin'. So Pepper got as far as the foothills in the Sierra Mojada. I wonder what the hell he did after he left there. I reckon I would give something to get a sight of Pepper.

"One day while this Pepper is away I go over to his hut," says Pedro. "Because I am a curious man who is interested in all things, I look around the hut. I search and find in one of his boots an identification card of the Federal Bureau of Investigation of the United States Department of Justice.

"Aha, I think to myself, the Señor Pepper is playing a little game. I think it is a coincidence that he and I should be the only people in this desolate district, and I conclude that he is there because he wishes to talk to me, and that maybe some diffidence on his part has prevented him from informing me of the fact, and also that he was a 'G' man."

This is a good one! It is not like Pepper to go carryin' his identification card around in his boot which is the first place that any guy who rides horses is goin' to look.

"So I await his return," Pedro goes on, "and when he comes back I hand him back the identification card and tell him that any knowledge that I have is at his disposal, providing a little money—say 5,000 American dollars, is paid for it.

"He tells me that he will go away and collect the money and return and pay it to me, and that he will be glad to listen to what I have to say. But alas he does not come back, and from that day to this I have not seen him.

"A charming man, Señor, a brave man, a *caballero*. . ."

"You're tellin' me," I chip in. "Nobody else ain't seen Pepper since then neither. He's just disappeared off the map."

He nods.

"Precisely, Señor," he says, "because I do not need to tell you that there are people in Mexico who are at this moment not very well disposed to members of a Department of the American Federal Service wandering about this country endeavouring to discover things which I have no doubt certain people do not want known."

He looks at me an' he smiles. I reckon that the look on his face is the same sorta look that a boa constrictor would have when it was lookin' at a rabbit, only in this case I reckon that I'm the rabbit.

He switches around an' puts his legs up on the bench an' lies there on his back with his arms behind his head lookin' at the ceilin'.

"I will tell you, Señor Hellup," he says, "exactly what I told to the Señor Pepper. Two weeks before I met him, which is about five weeks ago, Señor, I am approached by a friend of mine called Ramon de Puertas. My friend Ramon, who knows that at this moment I do not wish my whereabouts to be known to the Government of this country, or to any of the police patrols in the vicinity, suggests to me that I may make myself a little money by undertaking to be responsible for the safety of an old gentleman and some friends of his who are living in a desolate and lonely *hacienda* in the Sierra Madre.

"This old gentleman, according to my friend Ramon, is a little bit mad. He is a scientist who apparently is conducting some ridiculous experiments which he considers would improve greatly the process used for blasting rock at the mines in the silver district.

"Ramon says that the old gentleman is wealthy, that he has money, and that therefore unless he is adequately guarded some of the bad characters with which that part of the country abounds, may endeavour to either despoil or kidnap him or his friends. He suggests therefore that I secure the services of three or four of my friends and that we go along to the *hacienda* and look after the old gentleman.

"The idea appeals greatly to me, Señor. I go to the *hacienda*. I meet this charming old gentleman—one Señor Jamieson—with whom I make arrangements. It is agreed that during the night myself and my four friends shall mount guard around the outer walls of the hacienda, that we shall live in a little *adobe* house on the eastern edge of the grounds; that we shall receive our supplies from the *hacienda,* and that whilst we carry out these duties I shall be paid 150 Mexican dollars a week for my own services and those of my friends.

"Understand, Señor, that I am quite happy. It is desolate country. We are away from the world. In this district the Rurales patrols— which I do not like at all—seldom penetrate."

He stops talkin', then he swings himself around, grabs another cigarette, lights it an' sits lookin' at me. Pedro is a good actor. The expression on this guy's face tells me that we're now comin' to the crux of the job.

"It is three nights afterwards it happened, Señor," he says. "During the evening some people arrive. I get this from the two Indian women who are servants at the *hacienda*. There arrives a lady and there arrives another gentleman whose name I do not know. It is soon after midnight, Señor, that I am standing looking out across the *mesa,* thinking that the world is after all a peaceful place for Pedro Dominguez, when I hear from the *hacienda* the sound of a gramophone. I hear the sound of the lady laughing. I think it is beautiful that there could be joy on such a night as this.

"At this moment I am attracted by the sound of a motorcar, and I observe an automobile being driven along the track that leads to the gates in the wall of the *hacienda*. I pick up my rifle and I walk towards this car to find out who this newcomer is, when, Señor, from the *hacienda* there comes the sound of a most terrible explosion.

"I am thrown over upon my face. I mutter a prayer to the Madonna, and I say to myself that it is unfortunate that the Señor Jamieson should select such a beautiful night to blow himself up with his ridiculous experiments.

"At this moment I see running down from the *hacienda* the young man who is the secretary to Señor Jamieson. He runs towards the car which was approaching and which I then observe to be driven by a young and very beautiful woman, and he explains to her the terrible calamity which has happened. This lady was apparently to be another guest at the *hacienda*."

An expression of great sadness comes over this guy's face.

He spreads his hands.

"How terrible this was, Señor," he says. "One half of the hacienda is blown down, the walls are blown out, the furniture is smashed to pieces. It seems that Señor Jamieson was explaining his new invention to his friends when this terrible accident happened. The two Indian servants are killed, as is Señor Jamieson, the lady and the young man. Only the secretary escapes and that because he had left the *hacienda* to observe the arrival of the young lady who should have been there hours before, and who can thank the saints that she had been delayed, otherwise she too would have died."

Pedro stubs out his cigarette an' stretches.

"We buried them as well as we could inside the east wall of the *hacienda,* Señor," he says. "Señor Jamieson was not recognisable. He was in pieces. The young man who was a guest was without a head. We could not even find the servants, we found only pieces of their clothes.

"I am very very sad, Señor, because I have lost what you call my meal ticket. You will realise that I do not wish to report this business to the Commandant of the nearest Rurales post.

"Next evening, Señor, regretfully, I and my four *amigos* mount and ride away over the desert."

He gives a big sigh.

"How beautiful life can be," he says, "and how sad. Señor, that is all I know."

He stretches himself out on the bench an' puts his hands behind his head an' looks at the ceilin' some more. I reckon it is now my turn to start playin'.

"O.K., Pedro," I tell him. "But that don't tell me a lot except that Jamieson an' the girl an' the other guys are all dead. Did you find any of the old boy's papers or things while you was pokin' about in the ruins?"

"There was nothing, Señor," he says, "nothing at all. Everything on that side of the *hacienda* was smashed to little pieces or burned. Naturally I searched to see if there was anything of value but I found nothing."

I light myself a cigarette.

"Well, that ain't a helluva lot of information for 5,000 dollars, Pedro," I tell him. "Is it now?"

He swings around off the bench an' looks at me.

"Señor," he says, "you insult me. I am not for one moment suggesting that you should pay me the money until I have taken you to the *hacienda* so that you may see for yourself. It is not an easy place to find; you will not find it unless you have an experienced guide—such as myself. The place is two days' journey from here. The country is bad at the moment and not safe for you. The sum I ask you is not much for what I would do for you."

I do a little quiet thinkin'.

"O.K.," I tell him. "Well, supposin' I trade with you? How're we goin' to get outa this dump?"

"That is not going to be very difficult, Señor," he says. "I know this guard here. He is amenable to reason. If we talk to him of a little money he will listen. Señor, here is my plan. We wait till to-morrow afternoon, because the morning is not a good time for there are people about the jail, but in the afternoon the place is deserted.

"Very well. When the guard comes in I will talk to him and in the early evening he will arrange so that the door here is left unlocked. You will go but I shall remain as security that we pay him his money—it will not cost much, say two hundred *pesos*. Very well. You will go off, you will go and get the money, but you must be careful to keep away from Tampapa. How long will it take you to get the money?"

"I got the money in my car," I tell him. "I parked it in some sage-brush dump out on the east side of the town before I come in. I can get there in an hour. But I'll have to walk back," I tell him, "because the car is no durn good. The carburettor is all jiggered up. She won't go a yard."

"Do not worry about that, Señor," says Pedro. "That is merely a detail. You will not need the car. When you have got the money you must lie low until nightfall. Then work around the outskirts of Tampapa and continue along the line of the road that leads past this jail towards the *mesa*. Two miles away you will find a desert road leading north. Follow it and presently you will come to a little house—a white *casa* in a small valley towards the Nazas country. It is a desolate place and you need not worry about being seen. The police patrols seldom penetrate there, besides which the guard here will probably have informed his friends of your generosity.

"At this house you will find the Señora Fernanda Martinas. Make your peace with her. Explain to her the fact that your rudeness to her was merely theatrical and part of our little scheme, because I do not wish to antagonise this lady of whom I am extremely fond, and who has the temperament of a tigress when aroused.

"She will make arrangements for the money which you will give her to be brought here to the jail. I suggest that you send two hundred *pesos* for the guard and another three hundred for the *Commandante*."

He stretches himself again. He looks plenty pleased with the way he is runnin' this business.

"Then," he goes on, "I shall be released. I shall immediately join you at the *casa* and we can make our own arrangements about setting out for the remains of the *hacienda* of the late Señor Jamieson in the Sierra Madre."

He looks at me with a big smile.

"Well, Señor," he says, "does it go?"

"It goes swell, Pedro," I tell him. "I reckon I won't forget how you've played this business when the time comes."

He gives a big yawn an' he stretches himself out an' goes off to sleep. It sit there smokin' an' lookin' at him. In a few minutes this guy is sleepin' like a baby.

I do some quiet thinkin'. Me, I do not know whether this Pedro is tellin' the truth or makin' it up as he goes along. I do not get this Jamieson stuff, and this explosion business, one little bit. Maybe

Pedro thinks I know more than I do know. What I want right now is some sorta information that is goin' to get me next to Pepper.

The moonlight is comin' through the gratin' an' fallin' on Pedro's face, makin' it look like a checkers board. I get to thinkin' about Fernanda.

Now there is a dame for you. How comes it that a palooka like Pedro who is nothin' but a two-by-four four-flushin' bandit should get for himself a dame like Fernanda? Maybe he is right when he says that she has gotta temper like a tigress when she ain't seein' eye to eye with you but a dame is often all the better for bein' that way.

I usta know a dame in Chattanooga who wasn't even good-lookin' until she saw you givin' the once over to some other honey after which she got so durn beautiful that you could only duck an' hope that she would miss when she started throwin' the cutlery about. It was only when I heard that this baby had cut the right ear clean off a Marine with a drop shot with a carvin' knife from ten yards that I remembered I had got a date in New York.

But apart from the knife throwin' act she was a honey an' very kind to animals.

Are dames funny? You're tellin' me. I reckon that if it wasn't for dames I should be doin' some other sorta job. The guy who said *cherchez la femme* didn't know the half of it. It's one thing to *cherchez* 'em an' another thing to know what you're goin' to do with 'em when you've found 'em.

Any dame who has got a face that don't hurt an' whose shape entitles her to credit in a swim suit advertisement is always goin' to start somethin' whenever she can, just to teach herself that she can still pack a wallop where the boys are concerned. An' anytime you run into a sweet bunch of trouble you can bet your next month's pay that you are goin' to find some baby sittin' right down at the bottom of it all lookin' innocent and packin' a six-inch knife in the top of her silk stockin' just in case she needs it for peelin' apples.

Which maybe is one explanation of the Pedro-Fernanda set-up.

I sit there thinkin' to myself that the sooner I get outa this jail the better for all concerned. I am in this country an' I got to look after myself because I reckon that a Federal identification card is about as much good to me here as a raspberry sundae to an Esquimo with frost-bite.

So what. I lay down on the floor an' stretch out. This can is as hot as hell in summer but I reckon that all things come to him who waits—all the things that the other guy don't want!

The sunshine is comin' through the gratin'.

While I am rubbin' the sleep outa my eyes I can see Pedro talkin' to the guard through the slot in the door. He is gesticulatin' an' wavin' his arms about an' talkin' plenty fast.

After a bit he comes over to me. He is grinnin'.

"It is all fixed up, Señor Hellup," he says. "Everything is going to be very well. At five o'clock this afternoon the guard will come here, open the door of the cell and enter. He will talk to me. You will slip out. Turn sharply to your right, keep along the passage until you come to the end and turn to your left. This will bring you directly to the side door of the jail. Outside run quickly around to the back of the jail and take the small path which leads back past the *estancia* where we met. Beyond there is the *mesa* and a dozen places for you to hide until nightfall, because you must realise that it will be necessary to make some show of searching for you. After which you must do what I have already told you."

"Swell, Pedro," I tell him. "You're doin' fine."

He goes back to his bench an' starts strummin' on the guitar. I reckon I am beginnin' to like this Pedro guy. He has gotta sense of humour.

Presently the guard comes back an' brings some lousy stuff that he calls coffee. We drink this, after which I tell Pedro to wake me up in time for the big act.

Then I lay down on the floor an' go off again, because I have found that if you have not got anything else to do sleep is a very good thing an' costs practically nothin'.

When I wake up I don't open my eyes or move. I just lie there wonderin' just what is goin' to happen to Lemmy Caution when the fun starts.

After a bit Pedro comes over to me.

"Wake up, Señor," he says. "In a minute the guard will be here. Prepare yourself an' do just what we have arranged. All will be well!"

"O.K.," I tell him.

I get up an' sit on the bench. In a minute I hear the guard comin' along the passageway outside. Then I hear him unlockin' the cell door.

"Now, Señor!" Pedro hisses at me. "Now is the time. You must make it look like an escape!"

The door swings open an' the guard comes. He starts walkin' towards Pedro an' the way to the cell door is clear.

I don't take it. I take a jump at the guard an' swing a right hook at his jaw that woulda busted a torpedo boat in half. As he goes over I grab his gun outa the holster on his belt.

Pedro is lookin' at me with his eyes poppin'.

"Señor," he starts in, "Señor . . ."

"Cut it out, punk," I tell him. "Do you think I ain't been wise to your bedtime fairy stories about how I was goin' to get outa here? You was goin' to play the same game with me as you played with Lariat, but it ain't workin'!"

I take a jump at Pedro an' I smash him a mean one over the top of the head with the gun butt. He goes down like he was poleaxed. I grab the key off the guard, get outa the cell, slam the door an' stick the key in my pocket.

I am standin' outside in the passage. Pedro told me to run right an' take the turn to the left. Well, I am just not doin' this because I reckon they will be waitin' for me an' they won't be sayin' it with flowers either.

So I turn left, gumshoe down the passage. At the end is a sorta guard room. Over on the other side over a sleepin' bunk is a frame window. I ease over onto the bunk, bust open the window and drop out.

I am in some little *patio* to the side of the jail. There is a doorway in the *adobe* wall over on the right. I go through this with the gun ready just in case somebody wants to start somethin'.

Away in the front of the jail I can hear plenty yellin'.

Out through the doorway is a pathway leadin' to a road through the scrub. I take this an' start runnin'. A hundred yards down the road I turn an' look back. There is a guy outside the *patio* wall drawin' a bead on me with a rifle. I take a flop the second before he pulls the trigger, an' as he fires wriggle around on the ground an' take a quick one at him. He decides to get inside the *patio* again.

I get up an 'start runnin' some more. An' it's durn funny how fast you can go when you wanta.

After a bit I ease over to the left an' take a path through the scrub. In ten minutes I am in the foothills east of Tampapa with the *estancia* layin' away behind me on the right.

Maybe I know a bit more about this country than Pedro was wise to.

I go on for a while an' then flop down by a cactus an' listen.

I can't hear a thing.

I sit there an' get my breath. I reckon it has come off. I reckon the bozos who was waitin' for me was out on the other side of the jail.

An' they will go for the place where I told Pedro I had parked the car on the east side of the town, an' they won't find it because it's in a gully due north—an' it's still goin'.

I sit there for a bit an' then I get up an' start lopin' off, workin' round to the north. I have not got any really good idea about what I am goin' to do but there is one thing that I am durn certain about an' that is that whatever I am goin' to do I ain't doin' it till night comes along. Me, I like the dark—especially when there is a good chance of some guy takin' a pot at you just to see if you are one of them guys who wriggles when a bullet hits him.

After a bit I get up an' work around to the gully where I left the car. I open up the bonnet an' look under the false bottom in the tool box. I have got the Luger there an' a quart bottle of rye.

I take a drink an' then ease off about a hundred yards away where there is a clump of cactus. I lie down with the Luger between my knees just in case some guy should happen around.

I think I will get myself a piece of sleep, because maybe I'm goin' to need it.

CHAPTER THREE
SWEET MOMMA

IT IS eleven o'clock when I wake up.

There is a sweet moon an' when I look around I see the cactus bushes an' joshua trees throwing funny shadows around the place. I reckon the Mexican desert is an odd sorta place at night—creepy as well. I give myself a cigarette an' start doin' a little thinkin' about Pepper.

I reckon it would be a nice thing for all concerned if anybody hadda known what Pepper was playin' at. You gotta realise that this Pepper is a great guy. He is a swell agent with a heart like two lions. As well he is a good looker an' dames go for him plenty. This boy is too smart to disappear off the face of the map without some good reason unless somebody has creased him.

All the information I have got is that Pepper was operatin' in the Arizona district. He telephones through to the Agent-in-Charge down there an' says he has gotta beat on some tough stuff that is happenin' over the border—somethin' hot. He says it is a helluva business an' that he would like two three weeks over there, after which he reckons he is goin' to have plenty to report. He says he ain't got time to say any more right then because things are poppin', which is a fact that tells me that whatever it was got Pepper along to the shack in the Sierra Mojada, where he ran across Dominguez, started on our side of the Line. But they got telegraphs and telephones even in Mexico an' when the Agent-in-Charge in Arizona don't hear anything from the boy he starts gettin' worried an' they send me over.

O.K. It is stickin' out a foot that if Pepper was playin' his hand as quietly as all that, there was some dam' good reason for it. That is why I have been callin' myself Mr. Hellup an' am supposed to be lookin' for a ranch for some Americanos.

I heard about this guy Dominguez. I been hangin' around the San Luis Potosi district an' workin' from there right away up to Juan del Rio across to Tamaulipas then down to Hidalgo, tryin' to get a lead on Pepper. The sweet baby I was tellin' you about, the one I met in Matehuala told me she had seen an Americano answerin' to the boy's description with this Dominguez an' a dame called Fernanda Martinas. This honeypot tells me that Dominguez is a small time bandit who will do anything for dough an' that the Fernanda jane is a woman who is stuck on Pedro but who ain't so very well known around those parts.

The thing is just how much of this stuff that Dominguez has told me about this Jamieson guy and the rest of it is true, and how much is just plain hooey. It is a funny sorta story an' it ain't the kind of tale that Dominguez woulda had enough sense to have made up, so I reckon there is some truth in it. I start thinkin' about Dominguez.

Two things are stickin' out a foot. One is that Dominguez knew that I had come inta Mexico to find out about Pepper. Directly I started talkin' to that waiter about him an' the dame he got the news. The rest was a frame-up. Dominguez had promised some bum policeman, who was short of a few dollars, some dough to get me inta that jail. Then they were goin' to pull the old one on me. The old "shot while tryin' to escape" stuff. If they'd got away with this, the U.S. Government mightn't have liked it, but what would they have done? I'd been pinched for gettin' myself inta a tavern brawl an' under Mexican Federal law if a prisoner tries to escape you're entitled to shoot him.

All of which shows you that this guy Dominguez has got *some* brains, because that idea he tried to pull across me about gettin' me inta the jail just so's we could talk was a sweet one.

An' that is the reason why I think that this stuff he told me was the truth. Why should he worry about tellin' me a lie when he thinks that before I have got ten yards out that jail I'm goin' to be so fulla lead that I look like a cannon-ball factory?

An' where do we go from there? I lay back there, smokin' with my shirt collar undone, because, believe it or not, it is so goddam hot that the sweat is runnin' down my face. I reckon I can do one of two things. I can go back to the car, start her up an' turn her around. I can ease back to San Luis Potosi just as quick as I can make it, see the Chief of Police an' flash my identification card. After which there will be some sweet explainin' as to why a Federal Agent has to operate in one of the Mexican districts without the knowledge of the Mexican Government an' callin' himself Mr. Hellup. You'll agree with me that this ain't so hot.

An' what is the alternative? I'm tellin' you I don't know what it is, because it looks to me like if I go on with this job I stand a very sweet chance of gettin' myself very nicely creased out an' believe it or not I'm not a guy who likes to be dead.

I start wonderin' what's happened around at that jail after I got out. Supposin' it was true what Pedro said that there wasn't many people around that jail in the afternoon, well in that case maybe Pedro an' the guard are still locked in that cell. I reckon they could bawl their heads off but nobody wouldn't hear 'em, that is unless the guard outside—the guy who took a pot at me with a rifle—was in on the game with 'em. But then I got an idea that he wasn't, because it stands to reason that the guard inside the jail who was in on the job woulda had to split the dough with the feller outside if the outside guy hadda known.

No, I don't reckon they told this guy. I reckon he was just standin' in his usual place on duty at the jail door an' that they expected that when he saw me ease out there he would just have taken a shot at me an' got me. Supposin' that ain't true? That he knew all about it, that he went back inta the jail an' found Pedro an' his pal locked up in the cell? Well, I got the key in my pocket, ain't I? If the *Commandante*, who I reckon is the guy with the duplicate key, don't come back until next morning like Pedro sorta suggested, then maybe they're still stuck there, which would be a nice break.

Here is the point I'm gettin' at. Me, I have got to do the things that Pedro will think I am not goin' to do. You will realise that I have told this guy a bundle of lies. I have told him that my car was hidden in one place which it ain't. I have told him that the carburettor was bust. He will believe this. I reckon that Pedro thought that directly I got outa that jail I started leggin' it as hard as I could over the *mesa* towards San Luis Potosi, because he reckons I think I'd be safe around there.

Well, he will have a sort of idea that the thing to do is to stop me gettin' there. So if he got outa that jail I reckon he got himself a horse an' is poundin' away lookin' for Lemmy Caution somewhere on the *mesa* just so's he can give him a coupla visitin' cards out the business end of a hand gun.

Here is the plan. Pedro told me where Fernanda's place was—a little white *casa* in the valley. He didn't mind tellin' me about that because he thought I'd never get there. I reckon that that is the last place that guy thinks I will go to. That being so I reckon that is the way I will play this thing, because if Fernanda ain't seen Pedro since I saw this guy last, maybe I can pull a fast one on her.

I get up an' shake myself. I wonder why the hell I always get this sorta job. One of these fine days I'm goin' to have one of those sweet cases around New York or some place where dames are dames an' like you to know same, an' where a man does not have to live on *chili con carne* all the time an' drink this *tequila* stuff that seems to make everything twice as bad as it was. What the hell?

I walk back to the car an' I bust the carburettor. If I ain't goin' to use this car nobody else is either.

From where I am sittin' behind a clump of cactus I can see the *casa*. It is a little one-story place away down on the left of the track that leads north. There is a corral fence round it, painted white, an' somebody has made a sorta ornamental pathway from the gate in the fence up to the door of the house. It looks pretty in the moonlight.

From where I am I can see that there is a light in the room that faces the road, a room with a sorta veranda outside. Well, whoever put this place up—an' it is pretty well built, Spanish fashion—musta wanted a job, because I reckon there ain't any other dump for two or three miles each side of it, an' then only single shacks. Maybe the guy who lived here wanted to do a Greta Garbo an' be alone.

Now I have got here I am not feelin' quite so good about this proposition. How do I know that Dominguez ain't sitting inside there with a drink in one hand an' a hand gun in the other, just sorta hopin' that I might show up.

But then again I don't reckon he will be. Like I said this guy is probably away on the San Luis Potosi road, thinkin' I am making for there, lookin' for me.

It is as hot as hell. I get up an' fan myself a bit with my hat, after which I take the Luger outa my hip pocket an' stick it inside my shirt, because I reckon if anybody is goin' to start any shootin' it's goin' to be me.

I ease away in the direction behind the house, keepin' in the shadow of sage brush an' cactus where I can. I work round to the back of the house, get over the fence an' crawl up. I listen but I can't hear anything. I stick around there a long time an' I reckon, as there is a light in the room on the other side of the *casa* that somebody is up. If they are they ain't talkin', so maybe Fernanda is on her own. O.K. Here we go.

I ease back the way I have come, walk along the road, go through the corral gate as large as life right up to the door of the house. The door is pretty good, heavy oak an' Spanish iron work, stuck in an *adobe* wall. I bang on it. After a coupla minutes I can hear somebody movin' inside. The door opens an' some Indian girl looks out.

"Look," I tell her, "is the Señora Fernanda in?"

She nods. Her eyes are poppin'.

"Is anybody else here?" I ask her.

She shakes her head.

"O.K.," I tell her. "You get inside an' tell the Señora that Señor Hellup is here an' he'd like to talk to her."

She goes away an' she leaves the door on the chain. After a coupla minutes she comes back again an' opens the door. I step inside. I am in a nice square sorta hallway. There are Mexican blankets an' things hangin' around the walls an' the furniture is O.K. While I am standin' there Fernanda comes out of a door on the right. She is smilin'.

I told you guys before that this dame was a looker, but I didn't tell you the half of it. She has got on a black lace loungin' gown an' she is wearin' a mantilla. She looks one hundred per cent good. She smiles at me, a slow sorta smile.

"You are welcome, Señor Hellup," she says. "I have been expecting you."

The smile goes off her face an' she stands there lookin' sorta sad. I do a quick think about this Fernanda. I told you before that I was wonderin' why a dame who has got what this dame has, should be playin' around with a guy like Dominguez. I am still wonderin' why. Maybe Dominguez has got something on her. All these dames have a story if you can get at it as the news hound said.

There comes through my mind the idea that I might even take a chance with this Fernanda. I put my hat down an' I go across to her. She turns an' walks inta the room. It's a long room runnin' the whole length of the *casa*. One side of it opens on to the veranda lookin' out across the *mesa* towards the road. The furniture is durned good. It's all good old Spanish stuff. There ain't one piece of Grand Rapids anywhere. The place has got class.

She pushes a big chair up towards the veranda, puts a little table by it an' signals me to sit down. Then she goes across to the sideboard an' starts fixin' some drinks. I can hear ice tinklin' an' I wonder how in blazes this dame manages to get ice around here. I am also very glad to see that she has gotta bottle of rye. I watch her while she is mixin' these drinks. She is one of those dames who is pretty to watch. She moves soft an' easy like a cat, an' with her white arms showin' through the lace gown she looks a million. I get to thinkin' that I reckon I oughta bring my mind back to the job in hand, an' when I think this I pull myself together an' wonder just what I am goin' to hand out to her.

She comes over with the drink an' puts it on the table beside me. She is still smilin'.

"I expected you before, Señor Hellup," she says. "Pedro sent me a message that I might expect you earlier. Did something go wrong?"

I pick up the drink an' start suckin' it down just to give myself time to think. I reckon Pedro sent her some sorta message some time when he was talkin' to the guard before I broke out, an' I reckon that he ain't been near her since. Anyhow she is probably lyin'. All of a sudden it comes to me how I am goin' to play this. I am goin' to take a chance an' do the thing that nobody would expect me to do. Maybe I will hand this dame a slice of truth mixed up with enough lies just to make the mixture right.

"Looky, Fernanda," I tell her, "I wanta talk turkey with you because I would hate to see a dame who is a swell looker like you get yourself in some sorta jam that she couldn't get out of—See?"

She looks at me. She has still got that sorta slow smile on her face, an' her pretty red lips are parted. Did I tell you this dame had sweet teeth or did I? Sittin' where she is they are shinin' like little pearls.

"There is a pretty good reason for me bein' late, Fernanda," I go on. "I bust outa that jail this afternoon, only I didn't go out the way they thought I was goin', because there was some guy waitin' with a rifle for me. O.K. I went an' got my car an' spent a coupla hours amusing myself findin' a telegraph office."

I am watchin' her like a cat. I see her eyes flicker.

"That bein 'so," I tell her, "an' havin' regard to the fact that by this time the Texas State cops know all about what is goin' on around here an' where I am, I reckon that you an' me can do a little straight talkin'."

She gets up an' she goes back to the sideboard an' she brings over a box of cigarettes. She gives me one an' strikes a match an' lights it. Then she lights one for herself an' goes back to her chair.

"Señor Hellup," she says sorta quiet, "I would like you to understand that as far as I am concerned all this is very mysterious. I do not quite understand."

"No?" I tell her. "How long have you known Dominguez, Fernanda?" I ask her.

She shrugs her shoulders.

"Not for very long, Señor Hellup," she says. "You must realise that Pedro is a person of ferocious nature. He is inclined always to take what he wants an' he seldom asks permission. I met him nearly three months ago and on two or three occasions I have tried to bring our—shall we call it friendship—to an end, but he is not inclined to do so. Also you will realise that Pedro has so much to answer for that another little thing like the sudden death of myself in the event of my not doing exactly what he wishes would not greatly trouble him."

I nod my head. Maybe she is tellin' the truth. Maybe that's the way it is.

"Yeah," I tell her, "an' I don't suppose that a little thing like me gettin' myself ironed out would trouble him either—hey, Fernanda?"

She shrugs.

"If you have telegraphed to your police in Texas," she says, "I think that you are safe. I do not think that Pedro would be so foolish as to do anything that might cause trouble on a large scale."

She leans back in the chair an' she puts her hands behind her head an' she looks at me. I have already tried to tell you guys that this Fernanda has got plenty appeal, an' sittin' like that lookin' at me with them big eyes reminds me of a dame I usta know when I was in a job in Sonoita. I get to thinkin' that maybe this Fernanda ain't so bad; that maybe she will play ball. Anyhow I have gotta trust somebody because right now I am walkin' around in circles tryin' to catch up with myself.

She gets up an' she comes over to where I am an' picks up my empty glass. She is so near to me that I can smell the scent that she is wearin' an' I'm tellin' you that it was the stuff—you know that sorta discreet, lingerin' perfume that some dames are clever enough to wear that makes you wanta get 'em in your arms an'—but why bring that up anyway? You probably felt the same way some time yourself.

She goes back to the sideboard an' starts pourin' me another drink. I get up an' sit on the arm of the chair watchin' her.

"Look, Fernanda," I tell her, "I'm in a spot, see, an' I've gotta trust somebody, so I'm pickin' you. But don't get me wrong, baby. Don't you get any funny ideas in that little head of yours that you can pull a fast one on me an' try to cross me up, because even if I was dead I reckon d see Lemmy Caution comin' back from the grave fulla big ideas about gettin' you where it'ud hurt most. . . ."

She puts the glass down. Her eyes are poppin'.

"Madre de Dios!" she says. "Lemmy Caution. . . ."

She gives a little gasp.

I grin at her.

"Maybe they told you about me?" I ask her.

She nods.

"Señor," she says. "A year ago I was at Hermosillo—you know, near Sonora. I was singing in the Café there. They were talking about you. They told me about the Madrale business—about the trouble in Sonoita. They told me how you shot Guarcho; how you brought Nendensino across the Sonora desert, through his own country, with all his people looking for you. I said to myself that if the saints were good to me maybe one day I should meet such a man as you.

"And here you are, in this room, smoking my cigarette, about to drink this drink which I bring you with pride. *Madonna*, what a man!"

I don't say anythin'. What the hell can I say anyway? If I knew how to start blushin' I would do it.

She comes over with the drink an' she puts it on the table, then she takes a step back an' throws me a curtsey like I was the King of Siam or somethin'. Then she says, sorta soft, that old one that they always pull on you when you arrive at somebody's dump in Mexico—that is if they got any class at all.

"Señor Caution," she says. "This house is yours—and all that is in it."

She is lookin' right inta my eyes an' somehow, she is right up close to me, before I know what this dame is doin' she is in my arms an' I am kissin' her like I was a film hero in a love scene after the director had told him off for not tryin'.

All the time somethin' is tellin' me not to get deflected an' to keep my eye on the ball, which is not easy when you have got an armful of a woman like Fernanda.

She makes a little noise an' wriggles an' I get it. The gun stuck inside my shirt is hurtin' her an' I grab it out an' put it on the table with the drink.

"O.K., Fernanda," I tell her. "That was swell an' maybe when we have talked a little business we can think up some more sweet ideas about neckin', but in the meanwhiles you get over to that chair an' sit down an' listen."

She don't say anythin'. She just goes back to the chair an' sits down. She is lookin' at me the way I have seen an East Side kid lookin' at a picture of Clark Gable.

"Here's the way it is," I tell her. "There is a guy called Pepper who is a Special Agent in the Bureau of Investigation. This guy is operatin' in the Arizona district. O.K. Well, he telephones through to the Agent-in-Charge that he is on to somethin' hot, that he is comin' over here inta Mexico an' that he reckons to be about three weeks or so. All right. Well, we ain't heard a thing about him since then, an' so after a bit I get sent over here to try an' find Pepper.

"I hang around the place an' try an' get a lead. Then some dame in Matehuala tells me that she has seen a guy like Pepper gettin' around with Dominguez. She says that you're with 'em an' tells me what your name is. I go back to San Luis Potosi an' I hear that you was up in Tampapa singin' at that one-eyed dump, an' I put two an' two together an' reckoned that if you was there Dominguez would be there too. Well, I was right.

"The next thing is that Dominguez tries to pull a fast one. He gets me inta that jail an' tells me that he has fixed that idea so's we can talk. He then gets another big idea about bribin' the guard to let me escape first an' him after, but I gotta idea that he is tryin' to get me ironed out whiles I am tryin' to escape. I was right too.

"O.K. Well, whiles we was stuck in that can he told me a lotta stuff about actin' as bodyguard for some guy called Jamieson at a *hacienda* in the Sierra Madre foothills. There was some more stuff about an explosion an' some dame arrivin' just too late to be in it.

"When the time come I made the break but not just in the way we fixed. I smacked the guard down an' bust Pedro one on the dome. I told him that my car was bust, an' I reckon that he thinks I would be leggin' it for San Luis Potosi where I would be safe an' I reckon that if he has got himself outa that jail he is goin' after me just for the purpose of stoppin' me from gettin' there an' talkin'.

"O.K. Well, here I am an' where do we go from there?"

Fernanda is still sittin' there lookin' at me like I was the best thing she has ever seen. She has got her little hands folded in front of her. Right then I get the idea that this dame is real class; that there ain't two bits worth of Indian in her, that she is real Spanish Señora an' one hundred per cent high hat if you get me.

"Lemmy," she says, "I will tell you the truth. I have been in the company of Dominguez because it was necessary for me. I have a husband—I was forced to marry him when I was very young. He was a very bad man. He made my life hell. At the first opportunity I tried to escape. He caught me, brought me back. Then I thought of Dominguez, of whom people are afraid because he is a killer. I paid Dominguez such money as I had to take me away. I knew that my husband would be afraid of following me if he thought I was with Pedro. I was right.

"But there has never been anything between Pedro and myself. No man has ever meant anything to me until now. Now I love you!"

She gets up an' she comes over an' she puts her little mouth on mine an' gives me a kiss that woulda made Rip Van Winkle wake up an' shake himself. Then she goes back to her chair an' sits down again. Everything this dame does is sorta slow and graceful and deliberate.

"I know little of Pepper," she says. "I knew that Dominguez went away with a young man who was an American. I knew nothing else. But Pedro has told me about the *hacienda* near the Sierra Madre. It is a long day's ride from here. I know nothing else."

She gets up an' grabs my glass an' goes back over to the sideboard. I notice that she ain't usin' the rye this time. She is fillin' it with lemonade an' ice. She is a thoughtful dame.

"Pedro sent me a message from the jail," she says. "He said that he would be here to-night. But I think that you are right when you believe that he thinks you are making for San Luis. He has gone after you to kill you. He would not wish for you to arrive there and talk."

She brings the glass over to me. Then she goes back to the sideboard an' stands there leanin' against it in the shadow.

"Consider, Lemmy," she says. "If Pedro is riding towards San Luis looking for you, he will not give up the chase until about this time. Then he will believe that you have escaped him. He will turn and come back here. Possibly he will think that you would be fool-hardy enough to go out to the *hacienda*. If he thinks this he must return this way. He will rest here and then go after you. Because now he *must* kill you.

"If therefore you desire to go to the *hacienda* and see for yourself what happened there you must go at once. If Pedro comes back I will arrange something so as to give you time to get to the *hacienda* and, when you have done what you want, to get away. But you must not stay in Mexico. You must go back."

"An' what about you?" I ask her.

She shrugs her shoulders.

"Perhaps one day when you are in New York I shall send you a little note. Perhaps I shall come and see you. Would you like that?"

I grin.

"You try me," I tell her.

I stub out my cigarette.

"O.K., Fernanda," I said. "I'm goin' to play it your way. I'm goin' to get a move on an' get out to this *hacienda* an' take a look around. Then maybe I'll blow outa Mexico an' maybe I won't. Maybe I'll come back here an' have a little talk with you."

I get up an' move over towards the veranda. I turn around when I hear her move.

She is comin' towards me an' her face is set. I wonder why until I see the little black automatic in her hand.

"You fool," she says. "So you believed me. The brave, the clever Lemmy Caution was fool enough to be taken in by a woman. Go, stand with your back to the wall!"

I do it. I will not tell you the names I am callin' myself. Me . . . to get sucked in by a dame like this. An' what the hell is she goin' to pull now?

I stand there leanin' against the wall facin' the veranda by the side of the sideboard. She moves until she is only a coupla yards away. She has got the gun pointin' at my guts. I can feel myself sweatin' around the back of my neck.

"I am going to kill you, Señor Caution," she says. "Where would you prefer to be shot? In the head, the stomach or the back? I believe that if one is shot in the stomach it sometimes takes a long time to die. Perhaps you would like to tell me."

She is smilin' at me like a she-devil.

My brain is workin' as quick as hell but I don't see any way outa this. Back of my head I am wonderin' just what it was made me trust this dame. Me, I am not very often wrong about dames.

Then I start callin' myself some more names. I wonder what the Bureau will say when they hear that the mug Caution got himself ironed out by a good-lookin' dame in Mexico, a dame who had pulled an old one on him an' got his gun away from him.

She comes a bit closer. She is lookin' straight at me an' the gun in her hand is as steady as a rock.

"O.K. baby," I tell her. "I was the mug. You shoot where you like because it don't matter much to me, but let me tell you one thing an' that is that the 'G' men will get you just as sure as you got that gun in your hand. Maybe this year an' maybe next but they'll get you all right."

"How amusing," she says. "Well . . . *adios*, Señor Caution!"

I see her finger curl round the trigger. I sorta brace myself for it. Well . . . here we go.

She squeezes the trigger an' the top of the automatic opens up an' a cigarette pops out. She offers it to me with a little bow. She is nearly dyin' with laughin'.

I stand there lookin' like the biggest sap that ever untied himself off his mother's apron strings. I don't even feel good when she comes an' puts her arms around my neck. I can still feel her laughin' fit to bust. Can this dame act or can she?

Then it gets me an' I start laughin' too. You gotta admit that this baby has gotta great sense of humour.

I take the cigarette an' she lights it for me.

"Lemmy," she says after that little interval. "It is obvious to me that you need somebody to look after you. So you will do what I tell you. Here is my plan. I will prepare some food for you. In the meantime you will go to the corral, at the end of the palisade. You will find a horse there. Saddle him and come back for the food and the water bottle which I shall have for you.

"Then take the desert road and keep due north. You will find the *hacienda* on this side of the foothills. You should be there by to-morrow night at latest.

"If Pedro returns here—and I think that he will—I shall have some false news for him. I shall tell him that you have been seen a long way off, making for Najos. He will go after you.

"When you are finished at the *hacienda*, return here. I shall be waiting for you."

She puts her face up to mine an' I can see that her eyes are shinin' like stars.

"Then you shall say *adios* to me before you return over the line," she says . . . "a long *adios*."

I grab her. I tell you that this dame is one hundred per cent what the doctor ordered.

After a minute she breaks away an' scrams off.

I go over to the veranda an' drop over on to the path. I reckon I will get this horse saddled an' ready to go before she thinks up somethin' else that might make me forget that I got a job to do around here.

Some guys are lucky and some guys are not. Me . . . I reckon I am one of the lucky ones.

I ease the horse inta a walk an' look around over my shoulder. I can see Fernanda standin' on the veranda lookin' after me, wavin' her hand.

Away in front of me is the desert an' somewhere ahead is the *hacienda*. I reckon that life could be a dura sight worse than it is.

Anyhow the palooka who said that a guy cannot mix business with pleasure was nuts.

So what!

Chapter Four
SO LONG, PEPPER

WHEN I see the location of the *hacienda* I get a shock, because whoever it was built this place musta been nuts. I have been thinkin' all along that it would be right among the foothills this end of the Sierra Madre where there would be shade an' water. But it is a helluva way from anywhere stuck right in the middle of the desert.

From where I am I can see the wall around the place like Pedro told me an' towards the top of the slope I can see the *hacienda*. It looks white an' creepy in the moonlight like one of the ghost towns you've read about. I can see that the right hand side of the place is bust in, but the other end looks O.K. Maybe it wasn't such a bad explosion as Pedro thought it was.

I tie the horse up at the gate an' go in. Everything is so still that you coulda almost cut the quiet with a knife.

I am tired as hell. This business of chasin' round Mexico don't please me too much. Why should it? As I get up near the *hacienda* I can see away down on the left standin' close to the wall the hut that Pedro an' his boys were livin' in when they were around here. There is a sorta pathway lined out with giant cactus, greasewood an' dead joshua trees, an' you can see where some nutty guy has tried to lay this place out an' give it some class. This makes me laugh because you might as well try an' paint the asbestos in hell. An' what this guy Jamieson coulda been doin' around here with this dame an' a secretary an' what-not is somethin' else I would like to know.

I walked on up towards the *hacienda*. There is a little flight of wooden steps leadin' up to the entrance with an *adobe* porch an' a coupla pillars, you know, Mexican stuff.

I kick the door open an' I go in. Believe it or not nobody ain't even worried to move the furniture away. The hall is furnished an' there is thick alkali dust over everything. Nobody has been there because there ain't a footmark in the place. The dust has just settled. I reckon this is one of them places that would give you the jitters if you was the sorta guy who got the jitters.

On the right an' left of the hallway are rooms. I go in an' look around. They are furnished all right an' there is the same dust lying about. I come out an' walk along the passage that leads from the hall away down to the back of the house, the part that is bust in. As I walk along my foot kicks against something an' I see it is the top of a gramophone case, one of them big ones. Maybe somebody was playin' it when the place blew up. At the end of the passage is a room. I reckon it was the biggest room in the house, the one they used for a lounge. The walls this side are O.K. except that they are scarred an' here an' there lumps have fell outa them, but on the other side there is just the air. Two sides of this wall have been blown right out so I reckon the whole gang was standin' maybe where the other corner of the room is, listening to this Jamieson guy explain his stuff maybe, when the balloon went up.

I walk back an' I sit on the porch steps. I light myself a cigarette an' start thinkin' about Pepper. I have got a sorta idea in my head that Pepper was around here when this business broke. I'm bettin' my last dollar that he wasn't hangin' around the foothills away in the Sierra Mojada unless he wanted to link up with Dominguez an' I am makin' a guess that the reason he had for doin' that was that he knew that Dominguez was comin' 'out here. Maybe it was this guy Jamieson that Pepper was interested in. All this stuff is funny anyhow, because you gotta realise that an Agent of the Federal Bureau of Investigation is not supposed to go leapin' off an' doin' things without somebody knowin' what he's doin', an' whiles it would be O.K. for Pepper to scram out inta this dump quick if there was a legitimate reason for doin' it, yet the first thing he oughta have done directly he got the chance was to get a report over somehow to the Agent-in-Charge of the Field Office in New Mexico, who is a good guy called Scattle.

An' where do we go from here?

I light myself another cigarette.

I wonder if I am the mug. Now I have got out here to this dump I would like to know just what I am goin' to do. I have always been a guy who was sorta keen on followin' his nose an' in a lotta cases I've been right. I get up an' I start wanderin' about this place right round it, lookin' for anything that strikes me as bein' odd or funny. I can't see a durned thing. I go through the rooms that are standin' up an' kick the furniture around a bit hopin' that something might sorta hit me, but nothin' does.

Standin' there in the hallway I get to wonderin' what really happened around this dump on the night of the explosion. Then I get an idea. They had to bury these guys somewhere around here, didn't they? I scram outa the *hacienda* an' walk down to the hut where Pedro an' the boys was hangin' out. Just near it there is a little flat sorta place with some scrub bushes round it right in the shadow of the wall. Over there I can see some wooden boards stickin' outa the ground which you can see has been disturbed. It looks to me as if I have found the graves all right.

I go over there. There are five head boards stuck up an' on each one is "Rest with God" in Spanish hacked out with a knife, an' there are the names underneath. So I reckon the names will be Jamieson, the dame, the other guy—the young feller that Pedro talked about—an' the two Indian servants.

Standin' there I start wonderin' about this buryin' business. You gotta realise that this guy Dominguez will be religious. All these guys are religious an' usually the tougher they are the more they get that way. I reckon it was funny that Pedro never said anything to me about tryin' to get a priest over here before they buried these palookas.

I give a big sigh an' I go back to the *hacienda* an' I start lookin' for a spade. I find one an' a pick stuck in a shed. I take my shirt off an' I go back to Pedro's cemetery an' I start doin' some excavatin' on the Jamieson grave. I am cursin' like hell, because believe it or not I do not like addin' grave-diggin' to such other accomplishments as I have got.

O.K. Well, I find plenty. When I have got down about two feet at the top of the Jamieson grave, just where the board is stuck up, I find that this grave is just a big fake. The ground has been dug up over about six and a half feet by four feet to look as if there was a grave there, but two feet down you can see that the diggin' has stopped. This grave is just a blind. I sit down an' give myself a rest an' a cigarette, an' do a little ponderin', then I start on the other graves.

It is an hour afterwards when I get to the last one an' that is the only real one that there is. All the rest of 'em is phony. But when I dig down a bit here I can see that this one is the goods. Maybe somebody is buried here, an' I reckon I will find out who. After another twenty minutes' diggin' I find a round board coffin. I'm gettin' a kick outa this, because when you are lookin' for graves it is sorta nice to find a real one, an' at the same time I am gettin' a nasty idea inta my head. Another ten minutes' work an' I have got the lid off this box an' I can see all I wanta see.

There is a guy in this coffin an' he is not very nice to look at because it is stickin' out a foot that when this explosion happened quite a lotta something hit him. His face an' neck are practically gone, but the clothes are American clothes. This guy was wearin' a belt—one of those Texas belts with leather pockets in 'em. When I look in the pockets I find the only thing there is on this guy. I find an Investigation Bureau identification card. It is Pepper's card. I reckon I have found Pepper all right.

I stick the identification card in my pocket an' put the boards back on top of the coffin. Then I shovel the earth back over it an' make it look as O.K. as possible.

I reckon I am sorry for Pepper, but it just shows you that you gotta be careful around here otherwise somebody blows you up at any minute.

When I have done this I ease over to the hut where Pedro usta hang out with his boys an' take a look around. There is just a few stools an' a table an' a coupla shelves, but there is a full bottle of *tequila* stuck on one of the shelves so it looks as if Pedro got out pretty quick, because I cannot see that guy goin' off an' leavin' a bottle of hooch behind unless somebody was on his tail.

I grab this bottle an' I am just about to get back to the *hacienda* when I see somethin'. Outside the door of the hut in the dust is a footprint with a small heel—I can see it plain in the moonlight—the footprint of some guy wearin' cow-boots with cuban heels. An' the prints are plain, there ain't very much dust in 'em so they're fairly fresh ones.

They lead off down to the gate in the wall an' over the scrub towards the Sierra Madre an' I lose 'em where the ground gets hard an' there ain't any alkali dust.

Well, it stands to reason that if this guy could walk so can I. Maybe there is some shack this end of the foothills an' some bozo livin' in it who can throw a spot of light on all this bezusus. I keep on walkin' for a helluva time an' then, from the top of a little hill I can see a board shack on the other side of the slope. Away to the right there is a horse staked out to a post.

I ease down the hill an' I get up to the shack sorta quiet an' look in through a cut-out window in the side. There ain't anybody in there. There is a bunk an' a wooden table an a coupla stools an' some bottles an' a coffee pot. There is a box in the corner an' some odd junk lyin' around. The place looks like a range-minder's hut, but as there ain't any range here I don't see why anybody should be tryin' to ride it.

I get around to the other side, open the door an' let some moonlight in. The place stinks of heat an' bad hamburgers, I go in an' look around. I open the box an' look at the things inside. There are some old pants an' shirts an' a coupla magazines an' a few pictures of women. These dames have got such pans that I do not wonder that this guy is livin' as far away from 'em as he can get.

I straighten up an' light myself a cigarette an' just when I am doin' this I hear the horse whinny. I ease over to the door an' look through the crack.

There is a guy comin' this way. He is a tall, thin feller in Mexican pants, a big sombrero an' a bolero coat over a blue shirt. He has got a gun belt on with an automatic stuck in it an' he is singin'.

I reckon I will talk to this guy.

I open the door an' step out sorta jaunty. I wave my hand to this bozo an' when he sees me he sorta starts an' then waves back. I start whistlin' a hot number an' start walkin' towards him nice an' easy, an' when he is good an' near I say:

"*Buenos Noches amigo*, I am from the *casa*—Señora Fernanda Martinas wishes that you should . . ."

The guy is close to me. I look over his shoulder behind him with a sorta startled expression in my eye. He swings his head around an' I bust him a mean one right on the edge of the jaw. He goes down like he was poleaxed. I pick him up an' swing him over my shoulder an' take him back to the shack.

I chuck him on the bunk an' take his belt off. I pull the gun out an' look at it. It is a .38 automatic with an F.B.I, mark on it. I will bet all the silver in Mexico to a hot sardine that this is Pepper's gun.

Outside around the back is a water butt with a skin carrier. I fill this up with the water that is as scummy as hell an' take it back an' throw it over this guy. He decides to come back to earth. He sits up on the bunk lookin' at me an' feelin' his jaw. Then he says some very rude words in Spanish.

"Listen, *gaucho*," I tell him, "I am sorta very sorry for you because I reckon that you are in a spot. It looks to me that a friend of mine has got himself very badly creased out around here an' that is a thing I do not like at all. My advice to you is to talk very fast an' plenty otherwise I am goin' to write my initials on your belly with bullets outa this gun. Sabe?"

He says he get it all right. Then he starts tellin' me a lotta hooey about how he is the sorta range-rider for the *hacienda*, that he is the feller who looks after the place, an' that he lives in this shack.

I tell him that he is a goddam liar because the water around the back is bad, an' that the horse staked out down the track has got no feed. I tell him that he has not even been livin' in this shack an' that it is a very good thing to tell the truth if he does not want to be ironed out *pronto*. I ask him where he got the gun from an' he says he bought it from a guy ten days before in Tortuala.

He starts walkin' up an' down the shack callin' on all the saints to witness that he would not tell me a lie even if somebody paid him a hundred *pesos* an' when he gets opposite the door he jumps sideways an 'scrams down towards the horse like he was bein' chased by lightnin'.

I jump outside the door an' take a nice, easy shot at this guy but I don't do any good because the gun is not loaded.

By this time this bozo has got to where the horse is staked. He unhitches the rope, swings himself on to the horse an' goes off bareback, ridin' like a fool, towards the foothills.

I watch him go an' then I start walkin' back towards the *hacienda*. This guy is a very frightened guy, an' maybe he was tellin' the truth when he says that he bought this gun in Tortuala. If he'd taken it off Pepper I reckon he woulda had a coupla clips of ammunition with it.

I get back to Pedro's shack an' grab up the bottle of *tequila*. I am not worryin' very much about this guy who has done the scrammin' act. I reckon he is a helluva way from anywhere where he could find enough of his pals to come back an' start somethin' with me. Anyhow it's a cinch that he is too scared to do anything much.

I grab the bottle an' get back to the *hacienda*. I go sneakin' around lookin' for water. After a bit I find a very cunnin' tank stuck in the inside hall wall. The tank is a quarter full an' the water tastes O.K. I fill up a pail an' a jug that I find an' go an' water the horse. Then I turn him loose on a long rope an' let him nose around lookin' for somethin' to chew on, while I sit down in the shadow by the wall an' do a little bit of quiet thinkin'.

It is a swell night. The moon is good an' everythin' around is bathed in a sorta white light. Me I get to feelin' poetic an' thinkin' about some honeypot dame I knew way back in '32 in the Texas Panhandle.

She was a sweet dame to look at an' there was only one thing wrong with her. She was such a bad-tempered baby that I have even known her try to slam a revolvin' door.

An' was that dame hard or was she? She was so tough that when I gave her a fright one night an' her heart came up inta her mouth it chipped bits off her back teeth.

But she taught me plenty. She wised me up to the fact that while a guy is sittin' around strainin' his brain tryin' to think out a situation an' act sorta logical a dame will just do some old thing right away just because her instinct tells her to.

An' she practised what she preached because whiles I was sittin' around one night lookin' sorta lovin' towards the room where I thought she was sleepin' like a bird, an' wonderin' just how I could ditch her without her raisin' the countryside, she was around the other side of the house puttin' rattlesnakes inside my ridin' boots, which will show you guys that the instinct of a woman is a thing you should not take a chance on, especially when she thinks that you have got sorta tired of her general outlines an' are seriously considerin' goin' in for somethin' with a little more streamline.

I do not wish to try an' teach any of you boys anything about dames because maybe you have been in trouble yourself but I wish to say here an' now that nine hundred an' ninety-nine guys out of every thousand believe that all the mommas they happen across are just sweet, soft an' lovin' babies, an' the thousandth guy is probably in prison anyway and would not believe in fairies even if he was out.

But dames are not at all like that. No, Sir! A dame is O.K. so long as she thinks that you are so hypnotised by what she has got that you are shavin' yourself three times a day an' wonderin' if even your best friends wouldn't tell you. But directly she gets the idea inta her little blonde head that you are thinkin' up some deep an' heavy plot for a quick shake-off, or if she even sees you lookin' at a railway departure list, then I am tellin' you mugs that this dame will get so taut that she will make William the Conqueror complete in chain mail, plate-armour an' wearin' the kitchen sink for luck, look like the big sissy who asked for a strawberry sundae at the Ironworkers' annual beer frolic.

Sittin' there with my back against the *adobe* wall, takin' a suck at the *tequila* bottle an' then havin' a go at the water jug, I start gettin' some slants on Fernanda, who looks to me like she has got a lot of instinct an' is a logical baby as well.

First of all as well as bein' a nifty looker she has got what it takes in brains. I start goin' over my conversation with her an' sorta wonderin' why she pulled that gag on me with the cigarette case that was made like an automatic. It might justa been fun but you would have to have a funny sorta sense of humour to pull that one on a guy who is thinkin' that maybe somebody around here would be likely to take a shot at him.

But supposin' you take another angle on it. O.K. Well, first of all Fernanda pulled that act right at the very time that I was liable to begin askin' her a lotta questions about this business, about the places that she an' Dominguez got around together an' about Pepper. But you gotta realise that when she pulled that fake gun act on me I got jittery—an' who wouldn't? It sorta put everything outa my head, an' from that time onwards Fernanda was playin' it the way *she* wanted. She was the one who was doin' all the talkin', tellin' me what she thought Pedro would be likely to do an' where he would be lookin' for me.

An' she wanted me to get out to this place quick. She was sorta keen that I should come out to this *hacienda* an' not stick around waitin' to see if Pedro come back again. She knew durn well that there wasn't any real reason why I shouldn't wait for this guy to come back. I had a gun too an' if it comes to shootin' I reckon I can be as good as Pedro any day in the week. In fact I would go so far as to say that I would shoot the pants off this guy with anything from a sub-Thomson gun to a little boy's .15 pearl-handled Special.

I'm goin' to tell you somethin' else too. I got away from the *casa* in such a hurry that I come away without my gun. You gotta realise I have left my Luger on that table where I put it when I took it outa my shirt. All of which goes to show you that a "G" man can be just as human as the next guy when it comes to a show-down, an' that Mark Antony wasn't the only guy who forgot to pack his artillery when Cleopatra got busy on him with one of them porous plaster kisses.

So what. Well, I reckon I got it doped out all right. Fernanda wants me to get out to this dump good an' quick. She don't want me to be around when Pedro shows up, but she wants me to get back there afterwards an' this can be for *two* reasons an' I'm goin' to allow for 'em both bein' right because you never know where dames are concerned.

First of all she mighta played it that way because she is really nuts about me an' she couldn't bear the idea of me gettin' shot up by the Dominguez guy. She mighta thought that she could get him off on some false scent by the time I come back so that we could go inta another huddle an' then I could scram back across the line inta New Mexico an' she would meet me later when I have got a little time for playin' around with a beautiful doll.

The other side of the story is that she wanted to get me outa the way because she thought that if Pedro come back I would either crease him or bust him one over the dome, rope him up, an' then get him over the State Line inta New Mexico to answer a few questions.

Because you guys are goin' to agree with me about one thing an' that is that the stuff she told me about the way she joined up with Pedro to get away from her wicked husband don't sorta ring true. First of all you guys will say that a dame who has got enough nerve to play around the way Fernanda handled me would not be afraid of her husband even if she was married to a bad-tempered alligator. That dame coulda dealt with the situation O.K. The second thing is that if she had enough dough to bribe Pedro to take her away then she had enough dough to scram inta the U.S. territory an' send a right royal raspberry to her husband by registered post.

All of which will show you people that just because I am kissin' a dame I am not always believin' the baby, an' if you pull a quick come-back that I should not kiss dames who I do not believe then I will tell you that I do not believe melons but I like 'em an' so I have 'em when I get the chance, an' what would you guys do, hey?

It is ten o'clock when I wake up an' the sun is boilin' up. I look round the *hacienda*. It is just the same as it was before. I reckon I have been a bit of a mug sleepin' in this place like this with an empty gun. Anybody coulda handed it out to me pronto if they'd wanted to. But then I have always been a guy who likes sleepin'.

I get to thinkin' about Pepper's gun. I take it out and look in the butt expectin' to find an empty space where the ammunition clip oughta be. Well, there ain't an empty space. The clip is there all right. When I try to pull it out I find it's sorta stuck hard an' I have to waggle it about plenty before I get it free. When I pull it out a bit of paper comes out with it. This bit of paper has been stuck between the side of the clip an' the clip-channel in the gun. It mighta been put there because the clip didn't fit tight.

I take a look inside the clip. There ain't any shells in it which is a funny thing because I can't sorta understand Pepper havin' an empty clip in his gun. Then I take a look at the bit of paper.

It's just a bit of cream-coloured paper that's been torn off the bottom of a sheet. It's about three-quarters of an inch wide an' there's a name written on it—*Zellara*. I get to wonderin' who or what Zellara is an' I reckon that maybe it is the name of some place around this country. Maybe Pepper made a note of it an' stuck it in his gun-butt because that would be a place where nobody would look. Still you woulda thought he coulda remembered the name without keepin' it.

Or maybe it was just any old bit of paper that he'd stuck in to keep the ammunition clip tight. I put it in my bill-fold an' stick the gun back in my hip.

I do a little calculation. I reckon if I get away now I can be back at Fernanda's place by night, although I do not like the idea of goin' across the desert at midday, when the heat is liable to burn the pants off you. However, that's the way it is.

I take a last look round, saddle up the horse, fill my water bottle from the tank at the *hacienda,* an' scram. Me—I am very glad that there was that water there otherwise I mightn't have been so good, because, although you may have read in books about travellers on the desert squeezin' the water outa cactus spines an' livin' on that, you can take it from me it ain't so hot. I've done it.

I have plenty time to think durin' the day. I get to workin' out all sorts of schemes that I am goin' to do if I get back to the *casa* an' find that Pedro is there or if he ain't. I have always found it a very good thing to do to work things out beforehand just so's you can do something quite different when the time comes.

It is near midnight when I sight the *casa.* I pick up the desert road about a mile from the house. Somebody is there now, because I can see a light burnin'. But I am the wise guy. I walk the horse— who is not feelin' so good himself—the last three-quarters of a mile, get off the road an' come up by the west side of the *casa.* I corral the horse around by some cactus clump an' I start doin' a big scoutin' act around the back, just seeing what is doin', an' right away I find something that is very interestin'.

There is thick dust there an' I can see that some guy has been by this way in a car. I reckon this car comes from Tampapa. I can see the tyre treads easy in the moonlight which interest me still some more, because I notice that the near side rear tyre is an odd one with a double diamond tread.

They've been usin' my car all right.

I do a little bitta quiet figurin' out. It looks to me like Pedro or some friend of his has found the car where I left her, an' has got some guy from Tampapa to fix her up with a new carburettor, after which they have driven it out here.

I take a look around to see if I can see any sign of it, but I can't see a thing. I get up an' start walkin' towards the back door of the *casa*. It is all dark there an' I can't hear anything. I get the sort feelin' that I would be very glad if I had a full gun on me because I am not quite certain as to whether Dominguez is goin' to be stickin' around there waitin' for me or not. I reckon he is the guy who brought my car along here.

There is a wire door in the back of the house. I push this open an' step inside. I listen. I still can't hear anythin' at all. This strikes me as bein' funny because I reckon I oughta hear that Indian girl snorin' somewhere around. I gumshoe along the passage until I can see the light shinin' under the crack of the door that is on the right of the hall, the door of the room that looks out over the desert road, where I was with Fernanda. I get up to the door an' I listen.

After a bit I get my hand on the door-knob an' start turnin' it very gently. When I have got it right round, I hold my breath an' give the door a little push. Then I wait.

I still can't hear anything. I push the door a bit more an' I get my head in. I look around. Pedro is sittin' in a chair with his back to me. He is asleep. I reckon this guy was sittin' there waitin' for me to come up the desert road. I can't see right in front of him so I don't know whether he has gotta gun in his hand. It looks to me durned funny that Pedro should be waitin' like that with a light on. The proper thing for him to have done woulda been to switch it off an' then he woulda seen me comin' an' I couldn't have seen him.

I think I will try a bluff. I pull out Pepper's empty gun.

"Take it easy, bozo," I tell him. "One move outa you an' I'm goin' to blow the top of your head inta Arizona. Just put your hands up an' keep 'em there."

Nothin' happens. He just don't move. An' all of a sudden I get a big idea. I get the idea that Pedro has got himself ironed out.

I walk around in front of the chair an' boy am I right or am I? He is lyin' back in the chair an' his eyes are lookin' out over the veranda onto the desert. He looks surprised, which is sorta natural because somebody has given it to this guy twice—once through the head an' once through the top of the chest.

Lyin' on the floor in front of him is my gun—the Luger that I left behind. I pick it up an' slip out the clip. There are two shells missin'.

I put the gun in my shirt an' I go over to the sideboard an' mix myself a little drink an' give myself a cigarette. Then I go an' sit down in a chair an' look at Pedro an' ruminate.

The first shot that went inta him was the one in the chest, an' it was a durn close range. There is the burn of the powder all around the bullet hole in his near-white shirt. I reckon that shot knocked Pedro over an' when he was gettin' up he got the second one through the dome.

Me—I think life can be funny because for the past eight hours or so I have been wonderin' about Pedro and who was goin' to shoot who an' I was just wastin' my brains because it looks to me like somebody else has done it an' I am takin' six to four with one an' all that this somebody was little Fernanda.

I look at Pedro an' I get sorry for him if you know what I mean. Here is a real bad man—a desert sheik. One of these self-made guys who have worked their way up from the bottom, where they haven't got anythin', to the top where they are still owin' themselves a bit.

I start doin' a big Sherlock Holmes act. I start a big reconstruction scene which is what the ace detective in the book always does when somethin' happens.

I think that maybe Fernanda was sittin' in the big chair lookin' over the desert wonderin' about me when she hears a car drivin' up around the back.

I see her gettin' up sorta wistful an' lookin' towards the door of the room when Pedro busts in. Pedro is all steamed up an' goes chargin' around the place like a prize bull on *fiesta* day, spillin' the beans an' sayin' what happened. He asks Fernanda if she knows anything about me.

Fernanda says you can search her but she don't know a durn thing, but bein' a wise little dame she plants herself right in front of the little table where I have left the Luger lyin'.

Pedro then asks whether anybody has been around here an' Fernanda says no there ain't been a whiff of anybody.

Pedro then says oh yeah an' that she is a so-an'-so liar because he has seen where some guy has got the horse outa the corral an' he can see the horse's trail all around the back in the dust. He tells Fernanda that she is a double-crossin' daughter of the devil an' that he is now goin' to slit her throat from ear to ear an' he don't mean perhaps.

Fernanda smiles at him sorta wistful again an' just as he is comin' towards her she puts her hand behind her, grabs the Luger, an' gives him a free ticket to the never-never land outa the business end.

Pedro flops over an' tries to get up so she gives him one through the hatstand for luck. After which she calls in the Indian girl an' they stick him up in the chair facin' the veranda.

Fernanda then gets around an' packs her grip an' scrams off in my car, but before she does this she goes around turnin' all the lights off except the one in the room where Pedro is an' she leaves that one on so's I can see, as I come ridin' up the desert road, that my little pal Fernanda has pulled one for Lemmy Caution an' ironed out the wicked Pedro for him, an' saved his life in fourteen different positions.

This is what they call a reconstruction an' is what the ace detective does, an' he is always right in the last chapter if you get as far as that.

An' don't you guys think that this reconstruction is swell?

If you do then all I can say is you must be nuts because I think it's lousy.

CHAPTER FIVE
THE BRUNETTE BABY

IT IS seven o'clock when I pull inta Scattle's Office in Phoenix, Arizona. I have called him on long distance directly I got over the Mexican line inta New Mexico an' he has been waitin' around for me.

I have already told you guys that Scattle is the Agent-in-Charge of the Federal Bureau Field office in Phoenix. He is a very intelligent guy an' don't waste any time.

He asks me right away if I found out anything about Pepper an' I tell him yes that Pepper is as dead as a cutlet an' is pushin' up cactus seeds under four foot of desert earth in a wooden box out at the *hacienda* near the Sierra Madre.

"All right," he says. "Well, take a look at this. It'll tell you plenty."

He throws a letter across the table to me. When I pick it up I see that this letter is addressed from "Mexico City." The second thing is that I see it is dated five weeks ago an' it is in Pepper's handwritin'. It says:

"Dear Scattle,

Have I run into something or have I! I reckon you thought I was nuts when I called you on long distance two days ago and told you I was making for Mexico and that I couldn't say anything else right then.

Well, I couldn't. And for the same reasons I can't use a telephone now but I'm on to something so big that it will make your eyes pop.

I'm getting action to-night and I hope to contact you within the matter of a week or so from the nearest telephone or telegraph office to the Sierra Mojada hills (Caliempo district). In the meantime you might help along by getting some dope for me on a guy called Jamieson. I do not know anything about this guy except that he is an Englishman and . . ."

The letter, which has been written in ink up to here, stops dead an' written underneath in pencil is:

"I've got to stop right now. I'll get an official report off to you to-night or to-morrow."

It is signed by Pepper. I throw it back across the desk to Scattle. He opens a drawer an' brings out a type-script report.

"Here, Lemmy," he says, "read this. Maybe it's going to tell you something."

I get hold of the papers an' I see that they are a duplicate instruction from the Director of the Federal Bureau at Washington to all Agents in Charge of Field Offices in Texas, New Mexico, South California and Arizona:

"Federal Government,
Telephone: Priority: Urgent.

The immediate and urgent attention of all Agents in Charge of Field Offices of the Federal Bureau of Investigation in the New Mexico, South California, Arizona and Texas districts is called to the following facts:

Under an arrangement made nine months ago between the Board of Admiralty of the British Government and the U.S. Government one John Ernest Jamieson, a scientific research chemist employed by the British Admiralty, was to work in contact with Hedley V.

Grearson, a research chemist in the U.S. Navy Yard, on a new war gas which had been discovered by these two gentlemen, and on the development of which their respective Governments had agreed they should work together.

The intensive danger of leakage regarding the experiments of these two chemists by agents of interested Governments was foreseen both by the British and the U.S. Governments, and for this reason it was arranged that the scientific work should be carried out in a district the least likely to come under the observation of such agents. Under the pretext that Mr. Jamieson considered starting a ranch, a hacienda and ranch lands were secured in a desolate desert spot in the Sierra Madre district.

Within ten days of arrival there Mr. Jamieson had disappeared. Mr. Grearson, the U.S. chemist who was on his way to join Mr. Jamieson, and who was last seen near the Texas State Line, has also disappeared. It is essential that whilst the news of these disappearances should be kept absolutely secret, Agents in Charge of Field Offices in the district should spare no endeavour to trace the missing persons."

The report goes on to give a lotta details about these guys, what they look like and stuff like that. Underneath there is a second instruction from the Director about me which says:

"To Agents in Charge of Field Offices of the Federal Bureau of Investigation in the New Mexico, Arizona, South California and Texas districts:

Special Agent Lemuel H. Caution has been assigned to proceed into Mexico ostensibly for the purpose of buying a ranch, under cover as an American citizen Wylie T. Hellup. His investigation will include the disappearance of Special Agent Pepper, who the Director now has reason to believe had probably contacted some angle on the disappearance of the chemists Jamieson and Grearson and had decided to investigate on his own account. Special Agents in Charge will therefore cease individual operations on this matter except in so far as they link up with those of Special Agent Caution.

Special Agent Caution who, on original instructions, will at some time contact a Field Office of the Federal Bureau of Investigation in any or all of the beforementioned districts, should be supplied with the enclosed information, such technical and financial assistance as he may require, and will thereafter report direct to Headquarters in Washington."

Scattle throws a cigarette across to me an' grins.

"I'd like to know how you're goin' to play this one, Lemmy," he says. "It looks a tough one to me. Pepper just disappears into thin air and so do these other boys and you've got the whole world to look for 'em in. Boy, I wish you luck!"

I don't say anythin'. I just do some quiet thinkin'. I reckon I got one or two ideas bustin' around in my head but I don't think that I'm goin' to discuss 'em right now, because I have always thought that when you got an idea you oughta sorta let it simmer around an' stew up for a bit.

"This is the idea I got, Scattle," I tell him. "I reckon that whatever it was started Pepper off on this business was somethin' he found out in Mexico City which you will allow is a place where anythin' can happen. So I am goin' to Mexico City an' take a look around. Also I am goin' as Mr. Hellup an' I am goin' on bein' Mr. Hellup until I get some idea that it ain't goin' to be too dangerous to be Lemmy Caution."

"O.K.," he says. "It's your job, Lemmy. You draw what money you want and beat it. Report when you want to direct to Washington."

"That suits me," I tell him. "I'll be seein' you."

I scram.

I have always had a sorta soft spot for Mexico City.

Last time I was here was when I was jumpin' around with that dame Paulette Benito who is right now doin' twenty years an' I hope not likin' it on that Palm Springs business.

It's a great place an' if you gotta have your wits about you, well, life is like that.

I get off the "plana" at the airport an' take a taxi to the Peranza Hotel which is a sweet spot to stick around in an' where the manicure dames are such honeys to look at that you would think that you had bust into the streamline department of the Garden of Eden on the boy friends' visitin' day.

I give myself a bath an' change my clothes. I have got a swell new custom-built suit an' some silk shirts that a dame in Chattanooga gave me because she said she always liked silk next her skin. By the

time I have had a shower an' got inta this stuff I am lookin' like all
the flowers in May and feelin' one hundred per cent.

I telephone down for a bottle of rye an' I sit around in my room
an' do a little figurin' out, because I reckon that note of Pepper's—
the one he wrote to Scattle—an' the report thing from the Director,
is givin' me somethin' to get my teeth inta.

Everythin' is not always what it seems as the lady said when she
poured the prussic acid inta her boy friend's sarsaparilla, but all the
same I am doin' a bit of heavy guessin' an' hopin' that I am goin' to
come out right.

You guys know as much about this business as I do. Maybe you
know more because perhaps you are brainy guys who are on to somethin' that I have missed.

Right now I am not worryin' myself about Pedro an' Fernanda an'
the stuff that happened down in the Sierra Madre. I am just concernin'
myself with what started Pepper off on this job.

First of all he was in Mexico City an' he gets a line on this business an' makes up his mind that he is goin' to take a jump pronto for
the Sierra Mojada foothills. He hasta do this so quick that he hasn't
even got time to write Scattle the full story. He just telephones him
in the first place that he is goin' an' then afterwards writes a letter
sayin' just the same thing and finishin' it off in a hurry.

Now this guy Pepper has got brains an' havin' called through
to Scattle in the first place he ain't likely to write a letter to say just
what he has said on the telephone again. No, Sir, he started writin'
that letter because by then he had found some more out an' he was
goin' to tell Scattle all about it.

But somethin' happened just when he was writin' the letter,
somethin' that made him close it down right then because he hadta
do somethin' very quick.

I reckon that somethin' happened that made Pepper scram very
quick outa Mexico City an' make for the Sierra Mojada pronto. Maybe
he hadta jump a train or somethin' like that.

But whatever it was made him take a run-out before finishin' off
the letter to Scattle happened in Mexico City, it musta done, so that
is point number one.

The second point is that I am bettin' a phony double eagle that
I have got that the thing he got out for was because he had heard

that Pedro Dominguez was in the Sierra Mojada foothills, hidin' up after his last bit of trouble, an' Pepper wanted to get hold of this guy before Pedro scrammed off somewhere else.

An' if I am right here then somebody in Mexico City musta known about Pedro bein' down there an' musta phoned through to Pepper or told him, an' told him that he's got to scram out quick if he wants to contact Pedro.

Now I suggest to you people that the story that Pedro told me about findin' Pepper's Federal Bureau Identification card in his ridin' boot is a lotta hooey. Pepper is not such a sap as to put his card there just where some mug is goin' to look for it. So maybe the same guy that told Pepper where Pedro was wised up the Dominguez bird that Pepper was comin'. I reckon Pedro knew that Pepper was an F.B.I. agent before he even saw him.

All we know after that is that Pepper got himself bumped off down at the *hacienda* by somebody or other an' that Pedro has got himself very nicely ironed out in Fernanda's *casa*, an' that it is all the beer in Harlem to a ten cent bottle of hair tonic guaranteed to grow hair on a castle wall that Fernanda was the baby who shot him, either because she wanted to stop him takin' a mean shot at me or for some other reason best known to that very swell an' exclusive baby.

We also know that Fernanda is a nifty piece of streamline carryin' a one hundred per cent range of samples in what it takes, that she can kiss like the dame who invented King Solomon's own correspondence course in "How to get your man without a false bust bodice" an' that she has also got so much smartness concealed behind that Spanish pompadour of hers that she woulda made President Roosevelt's brain trust look like the annual general meetin' of the International Half-Wits Society.

So what!

Well, I figure it out this way. I figure that Pepper was just blowin' around Mexico City an' that he got wise to somethin' an' if I know anythin' of Pepper's technique it was through a dame an' if I know anythin' about dames it is that the ones with the most distinguished *chassis*. who are next to the bad men, are the little ladies who play around the big night spots.

So it looks to me as if Lemmy Caution otherwise Mr. Hellup is goin' to be a big play-boy runnin' around an' seein' if he can find a dame who has got one more curve than the rest of 'em.

An' I am tellin' you guys that maybe my system is all wrong. Maybe if I was the big detective I would sit down an' concentrate an' work out a clue that would be so hot that you would haveta handle it with tweezers, but I am not like that. When in doubt I always do the thing that is stickin' out right in front of my nose an' the thing I can see there at the moment is the telephone. So I grab it an' tell the hotel desk to send me up a very intelligent manicure to do my fingernails because I have always found that what the manicure dame don't know about a dump could be written in shorthand on the edge of a dime an' even then you couldn't see it.

It is twelve o'clock an' a sweet night, an' I am walkin' down the main stem ponderin'. The little manicure dame who fixed my finger-nails wised me up plenty. This dame has told me that the big night spot is the Estancia Elvira which is the tops in its line.

This Elvira is a helluva big show with gardens, an' two hot restau-rants, a coupla big time bands and a ritzy floor-show. There are plenty dames of all sorts an' sizes around there, but they are not the ordin-ary run-around girls. Not on your life. They are dames who are nice an' cultured. They have got class an' even if one of 'em does pull a fast one now an' again—well, it always amuses the other guys—the ones who don't get stung.

As for the dames in the floor show all these are hand picked mommas who are such nifty-lookin' honeybelles that they get married about four times a year. The manicure girl tells me that one of these babies has been married so much that every time she brings home a new husband the housekeeper asks this guy to put his name in the visitors' book.

I ease along nice an' quiet. It's a helluva night an' Mexico City is just wakin' up. The roadway is full of cars an' guys, an' the women in the autos are such swell-lookers that any time I can get some vacation I am comin' around here just to get my throat cut quick for nothin'.

Away on the right standin' back in a big sorta courtyard place I can see the Estancia de Elvira with the electrics twinklin' outside.

I walk down there an' turn in. As I am walkin' across the big *patio* missin' the cars that are comin' this way for the supper show I look up at the front of the place an' I stand there with my mouth open just as if somebody had smacked me a hot one across the pan with a wet fish.

An' why not! Because stuck up in electric lights right across the front of the place is the name of the dame who is starrin' in the floor show an' that name is *Zellara*—the same name that was written on the bit of paper that I found in the clip chamber of Pepper's gun.

Boy, this is my lucky day.

I go inta the restaurant an' sit down at a table an' order a hot dish an' some lager beer an' I start doin' a big reasonin' out act with myself.

Here is what I think. You gotta remember that I said I thought it was funny for Pepper to keep that bit of paper with the name on it when he coulda remembered it easy—you can't very well forget a name like Zellara—well now I reckon that I know why he did keep it, an' I will soon know if I am right or wrong.

I reckon that Pepper knew this Zellara. He probably contacted her right here in Mexico City an' maybe she was the dame who gave him the hot tip that sent him runnin' inta Mexico without time to finish writin' that letter to Scattle.

But whether or not she knew that he was an F.B.I. agent I don't know, an' I can't take a chance on that. I have just got to go on bein' Mr. Hellup an' try to find out what's goin'.

I sit there rackin' my brains to find out some angle for gettin' next to this baby an' gettin' her to talk very cold turkey to me but you gotta realise that this ain't an easy thing when you don't even know the dame.

I get the idea that this Zellara mighta been a bit stuck on Pepper or that he thought she knew somethin' an' made a play for her and worked a big sex-appeal act which came off one hundred per cent.

The thing that I wanta find out is whether this Zellara dame knew Pedro, but it ain't very much good askin' her because if she did an' is not on the up-an'-up she ain't goin' to tell me is she?

Then all of a sudden an idea hits me right in the back of the dome like I was struck by lightning. It is a nervy sorta idea an' one that might work very bad for me if it don't come off. But if it does come off . . . oh boy. . . .

I reckon I am goin' to take a chance on two things. I am goin' to take a chance that this Zellara baby is like all big floor show babies an' gets around the frontier towns so much an' meets so many guys who fall for 'em that they don't even remember ten per cent of the mugs. I am goin' to be one of these mugs.

The second thing is that I am goin' to take a chance that Pepper did a vampin' act with Zellara to get information outa her. Maybe she was a bit stuck on him. Anyhow I am goin' to play it that way an' trust to luck.

I pay my bill an' ease outa the restaurant an' go onto the dance floor. The place is a honey of a place, all white an' green an' gold, with soft shaded lights, an' the dames are an eyeful. Boy, I would like to have time on hand an' about ten thousand smackers, an' just stick around a place like this seein' which dame knew most of the answers.

All the men are wearin' tuxedos but they still look like tough babies, an' there is that sorta soft undercurrent of chit-chat that you can always hear in a dump like that.

I sit down an' order myself a drink an' make a signal to some guy who looks like one of the floor managers. He comes over.

I start talkin' nice an' easy to this bozo. I tell him that this is the first time I have been in Mexico City, an' that it is certainly just what the doctor ordered. I tell him that I been doin' some odd cattle an' horse tradin' around the Sierras an' that things ain't so good an' that I reckon that I might as well take it easy an' spend a little dough an' take a peek at a doll or two.

He says why not?

I ask him about the floor show an' he says it is very good an' then I ease the conversation around to Zellara. I say that I saw a dame with the same monicker singin' in some small towns around the Aguas Calientes an' he says that this is certain because she has worked all over the place in all sorts of dumps an' that she ain't been in the big-time for long. He says she is one helluva success.

Then I say I got it. I say that I saw this dame doin' a swell act in Manzanillo when I was in the banana business an' he says that is O.K. because she was workin' here at the Casa Mexicali when he was assistant manager there. I say ain't that funny an' don't it just show you how small the world is an' he says you bet it does an' scrams.

The place has filled up; the band—an' those boys could play I'm tellin' you—is handin' out some hot stuff, an' waiters an' people are rushin' about the place an' some of the dames who are comin' into this dump have got some frocks on 'em that would make a Chicago fence jump in the lake outa sheer rage.

Then, all of a sudden, there is a roll on the drums an' a helluva chord on an' the floor-show starts. The big curtain that is swung across the dance floor goes away to one side an' one of the niftiest legged choruses I have ever lamped starts in to work a number that would have woke up a corpse.

Me . . . I am gettin' very interested.

I sit back. After a few minutes the first number is over. Some little curtains at the back part an' out comes Zellara. Here is a dame who has got somethin'. She is a real Mexican. Little, slim an' made like a piece of indiarubber. She has got a swell shape an' a lovely face with a pair of the naughtiest lookin' brown eyes I have ever seen in my life. She sings a song an' goes into a rumba dance. This baby has got what it takes all right.

Me, I have seen dames swing it before but I reckon that if this Zellara hadda been loose in the Garden of Eden, Adam woulda taken a quick run-out powder an' the serpent woulda been found hidin' behind the rose bushes with his fingers crossed. At the risk of repeatin' myself I will tell you guys that this dame is a one hundred per cent exclusive custom-built 1939 model fitted with all the speed gadgets an' guaranteed not to skid goin' round the corners. Me, I have often thought that if I hadda dame like this Zellara. . . .

But why should I bring that up?

When she dances over my way I look her over carefully. There is a lotta intelligence in her face an' she's got a nice, firm little jaw. I reckon this dame could be a bit tough if she wanted to.

Well, I will try anythin' once.

I nod to a waiter who is standin' near my table an' ask this guy to bring me a piece of paper and an envelope. Then I write her a note:

"Dear Zellara,

Maybe you'll be surprised to know that an old friend of yours, nobody else but Wylie T. Hellup who met you in Manzanillo when you was working at the Casa Mexicali is sitting here in front bursting with admiration for your show.

*And not only that but I've got something durned important to
talk to you about—something serious. Can I see you tonight?*
Love and kisses,

Wylie."

I stick this in the envelope an' address it to her an' ask the waiter
guy to send it around back when her number's over. I give him a
dollar bill an' he says O.K. he'll look after it.

Pretty soon she finishes her number an' hops off. I give myself
another drink an' stick around. After a bit the waiter guy comes back
with a note from her. I open it. It says:

"Amigo,
*How marvellous to meet any of my old friends from Manzanillo.
I have to do another show in half an hour's time, but after that if
you like to give me supper somewhere else that would be wonderful.*
Adios, Zellara."

I slip the waiter another two bucks an' think it is cheap at the
price. I get up an' go inta the men's room. There ain't anybody there.
I take out my billfold an' slip out the piece of paper that I found in
the clip chamber in Pepper's gun. I compare it with the note I have
just got from Zellara. The handwriting is the same!

O.K. So now we know why Pepper kept that bit of paper. He tore
it off a letter or a note that he probably got from Zellara, an' he kept
it so that some time in future if he wanted to he could check on her
handwritin'; an' the only reason he would wanta do this would be
because he would think that somewhere in some police record there
would be a specimen of this baby's handwritin'!

I get my hat an' I go out. I walk back towards the hotel an' do a
little quiet thinkin'. I have gotta move from now on. I reckon it is no
good beatin' about the bush. It is stickin' out a foot that this Zellara
had somethin' to do with Pepper's goin' down inta the Sierra an'
meetin' up with Pedro, an' you can bet your sweet an' holy life that
she wasn't in this job on her own, that there was somebody behind
her an' there is only one way that I reckon I can find this out.

When I get back to the hotel I go to my room an' telephone for a
bell-hop. After a bit a guy comes up. He is not a bad lookin' guy. He
looks smart. I tell him that when I blow outa Mexico City I am goin'

way up inta the silver district, an' the spot I am goin' to is not a very healthy spot. I tell him that I wanta get me a little hand gun, one of them very small ones. Does he know where I could get a gun like this? He says yeah an' he tells me the name of a dump where I can buy one. He also says if it will be any use to me he will ring through to this dump which is owned by a pal of his, an' tell him I am comin' round. I say this is swell.

I then slip this guy five bucks an' ask him if he has got some other pal in Mexico City who is a very intelligent guy an' who maybe is in the garage business, the sorta guy who does not ask too many questions an' who would like to earn himself fifty bucks. He don't haveta think at all. He says sure he knows a guy an' that it is his cousin, a feller called Starita, who is a nice guy an' has a garage on the Calle Ferdinando. I say O.K. an' that after he has phoned through to the gun guy he can telephone through to his cousin an' say I'm comin' round to see him. He says O.K. an' I slip him another five spot.

I go downstairs an' I ease around to this place he has told me an' I get the gun. It is a little blue steel .22 pop gun—a seven shot automatic, a very nice little gun provided you hit the feller in the right place with it, but small enough for what I want.

I go back to the hotel, an' strap on my shoulder holster with the Luger in it under my arm. Then I ring the desk for a piece of adhesive tape. When the bell-hop brings this up an' scrams, I take the little .22 automatic an' I stick the barrel end in the top of my sock so that my garter grip goes over it an' holds it. I cut a thin piece of the adhesive tape off an' stick it over the butt end of the gun an' on to my leg on each side so that I have got it fixed so that while I can walk with this gun all right an' nobody would know it was there, I can grab it out just by pullin' my trouser leg up an' maybe tearin' a piece of skin off in the process.

I then ease around an' see the garage guy on the Calle Ferdinando.

This guy is intelligent all right. I tell him just what I want him to do an' make him repeat it so's he knows it an' don't get anythin' wrong, after which I slip this guy twenty-five bucks an' say that if he will come round to my hotel tomorrow mornin' he will find another twenty-five in an envelope at the desk if he has done the job properly. He says O.K. he will fix it.

He ain't a bit surprised because no guy in Mexico City is ever surprised at anything.

You're tellin' me!

CHAPTER SIX
CAN I TAKE IT?

IT IS two o'clock when I blow back to the Estancia de Elvira an' go around to the artistes' entrance an' ask for Zellara. When I go inta her dressin' room I get wise to the fact that this Zellara is as good a looker off stage as she is on.

One time when I was in England on the van Zelden case some guy said a dame was a "pocket Venus." Well, I reckon this Zellara is a "pocket Venus." She is like a little statue of the real thing; but boy, is everything in proportion or is it?

As I stand there lampin' this baby I don't think that I have ever seen so much honey done up in one bundle before. I reckon Zellara would start some biological urge workin' in the old gentleman who said that he would rather get married to a rattlesnake than a dame.

She has got her hair done up in Spanish fashion with a high comb an' a mantilla, an' she is wearin' a flame coloured frock that would knock your eye right out.

You gotta realise that I am a bit jittery myself because as you guys know I have never seen this dame before to-night in my life an' this fast stuff I have pulled on her about meetin' her in Manzanillo is all very well providin' she don't remember that she didn't.

She looks me over very slow an' quiet, an' then she looks up at me with one hand restin' on her hip an' she says:

"Wylie, honey, is eet so good seeing you again?"

I told you that she has a sweet little voice that is like a bird f an' when she calls me Honey I feel that sorta shivery feelin' I have when I get the idea that I have registered with a dame. I go towards her an' I put my hand out sorta casual in case she just wants to shake hands. But she don't. She gets hold of my hand an' she sorta pulls herself towards me, an' the next thing I know she has got her face up against mine an' I am kissin' her like I was a Robert Taylor close-up.

I am tellin' you mugs that it was such a helluva kiss that when she took her mouth away from mine it was like tearin' porous plaster off grandpa.

"Well, kiddo," I say, "is this good or is it, seein' you again like this? I reckon they was good times we had in Manzanillo."

I She takes a gold cigarette case off her make-up table, gives herself a cigarette an' throws one to me.

"Ver' good times," she says. "You remember the night, Wylie—the night that eet took t'ree four beeg men to t'row you out of the Casa Mexicali, wiz Zellara ronning round next morning to the police station to get you free." She raises her eyes an' looks up to heaven. "*Caramba!* Were you a madman!"

I think I'd better turn this line of conversation off, otherwise I am goin' to get myself in bad.

"O.K., baby," I tell her. "Those days are gone but the present is always with us, so where do we go from here?"

She puts her head on one side.

"There is a ver' nice place I know, Wylie," she says. "El Doro. We go there. We eat, we drink, we talk about . . ." she looks at me sorta arch—"what we shall do to-morrow."

I grin at her.

"That's O.K. by me," I tell her, "although I'm more interested in what we're goin' to do before breakfast."

"Come, beeg boy," she says.

We grab a cab outside an' drive round to this El Doro. It looks to me as if everythin' is swell. If I have a bitta luck to-night maybe I am goin' to get next to something.

I start working out a sorta time-table in my mind. It is just past two in the mornin', an' while two in the mornin' don't mean a thing in Mexico City, I don't want to leave things too late, because people get sorta tired an' when they're tired they don't do the things they do when they're feelin' good.

When we get around to El Doro the Manager, who knows Zellara, rushes around gettin' us a table in a corner away from everybody. This is a quiet, swell place with a very nice guitar band up on a balcony that don't disturb you when you wanta talk.

I order a meal, some champagne for Zellara and a bottle of rye for myself, an' while we're eatin' it we talk plenty. She tells me what she has been doin', about the places she's been playin' in. I just listen an' don't say much.

Lookin' across the table at this baby I see that there is something very attractive about this Zellara.

First of all she is a natural sorta kid. She eats an' drinks an' laughs an' looks you straight in the eye. In point of fact I will go so far as to say that this baby is the sorta baby that any guy would say was one hundred per cent on the up-an'-up. He would say to himself that this was a dame who could be trusted, that this is the sorta jane who would not pull a fast one on anybody, just because she is one of them straight-thinkin' natural sorta children of the sun, who just goes along dancin' an' singin' and takin' what's comin' to her on the chin.

Boy, am I poetic guy or am I?

Well, that is what the ordinary bozo is goin' to think about Zellara, but me, I have met too many dames to be taken in by what they look like. I have found that you can very often know a lot about a dame by lookin' at her face an' her ankles. If a dame has got a swell face an' one hundred per cent ankles she *always* gets inta trouble, an' if she has only got sweet ankles she is still a potential menace to a lotta guys.

It is the good lookers who cause the trouble, the reason being that they are good lookers, because you have probably figured out for yourself that the dame who has got a pair of legs like stove-pipes, the same size all the way up an' down, is the dame who is what they call a *good* dame, the one who leads the *"Down with the Men"* campaign, an' spends her off-time lookin' through the keyhole inta the kitchen to see if the cook is takin' a tumble with the ice-man.

I am just in the middle of these great thoughts when Zellara folds her hands under her little chin an' looks over at me an' says:

"*Cara,* tell me, what ees this serious business you wan' to talk about?"

I look sorta serious.

"Oh that," I tell her. "Well, here's the way it goes, honey. You remember when I was playin' around in Manzanillo in that banana business of mine, there was a guy—a nice guy, a sorta assistant to me—a feller with the name of Pepper. You know, baby," I go on, "I always had an idea in my head that Pepper was sorta keen on you."

She don't bat an eye-lid. Her eyes don't even waver or flicker for a second. She just goes on lookin' at me with the same little smile around her mouth. I tell you this dame is good.

"*Si-si,*" she says, "I remember. Peppere was a nice *hombre,* ver' nice, ver'—what you say good-looking."

"Sure he was," I tell her, "I suppose you know what happened to Pepper after he left the banana business?"

"No," she says, "I don' know. Tell me, Wylie."

We have both got our chins restin' on our hands an' we are both lookin' at each other an' we both know we're a sweet pair of goddam liars, but we're both doin' it very well.

"I'm goin' to tell you, Zellara," I go on. "This guy Pepper was what I call the big mug. He wasn't a guy like me who has got sense. He is always lookin' around for adventure. You know, he was one of them guys who was nuts about dames, he wanted to be Robin Hood, Paul Revere an' Custer's Last Stand all rolled inta one. So what does the big sap do? I'm tellin' you he joins the F.B.I.—the Federal Bureau of Investigation. He becomes a Special Agent—a 'G' man, see?

"Now can you imagine a thing like that? Just as if there wasn't enough trouble knockin' about for a guy like Pepper but he has to go an' do a thing like that."

She nods her head. I can see she is thinkin' fast an' plenty. She is wonderin' how the hell she is goin' to handle this proposition. I stop talkin' an' she don't say anything. We just sit there lookin' at each other for a coupla minutes. Then:

"*Cara,*" she says, very soft. "So what?"

"So nothing, honeypot," I tell her. "So just this. I'm lookin' for Pepper, You see I've gotta big sorta interest in Pepper. I wanta find where this guy is. I tried all sorts of things but I ain't had any luck an' then when I blew in here to-night an' I see your name up in neon lights outside the Elvira, I thought well this is funny, because I bet anything I got in the world that Pepper would have tried to see you some time, some place, because I gotta hunch he was blowin' around these parts."

She takes the bottle of champagne off the table before I can get my hand out to do it for her, an' she starts fillin' her glass up. She does it very slow an' she's doin' it so she can give herself time to think what she's goin' to say to me. I am doin' a big grinnin' act inside. I have put this baby on the spot an' she knows it. When she's filled the glass she takes it up an' she looks at me across the top of it, an' she says:

"*Cara,* why don' you be a sensible man? Why don' you see that when Zellara ees with Wylie she does not want to theenk about Peppere or any man?"

"Baby," I tell her, "you are a swell kid, an' while I could go for you one hundred per cent an' then plenty, at the same time this guy was my pal an' if you can say anything that will give me a line of him there's nothing I won't do for you."

She puts her little hand out an' puts it over my big one.

"Dear Wylie," she says, "as eef you didn't know that even in Manzanillo you were the only one who has ever meant anything to Zellara."

She gives a sigh, a little soft sigh, an' just for the sake of appearance I give one too, although not being good at it my sigh sounds like a whale comin' up for air. She picks up her wrap.

"Ver' well, Wylie," she says, "you wan' me to talk to you about Peppere, so I tell you about 'im. I did not want to do thees, because Peppere has done something to me which was unkind. But I do not want to talk 'ere. Come back to the apartment"—she gives me an arch sorta look—"we dreenk some coffee and I will tell you anyt'ing you want to know. Now, you will plees excuse me while I powder my nose?"

I tell her that's fine an' I watch her makin' for the woman's cloak-room, an' I do a quiet grin because I know that the amount of nose powderin' that this dame is goin' to do is just a minus quantity. She is goin' to do what I thought she was goin' to do. She is goin' to call up the boy friend!

One of these days when I am gettin' a bit long in the tooth and when the dames are beginnin' to tell me that they like me because of my brains—you know the stuff they pull when you get to the age when women can trust you which is a shockin' thing to happen to any guy, I reckon I am goin' to get myself a place like this dump of Zellara's. I'm tellin' you that the guy who threw this love-nest together certainly knew his pineapples. It is a big four-room street-level apartment with gold Spanish iron-work doors in between the rooms. The furniture is marvellous an' there is a heavy perfume hangin' about the place that sorta gets you. I'm tellin' you that this place has got atmosphere.

I am standin' in front of the big gold curtains that are hung in front of the double windows, an' Zellara is sittin' in a big chair on the other side of the room fiddlin' with the radio knob. She has got out a very good bottle of rye an' a Spanish cigarro that makes you think you are smokin' a piece of carpet, an' I would be very happy only I have got a coupla things on my mind.

She turns off the radio an' she says:

"Wylie, you are a ver' strange *hombre*. Maybe that ees why you fascinate me."

I grin.

"O.K., baby," I tell her. "Well, maybe before I'm through, you'll think I am a bit more strange but not so fascinatin'. Now we're here I'm gonna talk cold turkey to you."

She sorta settles herself in her chair. She has got a nice pleasant smile on her face.

"So thees ees the business," she says. "You go right a'ead, Wylie."

I throw the cigar stump away an' give myself a cigarette. When I am lightin' it I see the name "Lucky Strike" written on it. I hope it's goin' to be that way.

"O.K.," I tell her. "Well, here we go. I'm not goin' to mince any words with you, Zellara, an' I'm tippin' you off here an' now that you'd better talk the truth an' plenty of it, otherwise I might not be so pleased with you.

"I told you Pepper was an F.B.I. Agent. O.K. He was operatin' in the Arizona district. He usta get around plenty—South California, Texas, New Mexico an' over the line inta Mexico. He was an Agent who worked on the border, running contraband guys, counterfeit bozos an' Federal mail bandits down.

"O.K. Well, this bozo gets a hunch. He gets a hunch that there is something breakin' in Mexico. He rings through to the Agent-in-Charge in Arizona an' says he's goin' over to Mexico to find out what it is. He can't say any more right then, he says, he'll write later. The next thing that happens is he comes down here to Mexico City. When he gets here he starts writin' a letter to the Agent-in-Charge, tellin' him what all this besusuz is about.

"O.K. Well, he don't finish that letter, see? Somethin' happens that makes him tail it off quick. I reckon he'd heard something or had a phone call, or had to get out quick, or something like that. Anyhow he scrams. O.K. Well, nobody hears anything more of this guy an' where he is to-day or what's happened to him nobody knows.

"Now there is a guy in Washington called J. Edgar Hoover, who is Director of the Federal Bureau of Investigation. He is a bit old-fashioned inasmuch as he does not like to have his Agents missin', so I get orders to jump around a bit an' find Pepper, because, baby, as you have already guessed you never saw me in Manzanillo. You knew I was an F.B.I. Agent directly you clapped your eyes on me. But you thought you'd play it the way I wanted it played. You thought you'd get some time to do a little thinkin'.

"O.K. I get over inta Mexico an' I've been runnin' up an' down that dump until I have got permanent tonsilitis through desert dust an' my stomach is still turnin' over an' over through drinkin' about four gallons of bad *tequila* a day just because you can't get anything else much. Also I do not like the desert women because they get sorta dried up in the sun an' I like dames to be sorta limpid.

"Well, I don't find out much. All I do find out is that Pepper has been seen kickin' around all sorts of places from the Sierras right down to the Aguas Calientes districts. So I go rushin' around the place lookin' for him.

"Well, I don't find him an' I think maybe that he's fallen for one of these hot mommas you meet over there, because I am afraid that Pepper is a guy who would always put a dame before his job."

She looks at me an' nods. I don't say anything for a bit because I'm sorta mentally apologisin' to Pepper for sayin' funny things about this poor guy, but this is the way this job has gotta be played.

"O.K., Zellara," I go on. "So I get a hunch. I remember that Pepper wrote that letter from Mexico City, so I think that I will get down here an' take a look around. Now, the funny thing is that while I was over in Mexico I have got one point to work on. I get inta some place where Pepper had been an' I found a bit of a letter with the signature on it.

"The signature was 'Zellara,' an' to-night when I was easin' around this dump the first thing I see is the same name Zellera in lights in front of the Elvira. So I do a big Sherlock Holmes act an' I think that maybe you are the dame who wrote this letter to Pepper an' I was right because when I look at your handwritin' on that note you sent me to-night I see that it was the same.

"So what, baby? So this: Pepper met you down here an' he knew you. You wrote letters to him. Maybe you took a tumble with him, I don't know. But what I do know is that you've been gettin' around

Mexico for a long time. You've only just made the big time in your business. You've been an estancia singer for years, croonin' around the Mexican sticks, an' I'm bettin' all the tea in China to a coupla sticks of canned asparagus that you knew a guy called Pedro Dominguez when you was there, this Dominguez bein' a two-by-four cheap, four-flushin' bandit who will do anythin' from a railway stick-up to prizin' out the gold stoppin' from a sleepin' baby's tooth.

"O.K. So we do a bit more deducin' an' we come to the conclusion that as Pepper linked up with Pedro Dominguez somewhere in Mexico an' as I reckon you know Dominguez, it looks like you are the dame who put Pepper on to him. Now it's your turn, so shoot, baby."

She don't say anythin' for a minute. She gets up an' draws herself up to her full height. I forgot to tell you that when this dame got back here she changed inta a fluffy sorta wrap, négligées I believe they call 'em, an' standin' there with that big console radio as a background she looks like a million dollars. There is a sorta hurt expression in her eyes. She walks across the room towards me very slow an' she puts her hands up on my shoulders. She stands up close to me an' she looks right inta my eyes, an' she says:

"*Cara*, don't you see? . . . Cannot you see . . .?"

Boy, I get it, this dame is now goin' to tell me that she loves me, an' I get to thinkin' that if all the dames in the American continent who have been in love with me for some bum reason best known to themselves was added up they would reach four times round the world an' have enough left over to start two Wanamaker department stores.

"Isn't eet plain to you?" she says.

"Kiddo," I tell her, "somethin' is plenty plain to me at this moment, an' that is that I am still waitin' to hear you talk. So you go over an' sit down in the big chair while you do it."

She sorta droops. She goes back to the chair an' sits down.

"Look, Zellara," I tell her, "maybe you've heard of me, my name's Caution."

She nods.

"I know," she says. She swings around. "Listen," she says, "here's the trut'. I met Peppere here. I liked heem, he was a nice boy. He asked me to do sometheeng for heem, he asked me eef it were possible for me to put heem on to Pedro. I said I try and find out where Pedro was, and eet was arranged that when I discovered this I telephone through to Peppere. In the meantime I got ver' fond of heem. He was a nice boy.

"One evening I get the information he desires. I ring through to his hotel. I tell heem where he can find Pedro. Next morning I get a note from heem. The note tells me that he has gone to the Sierra Mojada, that when he comes back he hopes to see me. That ees all I know."

I do a quick think. Is this dame tellin' the truth or is she? How do I know?

"Look, Zellara," I tell her. "I'd hate to take you down to the office of the Chief of Police here an' flash my card at him an' start something that wouldn't do you any good. You wouldn't hold out on me, would you?"

She looks at me.

"Come here," she says, "and look into my eyes and tell me eef I am lying to you."

I go over an' take a look at her. Her eyes are all wet with tears. I start to think that a dame looks very good when she looks like this. Then I see that she is sorta smilin' an' lookin' past me.

Here we go!

I spin around an' stick my hand up in my coat for the Luger, but I am too late. Standin' in the doorway between this room an' the next one are three guys. They are very big guys an' they are wearin' tuxedos an' they are not nice guys. I can tell this because one of 'em has got a .45 Colt automatic pointin' straight at my guts.

"Take it easy, pal," he says.

He comes over to me an' takes the gun outa my shoulder holster an' puts it in his tuxedo pocket. He runs his hands down the side of my coat an' round my hips to see if I've got another one. Zellara has walked up to the table an' got herself a cigarette. She is grinnin' like a yellow cat. I reckon this dame feels pleased with herself.

"O.K.," says the big guy with the gun. "Come on, boy, we gotta nice yellow speed tub outside. Maybe you'd like to come for a little ride."

I look this guy over. He is about six feet, an' American. The two other guys are Mexicanos. I put up a weak sorta grin.

"It looks to me like this is where I hand in my dinner pail," I tell him. "I sorta feel you boys are goin' to be rough with me."

"You're tellin' me," he says. "I sorta reckon that we are. In fact," he says, "by the time we are through with you your sister wouldn't change what's left of you for an old pair of pants. Get goin', flatfoot! This way!"

He pushes me out through the door inta the other room. As I'm goin' through I turn my head over my shoulder.

"*Adios, carissima mia!*" I say. "If I have any luck I'm goin' to get at you one of these days an' when I do you won't sit down for sixteen years an' even then you'll need an air cushion."

She says a rude word at me.

They push me out. On the other side of the room we get inta a passage. We go out along to the back of the apartment block. There is a car waitin' there. They stick me in the back an' the big guy with the gun sits beside me. The other two guys get in front. They start the car an' we swing out on to the main stem an' go plenty fast through the city.

The guy on my right has got the muzzle of the gun stuck right inta my ribs. With the other hand he gets himself out a pack of cigarettes an' gives me one. I take it.

"Have a few puffs of that," he says. "Maybe you'll have time to smoke half of it. There's a sweet waste dump about five miles outa this city an' that's where you're goin' with a half a dozen slugs in your guts, and how do you like that, sweetheart?"

"I don't like it," I tell him. "I don't like it at all. But ain't you guys ever considered that you might be makin' a big mistake?"

He grins. He's got nice teeth, I can see 'em flash.

"An' just what do you mean by that crack, sucker?" he says.

We turn down one of the inter-sections an' now we're on one of the main boulevards leading east outa Mexico City. The night is nice an' quiet. I look around at him an' grin. While I am doin' this I start pullin' up the left leg of my trousers very quietly.

"Wise guy," I say to this palooka. "Just take a look behind you outa the rear window of this car an' you'll see a police car. Did you think I was mug enough to fall for a stunt like that put up by your girl friend? That car's been tailin' me the whole evenin', mug, an' if you an' your friends try any sorta rush-stuff you will find yourselves hangin' up until your neck is long enough to go fishin' with. Take a look, muggsy!"

He swings his head round an' sure as shootin' he sees that fifty yards behind is the car. Just for a moment he drops the gun muzzle.

I have got my trouser leg up an' I snatch the little .22 automatic off my leg an' I stick it inta his guts.

"You drop that rod, baby," I tell him, "an' quick."

The two guys in front have just got wise to the situation. I talk fast.

"Stop this car," I tell 'em, "an' anybody who as much as moves their ears is goin' to get it, an' if I've gotta shoot I'm goin' to shoot so's it'll hurt plenty."

They stop the car. I pick up the Colt that the guy on my right has dropped on the floor of the car, an' take my Luger outa his pocket. I get 'em out. Behind us the other car has also stopped. It's waitin' fifty yards down the road. I line these guys up against the side of the car an' I don't waste any time. I can see that these guys are already surprised that cops ain't disgorgin' themselves from the car. I act very quick. I bust 'em one each with the butt of the .45, an' when I say bust, I mean bust. You can almost hear their skulls crack.

I open the car door. I pick 'em up an' I push 'em in the back. I take two guns off the two guys who were sittin' in front. Then I light myself a cigarette an' walk down the road to the car that is waitin'. The garage boy sticks his head out.

"Sweet work, buddy," I tell him. "Here's the other twenty-five bucks I promised you."

I stick the Luger back in my shoulder holster, an' I give the other three guns an' the little automatic to the garage guy.

"You give these to your cousin round at the Peranza Hotel," I say. "Maybe he can do a deal with that pal of his who runs the gun shop."

He says that is swell business an' can he do anythin' else. I tell him he can drop me off way down the main stem near to where he was waitin' to pick up the car after we left Zellara's place.

I get inside an' we scram.

When we get to where I want to get out.

"So long, mister," he says. "I ain't bein' fresh or anythin' but I bet you're a cop."

"Don't be silly, kid," I tell him. "I'm a banana merchant from Manzanillo."

"Yeah?" he says. "An' I'm my girl friend's best pajamas. Good-night, boss!"

He drives away. I reckon he is a good kid.

The lounge room window—the one with the gold coloured curtains—is open around at Zellara's place. I reckon she thinks the night is goin' to be a hot one. Maybe she's right.

I ease through an' go across an' through the other room—the one where we was before. On the other side is the door that leads to her bedroom—the one she went through to change her frock.

I open it nice an' quiet.

Zellara is sleepin' in a big white satin bed on the other side of the room. The moonlight is comin' through the window an' shinin' on her face. She looks pretty swell to me—you know, like a little angel from heaven—wearin' a frilly pajama jacket with one little breast peepin' out as if it was sorta curious.

I heave a big sigh. The trouble with me is that—as you guys have probably figured out for yourselves—I am a very poetic sorta cuss an' I am always on the look-out for beauty an' sweetness, that is of course when I am not chasin' after some thugs or tryin' to ditch some hot momma who is tryin' to get a double half-nelson strangle hold on little Lemmy.

Standin' there I get to thinkin' that one of these fine days if I am lucky I shall get myself a dame who looks like Zellara looks but who is not all the time tryin' to issue me with a one-way ticket to the local graveyard.

Just then I let go a sneeze that you coulda heard in Iceland. I switch the light on quick just as she sits up in bed an' blinks. This dame's eyes are poppin'. She opens 'em wide an' takes a big look at me. Then she says something in Spanish that is so rude that I wouldn't even tell it to my deaf grandmother.

"Hey, Snakes Hips," I tell her. "How're you feelin'? Me, I am the ghost of Lemmy Caution callin' on his old girl friend Zellara the Manzanillo Nightingale, an' I am comin' around here every night at midnight to haunt you with my dyin' moans an' to cane the pants off of you with a handful of stingin' nettles. An' how do you like that, you cheap, double-crossin' little chisellin' daughter of a gaucho love-child?"

She starts in.

I would just hate to tell you guys the things she said. I have always liked Spanish because it is a very expressive sorta language but I'm tellin' you that the words that this dame was sayin' woulda done credit to a Mexican railway plate layer who was havin' his leg sawn off by cannibals. I have known top sergeants in the Marines who woulda given four months pay to get a vocabulary like this dame has got.

I go over to the bed an' stand lookin' at her. She is so burned up that she could even cut her own throat if somebody would pay her for doin' it.

"Look, Precious-Heart," I tell her. "I just couldn't keep away from you. I have come back because somethin' is pressin' on my heart an' I reckon it's either the cucumber or else it is your double-crossin' pan which is makin' me feel sick in the stomach."

She makes a gaspin' noise.

"An' just to imagine that you thought I was such a sap as to fall for you," I tell her. "Boy, I had a car trailin' me ever since I picked you up at the de Elvira before we went to the Doro. An' it was just too bad for your boy friends too.

"O.K.," I tell her. "Now I reckon I know the Chief of Police around here an' if I take you down there they ain't goin' to be too nice to you, are they? You tell me somethin'. What was your boy friend's name—the American guy, I mean?"

She tells me. Directly I hear the name I know plenty. This guy works for a mob in Chicago, as sweet a bunch of thugs as ever tried to play times on a copper with a tommy gun.

She looks at me.

"What you goin' to do wiz me?" she says.

I take a long look at her.

"Nothin'," I tell her. "Because I'm very particular about the sorta dames I get around with, an' you remind me too much of a boss-eyed rattlesnake I usta know when I was a boy. But," I go on, "you can get up pronto an' put some clothes on because you are goin' to send a little wire to your boy friend's boss in Chicago—the guy who paid you to put Pepper in touch with Pedro Dominguez, the guy who paid you to get Pedro to bump him off.

"After which," I go on, "you can stick around here just as if nothin' had happened. When your boy friend's boss in Chicago gets the wire you're goin' to send he's goin' to be steamed up plenty. He's comin' through on the long-distance to ask what it's all about.

"An' your boy friend will be around here askin' you about it, that is when he's got over the smack on the nut that I handed out to him not so long ago.

"So you just stick around an' tell 'em what they want to know, after which you can go on amusin' the customers at the Elvira each an' every night with that Mexican wriggle of yours. Get goin', baby!"

She looks at me as if I was nuts. Maybe she thought I was goin' to take her along to the cops here which is a thing I would not do for a million bucks.

While she is gettin' ready I do a little quiet thinkin'.

It's been a nice evenin' after all.

CHAPTER SEVEN
SPILL IT, TONY

MAYBE, one of these days, I am goin' to get some place on this Pepper-Jamieson business an' who am I to say that it ain't goin' to be a bit sooner than I expect. These jobs have gotta sorta way of takin' a turn for the better just at the sorta time that you think they're dyin' on you.

I'm on my way an' Mexico can have my smoke an' keep it. After I pulled that last seance with that hell-cat Zellara, I do not waste any time in ponderin' about things because I have always been a guy who believes that the great thing to do is to keep movin'.

Me—I do not believe that there is any good in stickin' around a dump after you have pulled a fast one, an' believe it or not I got the idea in my head that I have pulled a fast one on these guys who ironed out Pepper.

Maybe you have been wonderin' why I have not wasted a lotta brains in tryin' to get some angle on this Jamieson-Grearson disappearance because it will already have struck you guys that whatever has happened to these chemists is tied right up with what happened to Pepper.

Pepper mentioned Jamieson's name in the letter he started to write to Scattle. He mentioned this name before the Federal Bureau sent out that instruction sayin' that Jamieson had disappeared from the *hacienda* where he was waitin' to meet up with Grearson. So Pepper was on to Jamieson for somethin' or other. Maybe he had heard that there was some thuggery afoot; that somebody was aimin' to iron out Jamieson—which is what I think has happened to that guy.

Maybe Pepper thought he could get some action an' muscle in on the job first. It looks as if he didn't know anythin' about Grearson—the U.S. Navy Yard chemist guy who was on his way to meet Jamieson an' who disappears off the map after bein' seen somewhere near the Texas State Line. Maybe somebody or other has knocked off this guy Grearson too, which only goes to show you that things can happen to chemists just the same as if they was anybody else an' that they do not spend all their time bein' nice an' safe an' makin' bad smells in laboratories.

Anyway any guy who is prepared to strain his thinkin' box a piece is goin' to see that these two bozos Jamieson an' Grearson was playin' with fire anyway. They have invented a new sorta poison gas—I reckon that by a coincidence they both got the same sorta idea at the same time—an' the British an' U.S. Governments think that the best thing that these boys can do is to go live in that *hacienda* dump in Mexico, miles an' miles away from anywhere, an' go ahead with their own particular stinks factory.

The fact that they was sent to this lonely place to do the job was because these Government boys got the idea that some foreign guys might like to muscle in on this racket. This shows that the Federal department concerned was scared of somethin' or other an' I reckon they was right.

You know as well as I do that the whole cockeyed world is nuts about poison gas. I reckon that if anybody could invent some new gas that is a bit worse than the ones we got—or easier to make, carry, or let off—then I guess that there would be a whole lot of not-so-hot bozos would take plenty chances to get their hooks on it.

O.K. Well, maybe some not-so-hot bozos did get to hear about this Jamieson-Grearson proposition. Maybe they aimed to give these chemist boys the works. Then maybe Pepper got to hear somethin' about it while he was playin' around in Mexico City an' he is got to contact Pedro Dominguez because he thinks that he can get somethin' outa him, instead of which all he got outa Pedro was a coupla slugs an' his face bust in.

Did I forget to tell you guys that I am sittin' back in a comfortable drop-seat in the San Antonio-Fort Worth airplane? An' that right now the air hostess, who is one little blonde bundle and a nifty proposition that I could go for in a very big way indeed if I was not otherwise engaged, is gettin' me a rye highball, an' that so far as I am concerned everything is hunky dory.

An' I'm not stoppin' for anythin' until I get around to Chicago because I gotta big idea way back of my head that the next act in this big drama is goin' to be played out in the Windy City an' I don't mean perhaps.

I am all set. I contacted the Federal Bureau office in Washington on long distance before I started on this trip an' gave 'em my report over the wire, this bein' a cunnin' habit of mine because I do not like writin' reports.

I have wised them up at headquarters about Pepper. I have told them all I know about him contactin' Zellara an' goin' over the line to meet Pedro. I have told them what I know about Pedro an' just how I found the *hacienda* an' the state the dump was in, an' I have sorta suggested that I should not be very surprised if Jamieson an' Grearson are not already nicely ironed out.

An' I have told 'em that I am goin' on to Chicago an' that I will report again as soon as I think that is the thing to do.

But I have not said anything about one dame. I have not said anything about that swell baby Fernanda Martinas, an' if you guys ask me why, I am goin' to tell you that I am ponderin' plenty about that honeypot.

Because I am not sure about this baby an' when I am not sure about a doll I just do not do anything at all much.

Because some wise palooka once said "When in doubt—don't."

So I won't.

Boy am I tired or am I? I am so tired of this air-trip that I do not even react when the hostess dame slings me one of them "Look-me-over-kid-I'm-hard-to-get" looks. These air hostesses have got somethin', hey?

I reckon we are on the last lap. I have changed planes four times since I saw you last just to make it a quicker job an' way down underneath I can see the lights of Springfield, Illinois.

We shan't be long now.

Maybe you think I'm holdin' out on you about that wire that I made Zellara send after I got her outa that white satin bed an' talked horse sense to that baby boa-constrictor.

Well, I am not. I wouldn't hold out on anybody except maybe a dame, an' I'd only do that because some blondes go for anticipation.

An' I do not want you boys an' girls to make any mistakes or get tanglin' yourselves up in phoney clues an' things which is a thing which does not help anybody.

Me, I hate clues. I just can't get along with 'em. A clue—in case you don't know—is somethin' that the ace detective always finds stuck in the linin' of the dead guy's pocket, or else it is somethin' he finds hidden away in the water butt an' in nine cases outa ten this clue hasn't got anything to do with anything at all, but it makes the ace detective feel good an' also amuses the children.

One time I met up with some sleuth who was so dippy that he couldn'ta found Central Park without a magnifying glass. This bozo who reckoned that he was big time, tells me that a detective who ain't got a clue to work on is like a guy who has got a big date with a ravishin' brunette an' who forgets to get his pants back from the pants presser in time.

Me—I do not see this argument because I reckon I would keep the date with the dame if my pants was pressed or not. Because I have always found that although a snappy crease in your pants is a great help with dames, yet that is not the thing that enables you to get a baby seein' eye to eye with you about anythin' at all. In fact I will go so far as to say that I have known guys who had creases in their pants that you coulda cut bread with an' yet the dames have treated these bozos just like they was a bad odour.

The only time I ever met a clue was up in Laramie, Wyoming. There was a guy up there got himself very nicely dead by some means or other and this palooka was found by his sorrowing wife lyin' face downwards with his head over the front steps.

While the local county detective—who was a depressed sorta guy—an' why not?—because he had got bad-fittin' false teeth, halitosis an' broken arches—which you will admit is not a help to any guy—was rushin' round, measurin' everything up an' lookin' all around the place with a magnifyin' glass, I sorta wandered in an' found a banana on the window ledge.

I am just about to eat this banana when the detective guy says I mustn't do this because the banana is probably a clue. He says that the fact that this banana is left on the window ledge means somethin'.

He also says that the deceased guy—who is still lyin' outside on the porch steps an' not interested in anything at all, was very partial to bananas, an' was always eatin' same, an' that maybe if I move this banana I will spoil the whole reconstruction as to how this guy killed himself by fallin' down the porch steps an' bustin' his dome open.

I do not agree with this detective that this banana is a clue. I think it is still a banana so I eat it, an' ten minutes afterwards the local sawbones is workin' on me with a stomach pump because this banana was filled up with enough arsenic to kill King Kong.

So the case was bust wide open an' we all got wise how the dead guy got dead.

All this will prove to you guys that when your wife gets tired of you you should either take a train to some other place very quickly or else give up eatin' fruit.

O.K. Well, here is the set-up. You are probably wonderin' why when those gorilla friends of Zellara's took me for that car ride an' I turned the tables on 'em, I did not hand 'em over to the law officers instead of just bustin' 'em over the dome with a gun-butt.

An' you are also probably wonderin' about the wire that I made Zellara send. Well, I told you that this dame had already told me the name of the American thug who was the boss of the three gorillas who tried to hand it out to me. She tells me that this bozo's name is Pinny Yatlin. I have told them that I know this guy is a rod-man workin' for a high class thug in Chicago by the name of Jake Istria who is a big pin-table an' numbers racket king with a record that woulda made Satan's life story look like a book of instructions for a first year infant welfare teacher's course.

O.K. Well, the wire that I made Zellara send is just this:

"*Jake Istria Hotel Depeene Chicago.*

I had to talk I tried to be careful but you can have too much Caution sometimes stop Take it easy and keep your nose clean stop Yatlin a total loss at the moment.

Zellara."

O.K. Well, after we have sent this wire I tell Zellara that she can scram. I tell her that I do not like her one little bit an' that I would have great pleasure in throwin' her into the Pacific Ocean only I have got too much regard for the sharks.

I also tell her that if I see her around again in any place where I am then I will get so rough with her that any time she tries to sit down she will think she is wearin' sand-paper step-ins.

I then scram outa Mexico City.

An' this is what I reckon is goin' to happen directly afterwards.

Pinny Yatlin—after he has got some guy to stick a lump of ice on the bump on his dome that I issued to him—is goin' to get himself several long drinks an' is goin' rushin' around to Zellara to ask her what the hell all this is about an' why she double-crossed him.

She is goin' to say that she did not double-cross him at all, but that I have stood the whole lot of 'em up for plenty an' that I have made her send the wire.

She will then tell Yatlin what the wire was.

Yatlin will rush around to the nearest drug store an' long distance Jake Istria an' tell him all about it. Jake Istria who will have got the wire will ask what the hell does the wire mean.

Yatlin will tell him that it don't mean anything much. He will say that it was Caution made Zellara send this wire but all Caution knows is that she sent Pepper to contact Pedro Dominguez, but that he can't prove anythin' else an' that he is bluffin'.

Jake Istria will then say to himself what the hell did Caution pull this one for? He will get sorta nervous. He will expect me to turn up in Chicago an' pull a big act, an' he will get all set for me. He will have some sorta set-up waitin' for me. He will have some phoney tale waitin' just in case I get tough. Because even a very nasty tough *hombre* like Jake Istria is goin' to get plenty scared if he thinks the "G" heat is on and that the Feds are takin' a personal interest in him.

But whatever that phoney tale, or set-up, is, well it is goin' to tell me somethin'. It is goin' to give me some start somewhere because when a guy gets ready to pull a phoney act on you he always does somethin' that gives him away. He is so keen on four-flushin' you that very often he double-crosses himself.

So now you know. Maybe I have given you a big clue.

An' maybe it's just another banana.

When I get out on the ground at Chicago airfield—havin' made a big date to meet the hostess baby some place, some time, when we are both feelin' like that—I ease across to a cab an' tell the guy to take me around to the Palissade Hotel—this bein' a very quiet an' comfortable place where I like to stay when I don't want everybody knowin' just what I am at.

I stand there with my foot on the cab-step talkin' to the driver an' keepin' a weather eye open just to see if anybody is takin' any interest in me.

Somebody is. There is a quiet lookin' sorta bozo in a well-cut grey overcoat an' swell shoes, standin' down the cab line an' pretendin' that the only guy he is not lookin' at is me.

I get in an' say that I am not in a hurry an' that bein' of a nervous disposition I do not like goin' fast around the corners, after which I look out of the rear window an' see that the guy in the overcoat has got himself a cab an' is comin' after me. So I reckon that this bozo is sorta curious as to where I am goin' to stay.

I check in at the Palissade as Wylie T. Hellup, an' go up to my room where I unpack my grip an' tell the bell-hop to bring me up a bottle of Canadian bourbon, after which I give myself a hot an' cold shower an' lay down on the bed with nothin' on at all, this bein' a very good way of thinkin' about things in general. I am considerin' about the palooka who came after me here an' who now knows just where I am stayin'.

After a bit I get up an' take a look out of the window. It is seven o'clock an' I can see the lights twinklin' down in the street an' the stars shinin' up in the sky. I get to thinkin' that this Chicago is not such a bad place if you take it as it comes an' take it easy.

I then have another shot of rye for the road an' proceed to dress myself in a swell tuxedo I have got. Just in case of accidents I slip the Luger under my arm an' I go downstairs an' ease over to the hallway an' stand there for a bit just so's the guy in the swell grey overcoat who was waitin' for me when I got to the airfield can see that I am around.

I then get myself outside an' take a cab to the post office. I go in an' I have a few words with the supervisor an' show him my badge, after which he fixes to send through a Federal-Secret wire for me to Headquarters in Washington. Here's the wire:

"Federal Government Secret
S.A./L.H. Caution
Identification 472/B to Federal Bureau
of Investigation Washington.
Records and enquiry Urgent Priority stop

Please advise me record background of Zellara Spanish Mexican artiste dance crooner now employed de Elvira floor show Mexico City stop Pepper kept specimen Zellara handwriting probably suspecting police record somewhere please check thoroughly in U.S. and Mexico stop Advise me point of contact if any between Zellara and Pinny Yatlin one time gorilla for Jake Istria of this city last seen by me Mexico City stop Advise me record background Fernanda Martinas Spanish Mexican fronting as estancia artiste in San Luis Potosi and federal districts of Mexico stop Co-operation of Mexican authorities will be necessary for this last seen by me Tampapa area Mexico stop Advise me if she is married if so record background of husband stop Operating strictly under cover no official contacts wire reply care of supervisor Roseholme Postal district special delivery in code stop End."

Me, I go for burlesque shows. I am not a guy who looks down on a burlesque show, because I have seen some very sweet sights in burlesque an' I am very fond of lookin' at allurin' legs. An' what about you?

Sittin' there in a comfortable loge I get to thinkin' that my old mother once told me that if I would spend as much time considerin' the superstructure of dames as I did ponderin' on their underpinnin' I would get some place.

An' when I told her that that was the idea she cracks back an' says that I am just like my father only worse, an' that many a good man had taken the road to ruin through goin' to strip tease shows an' gettin' excited an' rushin' home an' knockin' his wife about just because she couldn't rate a streamline like the dame at the end of the front row—the one in the black silk tights an' pom-poms.

Because when you come to think of it Nature is a very wonderful thing an' I am prepared to go so far as to bet a coupla bottle of the best bourbon against a busted flush in a snide poker game that when Nature issued out swell an' taperin' legs to dames she knew what she was about. An' if she didn't then all I can say is that Nature is a swell guy for mischief because believe it or not if it wasn't for the swell shape that some dames have got there would not be half the trouble in the world that there is to-day.

I have never yet know a guy go bad or start hittin' the spots, stickin' up the local mail-cart or declarin' war on the Chinese just because some dame with a face like nothin' on earth an' a contour that looks like the shortest distance between two given points has asked him to.

No sir, because it is the heavy blonde or the mysterious brunette with the big eyes, straight nose an' little mouth, the one who is put up in a shape like the boys' first problem in circular geometry an' who knows how to swing it, is the baby that makes the cops work overtime. Because why? Because she is always tryin' to prove that she can get guys to do anything at all for her an' like it, an' in nine cases outa ten she is one hundred per cent correct.

All the while I am considerin' these heavy propositions I am keepin' a very quiet eye on the bozo in the grey overcoat an' the swell tan shoes who is standin' against the wall at the side of the theatre keepin' a quiet eye on me.

Presently two guys at the end of my row get up an' go out. I ease along inta the end seat so that I am next the guy in the grey coat.

After a bit he drops his cigarette lighter on the floor an' when I stoop down to pick it up for him he says outa the corner of his mouth:

"I wanna talk to you, Caution, an' I wanna do it nice an' quiet. Maybe I can make a deal with you."

I grin.

"O.K.," I tell him. "I'm goin' back to the Palissade. You better string along after me, but don't bring any friends with you, mug, otherwise I might feel hurt."

"I'll be there," he says.

He goes out.

I light myself a cigarette an' smoke it quietly. Maybe somethin' sweet is goin' to break.

When the cigarette is done I get outside an' buy myself a cab. I drive straight around to the Palissade an' when I get there I can see the grey overcoat guy standin' over by the elevator reading a news-sheet. I go over an' when the elevator comes down he steps in with me.

Lookin' him over in the elevator it sorta hits me that this guy is scared.

He takes off his overcoat an' I give him a grass of rye straight an' a chaser. His clothes are swell an' nicely pressed. By the look of his pan, which is long an' straight an' hard, he might be anything from a successful mortician to a boy in any one of the quieter rackets.

He sits down an' lights himself a cigarette. I am standin' over by the window, sayin' nothin'.

"I reckon I can make a proposition, Caution," he says. "Are you talkin' turkey?"

"Nuts, sweetheart," I tell him. "I am not stickin' around here to make bargains or cop pleas. I am listenin' an' if I like what you say then maybe I will not smack you on the snout when is the way I am feelin' right now.

"I would also like you to know," I go on, "that I am not a guy who is propositioned at any time by any smart Alec with a long beak like you have got, an' I am also very inclined to get steamed up with people who get me out of a swell leg show for the purpose of tryin' to make deals for themselves. So spill it."

He thinks for a bit an' takes a drag at his cigarette. He looks worried.

"I'm takin' a big chance in talkin' to you, Caution," he says. "I heard you was pullin' in an' I reckoned you'd come by plane. I stuck around at the airport an' followed you in. I came on here after you. When you went out to-night I tailed you to get a chance to make a contact that was nice an' quiet."

"So what?" I tell him. "I knew all that. Me, I have been tailed around for the last six years by so many guys that if somebody wasn't doin' a big shadow act on me I'd feel nervous. O.K. Well, now you're here"—I try a fast one—"I suppose you're goin' to tell me that Jake Istria wants to make a deal."

I think this guy is goin' to pass out. He looks around him as if he thought somebody was behind him. Then he runs his finger around his collar an' breathes hard.

"For Pete's sake," he says. "I'm tellin' you, Caution, that if Istria knew I was talkin' to you or anybody else he'd get me before I got back home. He'd stick me in a paraffin bath an' light it—an' I've seen him do that to a guy. He'd tear my eyes out."

"He sounds like a nice guy to me," I tell him. "All right, so Istria don't know you're here. So then what?"

He swallows the rye an' starts to pour himself another one. I can hear the bottle tappin' against the top of the glass.

"I'm scared," he says. "The game's gettin' too goddam hot for me. I wanta get out an' I'm scared to get out unless I get out good. I'm tellin' you that no guy has ever taken a run out on Istria without wishin' he'd shot himself nice an' easy first. He'd go quick that way anyway."

"Listen, punk," I say. "What is all this Istria stuff? It looks like this guy has got you plenty scared. But I'm gettin' bored. I reckon I heard of these big-time racketeers before. They usta tell me stories about 'em to frighten me when I was in short pants."

I light myself a cigarette.

"Cut out the drama, buddy," I tell him, "an' start talkin'. Otherwise I'm goin' to get the bell-hop to lead you home an' tell your mother to cut your candy ration down."

He runs his tongue over his lips. I'm tellin' you this guy is frightened good an' plenty.

"All right," he says. "Well . . . I'm gonna take a chance an' here it is. You know that things haven't been too good for guys like Istria since the 'G' men have been gettin' around these parts. The rackets are gettin' washed up. Ever since repeal the gangs have been takin' the knock one after the other. Hooch is all over an' done. Kidnappin' is a lost art an' if you tried a snatch these days they'd get you before the stamp is stuck on the ransom letter.

"So what's left? There ain't much, is there?

"O.K. Well, Istria's been doin' everything to keep the boys together an' get some jack, but it ain't easy. I know because I been workin' for him for five years. The vice trade is lousy in Chicago an' there's damn little in the pin-table an' numbers game now. People ain't scared to squeal to the cops any more.

"So Istria reckons to pull a helluva fast one. He's got some guy, name of Pinny Yatlin, who collects for the vice houses in Istria's district. This guy is hot an' the cops are lookin' for him, an' so he scrams off on vacation to Mexico City until the heat's off."

I open up my ears.

"While he's down in Mexico City Pinny gets on to somethin'," he goes on. "He gets Istria on the long-distance an' he tells him that he's wise to some business about two chemist guys—one of 'em an English fella an' the other a guy from the U.S. Navy Yard. These guys have got somethin'. They gotta new poison gas that is the berries.

O.K. Well, Pinny says that the two governments aim to have these two work this thing out somewhere where anybody ain't gonna get wise. The idea is that they go to some dump in the Mexican desert an' work out this gas thing together.

"So Istria gets busy. He reckons that if somebody bumps these guys he's got something. An' he would be dead right, wouldn't he? He reckons that nobody is goin' to make things hot for him whiles he's got those formulas for makin' the gas. He reckons that the U.S. Government will be plenty ready to forget about the two chemist guys bein' bumped—because they can always say that it was Mexican bandits pulled that trick—providin' Istria sells 'em back the formula."

I nod. It sorta sounds sense to me.

"Istria reckons that the Feds wouldn't be able to make any stink about it at all. If they start shoutin' their heads off that these chemist guys are dead an' makin' things hot for Istria, then other people an' other countries are goin' to hear about that gas. Then what's goin' to happen? Directly foreign guys know that there is a one hundred per cent better gas they're goin' to bust themselves gettin' their hooks on it by fair means or foul, ain't they?"

I pour myself out another shot of rye. I am doin' some quick thinkin'.

"Istria reckons that once he's got his hooks on that formula he's properly in the red. He reckons he'll be holdin' five aces cold an' he can blow raspberries at one an' all because if they don't come across then he can always sell out the formula to some foreign guys. Have you got all that?"

"I got it," I tell him. "And where do we go from there?"

He runs his finger around his silk collar some more. Then he gives himself another drink. When he lights his cigarette I can see his fingers tremblin'.

"Here's where we go," he says. "Istria an' Pinny get busy. Pinny has got some right guys workin' for him in Mexico, but at the last moment things get a bit mixed. The English guy Jamieson went along to the *hacienda* O.K. an' he got his all right. They bumped him, but they was nuts to do it. They oughta waited until Grearson, the U.S. Navy Yard chemist, got there. This bozo Jamieson had only got *half* the formula—the part *he* was workin' on. Grearson had got the other half an' Grearson never arrived at the *hacienda* dump. Last time he was seen was on the Mexican border, an' Istria don't know where he is, nobody knows where he is except maybe two people. . . ."

He sorta pauses. He takes another drink an' he looks at me. I can see him sweatin' across the forehead.

"O.K.," I say. "An' who are the other two people?"

He gulps.

"I'm shootin' my mouth plenty," he says sorta thick. "An' I'm a guy who has never talked to coppers an' has always kept his nose clean, but I gotta do it."

He lights himself another cigarette.

"Istria's a devil outa hell," he says. "But I wouldn't rat on him for that. You gotta be tough if you're in the rackets. It's them or you, but there's one or two things I don't see eye to eye with him about. He's given me a square cut an' I've always had my dough on the line, but it's somethin' else. . . ."

I grin.

"So it's a dame?" I say.

"Yeah," he says, "but not the way you think. . . . It's my sister . . . Georgette."

He pauses for a minute. I reckon that this guy is now goin' to get sweet an' sentimental.

"I got her outa U.S. into a French convent when she was a kid of three months," he says. "I didn't want her stickin' around here an' gettin' mixed up with the mobs that I was playin' around with. She's had a swell education an' she's practically French. O.K. Two years ago she comes over here on vacation an' naturally I wanta take a peek at her. She don't know I'm her brother.

"So I get around with her a bit. I go to some shows with her an' take her around. I tell her I'm a friend of her father's.

"Well, Jake is nosin' around an' he sees her. She was twenty-seven then an' what a peach. I might have known that that dirty so-an'-so would pull a fast one on me. One day he sends me up to Denver on some fake business an' when I come back do I get a shock?"

"So Istria makes the dame?" I ask him.

"Yeah," he says. "That lousy heel had sorta rushed her off her feet an' married her. Pulled a lotta big-shot stuff on her."

He shrugs his shoulders.

"O.K. Well, he's given her a plenty lousy time," he goes on, "an' if I'd had the nerve an' it woulda done any good I'd have bumped him. But what woulda been the use?"

"An' she's wised you up to all this?" I ask him.

"Sure," he says. "Jake trusts her. He talks to her, that is when he ain't bustin' her about, or flauntin' his cheap dolls at her. So she got an idea. She got a big idea."

"I'm still listenin'," I tell him.

"She's got an idea where Grearson is," he says. "She's got an idea that Pinny Yatlin has been playin' a double deck game on this Mexican end of the business, that he snatched Grearson, knowin' that without his part of the formula the stuff that Jake has got ain't worth nothin'. She reckons that Pinny is aimin' to hold out on Jake until Jake cuts him in with a half share, then he'll play ball again."

He gets up.

"Jake got a wire from a dame we got workin' in Mexico City. It steamed him up plenty. Then he got a long-distance call from Pinny. Pinny said that you were in on this job an' believe it or not the mobs have gotta certain sorta respect for you. Jake wasn't feelin' so good. But he still thinks he holds all the aces.

"He blows all this to Georgette an' she's scared of the whole goddam business an' so am I. I tell you that she was never cut out to string along with a cheap chisellin' mobster like Jake. She was talkin' to me about it an' your name come up. I reckon she thinks you're one helluva guy."

He picks up his hat.

"Then she gets the idea—the big idea," he says. "An' I'm tellin' you that that girlie has got something."

"Yeah," I tell him, "an' what's she got?"

He looks me in the eye.

"That dame is the loveliest dame that you ever set eyes on, Caution," he says. "She don't know that she's my sister but she's such an eyeful that I'm sorta proud just to think about that fact sometimes. She was never cut out to be a racketeer's pet. She's got class an' she would melt the heart outa a brass monkey.

"An' she thinks you're the berries. She remembers how you bust up the Jeralza mob—that cost Jake a bit, he was in with 'em—an' she's lookin' for a real man who's a straight shooter an' she's got proposition that even you'll be glad to listen to."

"O.K.," I tell him. "So what? So she's a lovely dame an' she's meltin' but where does that get me? What about the proposition?"

"She'll handle that herself," he says. "She'll talk to you personal or not at all. She's like that. She's as straight as they come."

I look at him.

"Where do we contact?" I ask him. "An' what's your name?"

"My name's Tony Scalla," he says. "To-morrow Georgette's supposed to go to an afternoon show. If you wanta talk she'll be in suite sixteen at two-thirty at the Louisiana apartments—an' she'll be alone."

"She better had be," I crack.

I light another cigarette.

"O.K., Tony," I tell him. "Maybe I'll string along with you. I ain't makin' any promises but if this thing works the way I want it maybe I can keep you an' her out of it. Maybe I can give you a break."

I go over to him.

"But let me tell you somethin', bozo," I go on. "If you try any neat stuff I'll cut your ears off. I'll send your lovely sister where she can be lovely all day and nobody won't even care. So long, mugsie, I'll be seein' you. Keep your nose clean."

He scrams.

I wander around the room a bit an' give myself another little drink an' a warm shower. There is somethin' about warm water that is sorta caressin'.

I reckon that life is funny, and what do you think?

I switch the shower on to cold. Standin' there I get to thinkin' about when I was hangin' around that lousy Tampapa job wishin' I could get myself a sweet job in the big-city. Well, here I am. I got it.

I get to thinkin' about this Georgette, an' maybe you'll allow that that's a sweet name, Georgette. I always thought that that was a sorta silk.

I reckon I'm like the dame who gave me those shirts, I always did go for silk next my skin.

CHAPTER EIGHT
GEORGETTE

I AM tyin' a new necktie in front of the mirror in my sittin' room an' I am thinkin' about this Georgette baby an' this brother of hers—the Tony Scalla guy. These bozos intrigue me plenty, and if you will do a little thinkin' you will see that there are some sweet possibilities.

First of all I think that this Tony Scalla is on the up-an'-up. I think he is playin' straight with me because you will allow he has spilled a lotta stuff. He has spilled enough stuff for me to grab off Jake Istria an' himself an' any of the other boys in the Istria mob, because I have practically got a confession from this Scalla that they was all in the plot to get these two chemist guys.

But it wouldn't do me any good. It wouldn't tell me where Grearson was; it wouldn't tell me anythin' about this formula that everybody is goin' so nuts about an' it would only mean that any of these thugs who are still operatin' on this job would close down. We shouldn't ever hear a durn thing more about Grearson, besides which some of the news-hounds might start somethin' an' the whole goddam story get blown in the press, which wouldn't do anybody any good—me in particular.

O.K. So just for the sake of the argument, as the professor said, I'm goin' to take it that Tony Scalla's story is on the up-an'-up. That bein' so we now know the followin' facts:

1. *That the guy who originally thought of doin' this job was Pinny Yatlin. Pinny Yatlin got the idea of bumpin' these two chemists and grabbin' off the poison gas formulas when he was down in Mexico City on vacation.*

I reckon that this was the time when Pepper first got the idea that there was somethin' blowin' up an' started to stick his nose in.

2. *Pinny gets through to Jake Istria an' tells him that this is one hell of a scheme for them to play. Jake, who is not doin' so well an' who is lookin' for some big-time stuff, says O.K.*

3. *Jake starts in with some quick organisin' an' through Zellara, who is workin' with Pinny Yatlin in Mexico City, gets inta contact with Pedro Dominguez who gets himself put in as guard at the hacienda. His business is to do the bumpin' off when the time comes.*

I reckon this idea of usin' Pedro for this is a swell one because Pedro is a guy with a bad record an' when the news of the bumpin' of Jamieson an' Grearson gets out it would be easy for anybody to think that it was just an ordinary Mexican stick up pulled by Pedro.

4. Zellara gets scared of Pepper. She suspects he is a Government man. She contacts Yatlin an' asks what she is to do. Yatlin says the thing for her to do is to play along with Pepper an' to give him just a bit of information, enough to get him curious. Zellara does this an' tells Pepper where he can find Pedro Dominguez—Pedro havin' already had instructions to take care of Pepper and bump him directly he gets him well into the desert.

5. For some reason that I don't know right now some trouble starts at the hacienda *before Grearson the American chemist gets there. This was a bad break because if Pedro— an' I reckon he was responsible for the killin' of Jamieson— hadn't been in such a hurry they would have been able to finish off the job properly. If they'd waited for Grearson they would have had both parts of the formula and they would have been as safe as grandfather at a Co-Eds ball.*

6. Whoever has got Grearson—alive or dead—has got his part of the formula which is just as much good as Istria's half is—that is no good at all without the other half.

7. Fernanda: I don't see where this dame comes inta the job at all. That is unless she was just stringin' around with Pedro because she didn't want her husband chasin' after her, like she said. Maybe we'll get some information on that honeypot in a minute. Anyhow, you gotta admit that Fernanda was a good dame so far as I was concerned an' she certainly ironed out Pedro which was maybe convenient for me just at that time.

8. Havin' regard to all this you can understand Tony Scalla an' Georgette Istria wantin' to get outa this business and keep their noses clean. Work it out for yourselves. Jake Istria has got the Jamieson half of the formula. Some unknown guy—or guys—has got the other half. Neither of these people can do any durn good for themselves until they get the other bit, an' that looks like a sweet set-up for a whole lotta warfare.

9. Besides which everybody will be playin' with dynamite because the Government is goin' to get very annoyed about all this business anyway an' if Istria was by some slip-up to get himself pinched, then it wouldn't be so good for Georgette, who everybody would think was the usual mobster's pet playin' along in the job. Also Tony Scalla would get pinched along with Istria. If I was these two I would certainly try to get myself out whiles the goin' was good.

I have put down these points so that you guys can see how I am thinkin' an' why I believe this dope that Tony Scalla has handed me out is the right stuff.

Anyhow that is what I think an' I am goin' to act as if it was right because a guy has gotta start somewhere.

This Louisiana apartment block is the berries. Me, I go for these places—grey and black carpets an' janitors in swell uniforms an' flowers an' all that sorta stuff. When I get around there I ask the reception guy if there is a lady waitin' to see Mr. Hellup an' he says yes.

While I am goin' up in the elevator I am wonderin' just what sorta dame this Georgette is goin' to be. I get to thinkin' about the other dames on this job. Fernanda is one helluva good looker an' I should say that dame has got plenty brains. Zellara was a honey too but she wasn't big time in brains. She was just a cunnin' little thing hangin' around I reckon with Yatlin an' doin' what she was told maybe because there was goin' to be a few grand in it for her.

An' now here's Georgette!

The bell-hop slings open the door an' I go right in. On the other side of the door I stand there with my mouth open like I was poleaxed. . . .

Oh boy!

I do not wish to bore you guys an' I do not wish to let my poetic feelin's run away with me, but I'm tellin' you that the dame who is standin' in front of the carved-out fireplace, with her hand on the overmantel, lookin' at me is the one hundred per cent super lovely of the whole wide world.

I have seen plenty dames. I have met up with honeys that woulda made you catch your breath an' gulp in all parts of the world. Standin' there lookin' at this Georgette there goes runnin' through my mind all the really big-time babies that I have run across since I been totin' a "G" badge an' a Federal Identification card.

Esmeralda van Zelden . . . Constance Gallertzin—she was a dame. That lovely dame Henrietta in Palm Springs, Paulette Benito in Sonoita . . . Mirabelle an' Dolores in the Federal gold snatch case

. . . Marella Thorensen an' that Chinese honey Berenice Lee Sam in the San Francisco job. . . .

Then there was Fernanda Martinas in this job, an' you gotta admit that Fernanda has got what it takes.

But I'm tellin' you that this Georgette baby knocks 'em for a row of skittles. She is the Queen-eyeful of the whole lot. I'm tellin' you that the movie fans would be glad to save up an' pay ten dollars to go in an' take one quick peek at her.

What a doll!

She is wearin' a black velvet frock with a lace tie at the throat, a three-quarter length swing Persian lamb coat that cost somebody some sweet dough an' no hat. She is wearin' beige stockin's so sheer that it almost hurts an' little patent shoes with Louis heels an' buckles.

When her brother Tony Scalla says that this dame has got something that bozo was only tellin' the half of it.

Her hair is honey-gold, an' if King Solomon hadda took one quick peek at this baby's figure he woulda sent out a riot squad to get the Court photographer to take a quick picture of her so's he could look at it when he was feelin' that he was gettin' past things generally.

Her eyes are that peculiar sort of blue an' they look straight at you an' they are sorta soft an' limpid. Her skin is like the cream on the top of the Grade A milk, an' she has gotta pair of ankles that woulda started a riot at a Coney Island leg contest.

An' she has got brains. Everything about this dame tells you that. The way she stands, the swell shape of her head, the expression on her face, everything goes to show that this baby can think when she wants to because she's got the material to think with.

So now you know all about Georgette.

I don't waste any time first of all because I am not a guy who likes wastin' time and secondly because I want you to get the fact that we are all workin' against the clock.

I wanta get my job done here an' outa this place pronto because now I've got the low down on what Istria is playin' at I do not want to stick around in Chicago one hour longer than I got to because some of these hot guys around here might recognise me an' somebody might start somethin'.

Another thing is that Jake Istria will think that I am goin' to start somethin' anyway. Makin' Zellara send that wire to Istria was a good

psychological stunt all right. It was responsible for gettin' Tony Scalla
frightened enough to contact me an' tell me what he knew about this
stuff, but it will also mean that Istria will have his eyes skinned for
me. He knows I'm goin' to do somethin' an' if nothin' happens he is
goin' to get suspicious an' start lookin' about him.

That's one reason I gotta be quick. An' here's another:

This dame Georgette an' her brother Tony are in a spot. They've
done the one thing that people who are tied up with the mobs don't
do. They've spilled the beans to a Government man. If Istria or any
of his bozos as much as got an idea about this business I reckon they
would tear these two in pieces. You heard how Scalla said that Jake
Istria once gave some guy a paraffin bath. . . .

So I gotta clean up quick. I gotta get Georgette an' Tony outa here
as soon as I can, an' I gotta get Istria quick.

She don't waste any time either.

"Please sit down, Mr. Caution," she says.

Her voice is just like you think it oughta be. Low an' soft an' she
pronounces her words properly like a dame who is educated.

"I'm supposed to be at an afternoon show," she goes on. "I went
in, took my seat and came out when the place was dark by a side exit.
I haven't got a great deal of time because if my husband even so much
as suspected that I was talking to a stranger there would be trouble."

She brings a cigarette box over to me an' I grab one an' light it.

"O.K., Mrs. Istria," I tell her. "We'll get down to brass nails. Tony's
told me a bit of a story, not much. He's told me that your husband's
got half the formula, the half that Jamieson worked out, but that
he ain't got the Grearson half. Tony thinks that somebody snatched
Grearson an' that's the reason why he never arrived at the *hacienda*.
Tony sorta suggests that you might know where Grearson is.

"O.K. Well, let me ask you a few questions first of all so that we
get this thing straight."

She sits down.

"I'll tell you anything I know," she says, "anything I can."

"All right," I tell her. "I reckon that somebody at the *hacienda* got
the Jamieson half of the formula off Jamieson after he was killed.
Who was it done this? Was it Pedro Dominguez?"

"No," she says. "Jake, my husband, did not trust Dominguez
because he was employed by Yatlin. Dominguez's business was merely

to kill Jamieson when the time came. On the night that Jamieson was killed two people arrived at the *hacienda,* a woman and a man. They were people who work for my husband. They were sent there to see that everything was carried out as it should be.

"But something went wrong. For some reason Jamieson was shot. He should not have been shot at that time. The plan was that Jamieson and Grearson were to be killed at the same time. Pedro Dominguez quarrelled with Jamieson and killed him. It was after this that my husband's people seized the Jamieson papers and immediately returned here to Chicago and brought them to him. They knew something had gone wrong."

"I got it," I say. "Jake Istria believed that Pinny Yatlin, who was handlin' the business in Mexico, was aimin' to pull a double cross, so he sends one of his mob an' a girl friend along just to keep an eye on things. He did this because he didn't trust Yatlin. Pedro has been tipped off by Yatlin to kill Jamieson before the arranged time so as Yatlin can get the Jamieson half of the formula. Yatlin wants this done quick because he knows that Grearson ain't even goin' to arrive at the *hacienda.*

"He knows this because he has already arranged to have Grearson kidnapped directly he gets over the Texas State Line inta Mexico. Yatlin knows that he will get the Grearson half of the formula that way an' then he's got the whole shootin' gallery in his own hands."

She smiles. Her teeth twinkle like little pearls.

"You're very quick, Mr. Caution," she says. "That is what happened."

"All right," I go on. "So your husband gets his hooks on the Jamieson half of the formula an' Yatlin snatches Grearson. Yatlin's next move woulda been to contact Jake Istria an' tell him that he wanted a bigger cut or else he wouldn't produce the Grearson half. But he don't have time to do this. He don't have time to see this plan through because I arrive on the scene down in Mexico City an' Yatlin thinks that him an' Istria had better stop arguin' with each other until they see what I'm goin' to start. In other words they gotta fix me somehow or another first. After which they can start their own private war again an' come to terms before they put the two halves of the formula together an' start doin' business with the U.S. Government."

She nods her head.

"Once again you are right, Mr. Caution," she says.

"All right," I say. "So up to there we know where we are. Now you do some talkin'," I tell her. "Where's Grearson an' his half of the formula, that's the first part of the question, an' the second part is how do you come to know where Grearson is? If your husband don't know how is it that you do?"

"I will tell you," she says.

She gets up an' brings me another cigarette. She brings out a little platinum an' diamond lighter an' she lights it for me. When she is standin' over me I get just a faint sorta suggestion of some perfume that this dame is wearin' an' I haveta take a pull at myself to stop my mind wanderin' off the subject in hand.

"Tony found it out," she said. "Tony found it out from a woman—a very charming woman in Mexico named Fernanda Martinas. This lady had left her husband and for some reason had become attached to the bandit Pedro Dominguez who, it seems, had a certain attraction for women. Pedro had been told by Yatlin that the plot was to kidnap Grearson directly he got over the Line into Mexico and it was Dominguez who arranged for Yatlin the kidnapping of Grearson and his transport across Mexico via Ascapulco to France where he now is."

I whistle. Here's a sweet set-up!

"You must realise that there was superb organisation," she says. "Yatlin had made perfect arrangements. He had a boat chartered at Ascapulco. He had already made arrangements for a certain Spanish-American gentleman who was partially insane to be taken to France to receive special treatment at the hands of a famous specialist there."

"An' Grearson was to be the Spanish-American who was nutty, hey?" I say. "How did they reckon they was goin' to get away with that?"

Her face goes sorta sad.

"I am sorry to say that Yatlin had said that when Grearson arrived at Ascapulco he _would_ be insane," she said. "They had arranged for that. Yatlin had said that once they had got the Grearson half of the formula safely in their possession they would 'get to work' on him."

I nod. I reckon I am sorry for this poor guy Grearson.

"Pedro told all this to Fernanda Martinas," Georgette goes on. "He boasted about how rich he would be, of how much money he was to receive from Yatlin. Fernanda Martinas became very frightened. She tried to persuade Pedro to give up this horrible scheme. Eventually, when she met Tony she told him the whole story in the hope that my husband might be able to stop the fearful plot against Grearson. I do not think that she realised that my husband is as bad, if not worse, than Yatlin."

I watch her and see her little mouth set into a straight line. I reckon she don't like this husband of hers much.

"But it was too late," she goes on. "Tony knew that it was too late. He knew that Yatlin would rush Grearson out of Mexico and to France as soon as possible. He knew that once Yatlin had Grearson helpless in France and his half of the formula in his possession he could make his own terms with my husband.

"Tony returned here to Chicago. He did *not* tell my husband anything at all that he had learned from the Señora Fernanda Martinas. He merely told him that Grearson had been kidnapped, that Yatlin was responsible and was holding the trump cards. But he told me everything.

"Then, immediately my husband received the wire from the woman Zellara; immediately he had talked on the long-distance telephone with Yatlin about it, and your name was mentioned, I thought of a scheme by which it would be possible for the Government to get back both halves of the formula, a scheme which would make it possible for me to escape from a life which I loathe and detest, from a man who is more wicked than anything I have ever thought possible, but a scheme which I would only have courage to carry out if I knew that a man of your sort was with me."

She stands there by the table an' she looks at me an' I can see that her eyes are shinin' like stars.

I get up an' go over to her.

"That's very nice of you, lady," I tell her.

She drops her eyes an' looks at the little diamond watch on her wrist.

"I must go soon," she says. "Otherwise Jake will wonder what has happened. On no account must he be allowed to become suspicious."

"O.K.," I say. "What is the scheme? If it sounds all right I'm playin'."

She draws her coat round her.

"Here is the scheme," she says. "Yatlin told my husband, when they had the long-distance telephone conversation, that Grearson was kidnapped and that you were investigating. My husband has heard nothing from him since. The reason for that is obvious. Yatlin, having done everything he wanted to do, is surely by now on his way to France. He will believe that he is quite safe there and that once he arrives in France my husband will have to agree to his terms. Yatlin will therefore suggest that my husband sends the Jamieson half of the formula to him and that he, Yatlin, will undertake negotiations with the U.S. Government for the return of the complete formula.

"These terms will include an immense sum of money and a free pardon for all concerned."

"I get all that," I tell her.

"Now, Mr. Caution," she says. "Supposing something happened to my husband. Supposing that he was very quietly arrested. So quietly that even his own gang knew nothing of it.

"Supposing that I, as his wife, got into touch with Yatlin and said that my husband had asked me to deal with him. That I was bringing the Jamieson half of the formula with me to France, that once there I, acting for my husband, would come to terms with Yatlin and together we would negotiate the deal with the U.S. Government. Well, what would Yatlin do?"

I Whistle. Boy, is this a scheme or is it?

"Yatlin falls for it like a sack of coke," I say. "He falls for it because once you go to France with the Jamieson half of the formula he's got both halves. He's got the whole durn lot. He's holdin' every card in the deck."

"Precisely," she says. "He thinks that the day I arrive in France he is in entire control of the situation."

A little smile comes round her mouth an' she looks right inta my eyes.

"But what he will not know," she goes on, "is that the person who accompanies me on this trip to France, the person who is supposed to be Tony Scalla, is none other than a gentleman by the name of Lemmy Caution. . . . Well, Mr. Caution?"

I look at her.

"Lady," I tell her, "I'm all yours. I'm sold. I'll tell you somethin' else. Tony said you had everything. That was only a quarter true. You are the original wonder. You are an oil paintin' to look at an' you gotta brain that just clicks like an electric clock."

I put out my hand an' she puts her little soft white fingers into it. "You can always reach me here," she says. "Telephone through to Mariette in the beauty saloon downstairs if you want to reach me. She is the one person I can trust."

She gives my hand a little squeeze. Then she walks over to the door. She stops there an' turns around.

"Wait ten minutes before you leave," she says. "That would be safer."

"O.K.," I tell her. "So long, Georgette, I'll be seein' you."

That little smile comes around her mouth again.

"*Au revoir,* Lemmy," she says.

It is five o'clock when the supervisor from the Roseholme post office comes around to the Palissade with the wire from Washington. I grab it, give him a shot of rye an' tell him to forget that he ever saw me. He says O.K. an' scrams.

I decode the wire:

"Federal Government Secret.
Headquarters F.B.I. Washington Identification 472/B
To S.A. Lemuel H. Caution via Supervisor Roseholme District
Postal Office Chicago for personal delivery
Urgent Priority stop.

Reference your enquiries stop The woman Zellara small-time Mexican artiste employed until recently in estancias in Mexico stop Originally common law wife of bandit Pedro Dominguez stop Zellara recently in contact with Pinny Yatlin in Mexico City stop Search for police record delayed as only means of identification is by photograph not yet secured stop Mexican authorities state Fernanda Martinas one time wife of silver mine proprietor Enrico Martinas stop She left husband after money quarrel then joined Pedro Dominguez stop Director F.B.I. urges you make every effort in Pepper Jamieson Grearson investigation stop U.S. and British Governments greatly concerned in regard to Jamieson Grearson formulas and research papers stop U.S. Government at request of Director F.B.I. has ordered all Customs and Port officials to minutely search all baggage effects etc. of every possible suspect or possibly concerned individual leaving U.S. territory stop British Government resting all action pending some definite report from

*this Headquarters stop In event of any suspect leaving U.S. terri-
tory British Government Secret Service awaiting to co-operate in
any capacity requested by you stop Secretary for War U.S. Government through Director F.B.I. states loss or knowledge of Jamieson
Grearson formulas to any unauthorised person might create appal-
ling situation stop Director F.B.I. authorises you to promise free
pardon to all or any criminal for any offence in return for assistance required by you stop Unlimited funds at your disposal through
any Federal or Federally associated bank stop In this and all other
connections in this matter your identity to be that of Zetland V. T.
Kingarry stop Any application for assistance by you in that name
to any Government Postal Telephone Cable State County District
or Local authority will be immediately available stop Read learn
destroy stop."*

Nice work, hey?

I give myself a cigarette an' one little snifter of rye. I got the
sorta idea in my head that this job is the big high-light in the life of
Lemmy Caution.

Standing there with the glass in my mitt, lookin' outa the window
at the dusk that is just comin' along I get to thinkin' about Ma Caution.
I remember the old lady sayin' one day that she reckoned that I had
enough brains to get myself some place, some time, if some dame
did not get at me an' tear me in pieces first.

I get to thinkin' that if I have gotta be torn in pieces I would like
this Georgette to be the dame.

Is that baby a whirlwind to look at or is she? Any guy who knows
his cucumbers would know that Georgette is one of them dames that
you come across once in a lifetime, because when they was plannin'
that baby they just gave her everything they got an' then doubled it.

So what!

I get my hat an' I ease around to a drug-store around the corner.
I go inta the pay box an' I ring through to Police Headquarters. I tell
'em that I am a guy called Zetland V. T. Kingarry an' that I would
very much like to meet the Chief of Police in the back-room of the
Welwyn Cigar Stand on Michael Street at Barry Avenue at eight
o'clock prompt.

CHAPTER NINE
EVERYTHING IS JAKE

IT IS seven-fifteen an' a sweet night.

I have had a ritzy dinner served up in my sittin' room because, as you guys will realise, I am not at all keen on showin' my mug around Chicago more than I have to. Maybe that won't be for much longer now.

I light a cigarette an' sit there stirrin' my *demi-tasse* an' wonderin' what the evenin' is goin' to produce. With a bitta luck I reckon I am goin' to be able to slide outa Chicago to-morrow.

Mind you that conversation that I had with Georgette around at the Louisiana apartments is givin' me plenty to think about. Maybe Pedro Dominguez has got more brains than I thought he had. Anyhow I haven't got to worry about that bozo any more. He got what was comin' to him an' how!

But I am thinking about Fernanda. I get to thinkin' that I been a bit tough on that dame—in my mind I mean—because when all is said an' done I reckon that she had done the best she could do with a bad job.

Here's the way it looks to me:

Fernanda has a row with her husband—this guy Enrico Martinas. Maybe this mug is one of them straight-laced so-an'-so's who likes to have his wife tied up on the end of a strings—Spanish fashion—an' maybe Fernanda don't go for that. She is the sorta baby who wants a little high life now an' again. I reckon too that this guy Enrico kept her short of money.

O.K. So they have one swell row an' Fernanda takes a runout powder on him. Then she goes kickin' around an' meets Pedro. I don't reckon that she was ever very struck on this guy, but maybe, like she told me, she thought that the fact that she was runnin' around with him would stop her husband startin' a lotta trouble an' goin' after her.

Also to some dames Pedro would seem a romantic sorta guy an' he's behavin' himself pretty well an' not gettin' into too much trouble with the authorities.

Then the next thing that Fernanda hears is that Pedro has got this job guardin' the Jamieson *hacienda*. I reckon she suspected that there was somethin' phony behind all that. I reckon she guessed that Pedro wouldn't be content just to be a sorta superior night watchman hangin' around that desert dump with four *amigos* to see that the rats didn't steal anythin'. If I know anythin' of that Fernanda baby she suspected plenty an' got to work on Pedro to find out what it was.

Pedro comes across. He tells her the works. He tells her how Yatlin is aimin' to cross up Jake Istria by pinchin' the formulas for himself an' then holdin' up Jake for a big cut before he comes across. He tells her how Grearson is goin' to be snatched on the border, sent across Mexico to Ascapulco where they have got the boat waitin' to take him around to France by the long route. Maybe Pedro—who is a cruel sorta cuss—told Fernanda just what Yatlin's boys was goin' to do to Grearson so that when he got to France he would be a first-class mental case an' no errors.

Then I reckon that Fernanda started to get scared. After all it's one thing to be stringin' along with a Mexican bandit—because after all that is a recognised sorta profession in Mexico—but it is a durn different can of beans to get mixed up with a bunch of first-class thugs who are indulgin' in hijackin' poison gas, drivin' fellas mad an' generally startin' a new high in skulduggery such as ain't ever been known before to man or beast.

Then, the next thing Fernanda knows is that I am blowin' around, that Pedro suspects that I am aimin' to find out what has happened to Pepper. An' right after that I get outa that jail plot that Pedro had worked out for me an' start talkin' very cold turkey to her.

O.K. Well, what is she to do? I reckon that she feels she owes some sorta loyalty to Pedro, that she's gotta play ball with him while she can, but she also feels that I am not such a bad sorta palooka after all an' so she tries to play ball with me too.

She sends me up to the *hacienda* pronto because she knows that that is the one place where Pedro will not expect me to go. Then she sits down an' waits for Pedro.

He comes back an' is plenty steamed up with the fact that I got outa that jail an' ditched him an 'that now I will be after him good an' plenty. Maybe by this time he is gettin' a bit scared himself an' he tells her that he is goin' to make a certainty of keepin' my trap shut by blastin' me down first time he sees me.

So then I reckon that Fernanda thinks she is in a spot. She has either gotta stand by an' see me bumped—an' it is a cinch that by now she has guessed that Pepper was bumped by Pedro too—an' then string along with the Yatlin-Pedro crowd, or else she has gotta do somethin' noble.

An' that somethin' is that she has gotta bump Pedro.

If she does this I will be O.K. an' if she scrams out quick before I come back she will not have to answer any questions an' put anybody else in bad.

So she shoots him an' takes my car an' scrams. She manages to contact Tony Scalla, who I reckon has been sent along by Jake Istria to find out just what the hell is happenin' around there, an' she tells him the whole works as she knows it.

But it is a cinch that she never said anythin' about me. The first thing that Tony Scalla knew about me was when he got back to Chicago an' Jake tells him about the wire they got from Zellara—the one I made that hell-cat send.

Then Tony is properly scared. He closes down. He don't tell Jake a thing that Fernanda has told him, because he is scared stiff, an' because he can see that this poison-gas formula pinch, with the murder an' mayhem an' stuff that is goin' with it, is goin' to be such a big-time schemozzle that he'd better keep outa it.

He goes along to Georgette an' he tells her the whole goddam story an' Georgette bein' the little girlie with brains wises him up to the fact that Caution, after makin' Zellara send that wire, will streak straight up for Chicago as fast as he can. She tells him that his business is to hang around the airport until I check in an' tail me so that he can contact me, wise me up an' take me along to her so she can give me the whole story.

All this stuff will show you that I am for thinkin' that the Fernanda baby is a better dame than I thought she was originally, that I am changin' my mind about Fernanda, but then I am a guy who plays the job as it comes along. I am not that ace detective bozo, who knows the whole goddam works from the start an' who can tell you that you had eggs for breakfast just because you got egg-shells stickin' to your whiskers.

An' what do you guys think?

I get myself a black fedora with a big brim, stick on a pair of horn-rims that the bell-hop gets me from a five-an'-ten, an' turn up my overcoat collar. I reckon that this way, with my hands stuck in my overcoat pockets an' my shoulders sorta hunched, I don't look very much like Mr. Caution.

At eight o'clock pronto I ease around to the Welwyn Cigar Stand an' walk straight through inta the little room at the back. This is a room that the guy who runs the cigar stand keeps for customers who have a date with some heavy blonde that they wanta keep quiet. The fact that Kreltz, the police chief, goes in there to wait for me will make this cigar guy stop anybody else goin' in there.

Kreltz is waitin' for me. I've heard that this Kreltz is a nice guy with a swell record as a cop. He is thin-faced an' keen an' is wearin' a nice blue suit with a flower.

I don't waste any time.

"Howdy, Chief," I tell him. "Maybe you heard somethin' about me. I'm a guy called Zetland V. T. Kingarry."

He grins.

"I heard plenty," he says. "There's a Federal Government Instruction about the guy Kingarry. He seems an important sorta cuss. In fact I've got a Government-Secret Instruction in my office on the authority of the Federal Secretary that if this guy Kingarry asks me to blow up the City Hall I've got to do it. So how-do, Mr. Kingarry. My name's Sam Kreltz, an' here's my badge."

He shows it to me.

"O.K., Sam," I tell him. "We gotta do some quick work. We gotta start somethin' to-night an' finish it to-night. We can't make any slip-ups an' we gotta keep plenty quiet."

"That's O.K. by me," he says.

He gives me a big cigar.

"Before we get to the main works," I go on, "I wanta ask you a coupla questions. First of all what do you know about a dame called Georgette Istria—that's the first question, an' the second question is what do you know about a guy called Tony Scalla?"

"That's easy," he says. "Georgette is the wife of our big-time bad-guy around here, Jake Istria. She's a bit of a mystery woman. There was a lot of talk that Jake four-flushed her into marrying him, that she's a high-hat dame who got sucked in by an act that Jake pulled on her, and hasn't been able to get out of it. If you know Jake you can understand that. He's as clever as a rattlesnake and about twenty times as dangerous."

He takes a drag on his cigar.

"You know how things have been," he says. "We've had a lot of trouble in this city one way an' another in the last ten years. Things haven't been easy for a police chief. Jake Istria has been a thorn stickin' in my foot for a helluva time, but he's been playin' it easy for some time now.

"I've tried plenty to get somethin' on him through Georgette. But no soap. Nothin' happened."

"I suppose she hasta rely on him for dough?" I say.

"I don't know about that," he says. "She's got plenty of jack of her own. She's got a box at the safe deposit with plenty in it, I'm told. She seems to me a nice sort of woman who's been makin' the best of a bad job an' that's all I can tell you about her.

"Tony Scalla is one of Istria's boys. He works for the mob. We got him once, two years ago, on a carryin' concealed weapons charge, but he got out of the can after six months on a parole that looked as if it was nicely framed for him. He's what I'd call a second-rate mobster who don't like bein' really tough."

"An' Pinny Yatlin?" I ask him.

He shakes his head.

"I'd give a year's pay to send that rat to the chair," he says. "He usta run a mob of his own here until Istria muscled in an' took it over an' Yatlin with it. Yatlin's poison. I had something on him a few months ago but I couldn't make it stick. Yatlin got out of Chicago an' scrammed off to Mexico or some place an' he hasn't been back since. I'm glad of it. He's a very tough gangster an' he's got brains too."

"That's fine," I tell him. "That gives me my bearin's. Now here's the thing:

"We gotta get Jake Istria to some place where I can talk turkey with him for a few minutes. He's gotta be there alone. He ain't ever goin' to leave that place except in a police wagon an' I want you to pick him up personally. When you throw him in the can he's not to see or speak to anybody. You ain't goin' to let him see a lawyer or any of his pals. He's got to be held solitary an' if there's any questions about a mistake it's goin' to be better to bump him off nice an' quiet than let him open his trap to a wrong guy. You got that?"

"I got it," he says. "But I'm tellin' you it's not goin' to be easy. Istria's been playin' things very quiet lately. He's been sellin' property he's got around the city. Everything looks to me as if that rat has been aiming to clean up an' get out. He's not goin' to any of the night spots he uses. He's just stickin' around his apartment an' taking things easy and keeping his nose clean."

"Who's he been sellin' his property through?" I ask him.

"He's got a lawyer," he says. "Calcismo. Calcismo is about the only guy that Istria really trusts although he's got some pretty swell mobsters workin' for him. An' Calcismo has got brains."

"An' where does this guy Calcismo stick around?" I say.

"He lives around at the Everglade Arms apartments off the Boulevarde," says Kreltz.

"O.K.," I tell him. "Well, supposin' Calcismo wants to have a quiet talk with Istria—where do they get together?"

"They got a meetin' place in the upstairs back room at the Old Virginia Club—that's about sixteen miles out. It belongs to Istria an' it's a hot spot. That's where they talk."

I think for a minute. Then:

"O.K., Kreltz," I tell him. "Here's how we play it. . . ."

I get ready to leave my room at the Palissade at ten o'clock, an' I'm tellin' you guys that I'm sorta excited because this is maybe goin' to be a big night an' maybe a rough one too—but if it does come off . . .!

I put on the fedora with the funny brim, stick my horn-rims on my nose, take a quick look at the Luger to see it is workin' nice an' sweet an' have one final shot of bourbon for the road. When I'm drinkin' it I wish myself luck.

I stick the gun in the right hand pocket of my overcoat. I grab off the telephone an' I ring through to the Everglade Arms apartments. I say I'm a special delivery clerk at Chicago main post office an' I have got a special delivery letter— registered—for Mr. Calcismo, an' will he be there to take personal delivery? The guy on the switch-board tells me to hang on. After a minute he says O.K., Mr. Calcismo will be in.

I hang up the receiver an' I ease downstairs. On the other side of the road is the roadster that Kreltz has had left for me. Five minutes later I go inta the Everglade Arms.

At the reception desk there is a very intelligent-lookin' guy. I go over to him an' show him my badge quietly.

"Look, baby," I tell him, "maybe there's goin' to be a little rough stuff around this dump. If there is you make it your business to see that nobody takes any notice. If you don't, I'll promise you a dirty deal for not co-operatin'. You got that?"

He says he's got it all right. I go up to Calcismo's apartment which is on the sixth floor.

When I get to the door I knock. After a bit some Japanese guy opens it. I reckon this is Calcismo's servant.

"Good-evenin'," I tell him. "I'm from the Telephone Company. There's a fault on Mr. Calcismo's line, but the house management downstairs want permission for us to fix it, from you. Will you come down with me an' see 'em?"

He says yes, he'll come. He shuts the door behind him an' comes down with me in the lift. When we get downstairs inta the entrance hall two plain clothes dicks—Kreltz's boys—come in like I arranged.

"Take him away, boys," I say, "an' tell him if he's good he'll be out in a month."

I scram back inta the lift, up to the Calcismo apartment an' play tunes on the door bell. I wait a minute an' the door opens. Standin' in the doorway is a middle-sized broad-shouldered guy with a clever face.

"You're ringin' plenty hard, aren't you?" he says.

"That's right," I tell him. "Are you Mr. Calcismo?"

He nods. I put my hand flat on his face an' give him a push that sends him cannonadin' backwards inta the hall. He busts inta the hatstand an' richo's off onto the floor. I step in an' close the door behind me. He starts to get up off the floor. He's white with rage an' he ain't one bit frightened.

"All right," he starts in. "What is this? I'll fix you. . . ."

"Look, Calcismo," I tell him. "I reckon this is serious business, an' just how serious it's goin' to be for you is up to you. Here's what you're goin' to do. You're handlin' some private sorta business right now for Jake Istria somethin' to do with sellin' property or somethin' like that? O.K. You're goin' to put a call through to him. You're goin' to tell him that somethin' very important has happened. You're goin' to tell him that he's to meet you at half past eleven to-night at the

Old Virginia Club, that he's just gotta be there an' that he's to wait for you in the back room upstairs as usual."

"Oh yes?" he says. "And who in hell are you? You can't pull this stuff on me, I'm a lawyer. I . . ."

I hit him once, after which I get to work on him. I bust him around his sittin' room until he don't know whether he's comin' or goin'.

The work I put in on this guy is just nobody's business an' believe it or not I am likin' it because I am just about sick of these cheap, chisellin' two-timin' rotten rats of lawyers who stick around, pull chestnuts outa the fire for mobsters, an' make circles round the police department any time it looks as if their client stands a chance of gettin' pinched.

I bust this bozo around the place until his face looks like an advertisement for sun-ripened tomatoes, then I chuck him in a chair. He lies there like a fish outa water gaspin' for air. I go over an' look at him.

"Sweet legal friend," I tell him, "you don't know a thing, but I'm tellin' you this much, that if you don't play ball with me, you're goin' to Alcatraz jail, an' you're goin' to stay there until you rot. You got that?"

He looks up at me. I can see his lips tremblin'.

"Looky, Calcismo," I tell him, "it's this way. There are some things that are so durned big an' important that they will even justify framin' a double-crossin' mouthpiece like yourself for somethin' he didn't do. Now you have it which way you like. You're goin' to do what I tell you, after which I'm goin' to throw you in the can. You'll be kept there in solitary for a month. After that they'll let you out. When you come out you'll keep your trap shut an' like it.

"That's what happens to you if you do what I want. If you don't, it's the other thing that I told you. Well, which is it goin' to be?"

He pulls open his shirt collar an' tries to stop his nose bleedin'. He takes another look at me an' sorta makes up his mind.

"All right," he says, "I'm listening, anyhow."

"Right, baby," I tell him. "You get your breath, an' then you do the 'phone call. When you've done it, we're goin' to walk outa here. We're goin' to walk across the street. On the other side there'll be a car with some cops in it. You'll get in nice an' quiet. You got that?"

"I get it," he says.

He starts gettin' up an' it hurts him plenty. He looks like he has been run over by a hundred truck 'bus fulla heavyweights.

I help him up. He gives a groan an' walks over to the telephone.

At half past eleven I swing the roadster round to the back of the Old Virginia Club. I leave it in a clump of trees by the side of the road. I ease across the road an' walk across a lawn at the back of the Club. I have got the geography of this place from Kreltz.

Away over on the right I find a gravel path leadin' to the service door, where the goods go inta the Club. The door is locked but it is one of those easy locks. I bust it off.

I step inside. I'm in a long passage with store rooms on each side. Away at the other end of the passage there is a door half open. I can hear a band playin' in there. I walk down the passage towards this door. Three-quarters of the way along is another passage leadin' off to the left.

I ease up to the half-open door an' look through. It is a little door leadin' to what looks like a band rehearsal room, an' I reckon on the other side of this is the Club floor. I pull the door shut an' lock it, an' put the key in my pocket. Then I walk back an' turn down the passage to the left.

Half-way along I find an iron circular stairway. I ease up nice an' quiet. It runs right up to the second floor. There is a passage at the top an' at the end I can see a light comin' through the crack under the door.

I gumshoe along the passage, push open the door and step in. It is a nice big room. The furnishin's are swell. On the other side of the room is a big mahogany desk an' sittin' behind it is Jake Istria. He is a big guy, nearly as big as I am. He has gotta square face an' a bald head. He looks to me like a first class rat—only I am insultin' the rat.

"So what?" he says.

I take off my horn-rims an' put 'em in my pocket. I pick up a chair an' I plonk it down on this side of the desk an' I sit down.

"So this," I tell him. "You're washed up, Jake, you're all washed up an' finished. I've been wantin' to have a little talk with you for some time. My name's Caution."

"Oh yeah," he says . "I reckon I heard about you."

"Sure you heard about me," I tell him. "You gotta wire from Zellara, the one I made her send. I sorta wanted you to know I'd be blowin' around. Now, I'm goin' to confer with you, Jake, so just put your hands flat on the table in front of you an' listen, an' don't make a move, otherwise I might get tough."

He does what I tell him. He looks sorta surprised. I get up an' go back to the door an' lock it. Then I walk back an' look at him.

"If it's any satisfaction to you, Istria," I tell him, "I know the whole works, the whole durned shootin' gallery. Just how I found out this or that is nobody's business, but before I do with you what I'm goin' to do with you, I wanta have a little talk. I reckon you're about the lousiest rat that ever walked on two feet. There is probably only one rat as rotten as you an' that's Yatlin, an' it looks to me he's so lousy that he's even crossed you up.

"Now I hate makin' deals with guys like you. I hate makin' deals with a guy who ain't content with the usual cheap thuggery, murder, blackmail an' vice rackets, that your sorta guy goes in for, a guy who has to start tryin' to make a world corner in poison gas. I suppose you got sick of dealin' with individual murder, you thought you'd like to do a little bitta trade in the wholesale stuff. O.K.

"But I tell you what you're goin' to do. Somewhere here in Chicago you got the Jamieson half of the gas formula. I want it an' I'm goin' to have it. An' when I say I'm goin' to have it. I don't mean maybe. I'm gettin' it either by nice sorta means or the other thing."

I look at him an' grin.

"You're the guy who's beefed about givin' other guys a paraffin bath," I tell him. "Well, I'm not goin' so far as that with you in the first place. I reckon I'll start off with a cigarette lighter held between the fleshy part of the fingers, an' see how you like that."

I give myself a cigarette.

"When you go outa here," I tell him, "Kreltz, the police chief, is goin' to pick you up. He's goin' to take you for a little ride, an' he's goin' to chuck you in a prison that you won't get out of. Just how rough he an' the boys are in takin' you there, whether you get there intact or whether you get half your ribs broken, an' your face lookin' like a sponge that's been trodden on, is up to you. Well, what're you goin' to do?"

He draws a deep breath, a sorta hissin' breath. Then he starts to smile. He looks to me just like a moccasin snake in a bad temper.

"I reckon Georgette's been talkin'," he says. "Nice dame that! I'd like to get my hands on her, the . . ."

"I wouldn't worry about her, if I was you, Istria," I tell him, "you ain't goin' to bother her any more."

"No," he says. "O.K. You know everything, don't you, fella? Say, have you gotta cigarette?"

I throw a cigarette an' my lighter on the table. He lights the cigarette.

"Look, Caution," he says, "you ain't really worryin' me when you said I was all washed up. You wasn't far wrong. Things have been pretty lousy around this dump an' this last cross of Yatlin's hasn't pleased me any. I'm sick of that too."

"An' now Georgette's crossed me too. I reckon that baby has just been waitin' the chance. Anyhow, I reckon I asked for it. A guy who trusts a dame to play along is askin' for what he gets, an' it looks as if I gotta take what's comin'. But I would like to get my hooks on that dame just for five minutes. I'd fix her nicely."

He starts grinnin' again. He looks like the guy who gave the devil his first correspondence course.

"If you've been talkin' to Kreltz then maybe you'll know I've been meanin' to blow outa this place," he goes on. "Well, I know I'm beat. If I hadda got both halves of that formula—the Grearson half as well as the Jamieson—I coulda stood the whole lotta you up, an' I know it. As it is I reckon this job's too big for me."

He takes a drag on the cigarette.

"But you gotta admit, Caution," he says, "that I can play ball nice or I can make *some* trouble about it. If you an' the police boys get tough with me I reckon you'll get the information you want, but maybe I'd last out quite a while, so how do we deal if I just cash in with it right away?"

"We don't deal," I tell him. "I ain't dealin' with you, Istria. You'll get what's comin' to you anyway, an' I reckon the best thing you can get is about fifteen or twenty years."

He shrugs his shoulders.

"Yeah, fly-cop," he says, "that maybe is so, but guys have gotten themselves outa the pen before now an' maybe I can do that too some time. Anyway I reckon I could do with a nice rest."

"Can it, Istria," I tell him. "Get talkin'. I'm sick of lookin' at your rat's pan."

"O.K.," he says. "There is a wall safe behind the bookshelves in the library of my apartment at the Depeene. Nobody knows where it is, not even Georgette. I moved the formula there this mornin'. The bell button on the right hand side of the book-case works the shelves so they can be pushed out. Behind 'em is the wall safe. The key to that wall safe is in the filin' cabinet over there under 'C.'"

"O.K.," I tell him, "you go an' get it."

He gets up, walks round the desk an' walks over to the filin' cabinet. I get an idea in my head that maybe all this has been too easy, that maybe this guy will still try somethin'. He will try somethin' because there ain't much hope for him anyway.

I put my right hand in my coat pocket. He gets to the filin' cabinet an' pulls down the steel door. Inside hung on hooks I can see a lotta keys. He puts his right hand out an' takes a key down, an' as he does it he shoots his left hand inta the cabinet an' swings round. I see the gun in his hand.

I throw up the gun muzzle in my overcoat pocket as he fires. I hear the bullet go past my left ear. I squeeze the Luger as he fires the second time an' takes a piece of skin off my ribs. I hit him clean in the guts. He goes down squirmin'. I give him two more both through the dome. He decides to be dead.

I go over an' take the key outa his hand. Downstairs at the back I can hear the noise of guys runnin'. I reckon Kreltz has heard the shootin'. I unlock the door.

Kreltz an' two boys bust in. He takes a look around.

"Well," he says, "so he tried the hard way an' it didn't get him any place. I reckon that was the best way to fix that baby."

He looks at me an' grins.

"When you come to think of it," he says, "this was just about the best thing that coulda happened."

"You're tellin' me, Kreltz," I say.

But I wasn't thinkin' of him or me. I guess I was thinkin' of Georgette.

It's just half past twelve.

I ease inta the Depeene Hotel, scram across inta the lift an' go up to the Istria apartments. I have put through a call that I am comin'. Georgette opens the door.

I take a quick look at her. She is wearin' a black sorta lace loungin' frock an' she looks like the dame who started the Greek Wars. Boy, is she a girl?

We go inside.

The place is one hundred per cent. I reckon that these mobsters know how to fix themselves. She goes over an' gets me a drink an' brings it to me.

"Look, Georgette," I tell her, "we gotta work fast. We *gotta* pull this business off. First of all I better tell you about Jake. He's dead. I made a tough deal with him an' he said he was goin' to play. While he was gettin' the key of the wall safe here he tries a fast one with a gun. I hadta give it to him. He went out like a candle."

She staggers a bit. I go over an' put my arm around her.

"Take it easy, kid," I tell her. "It was the best thing for you. Maybe you'll get a break now."

"I know," she says. "I know . . . but it's still a shock. . . ."

She puts her arms around me an' she starts cryin' like a kid.

I put her in a big chair an' I ease over to the sideboard an' mix her a drink. I take it over to her.

"Look, Georgette," I tell her. "You cut out that little girl stuff. You're doin' a man's job now, so get busy an' turn off the waterworks. I don't like my assistants to be big sissies, see?"

She throws me a little smile. I'm tellin' you this dame is sweet.

"What do you want me to do, Lemmy?" she says.

"Here it is," I tell her. "Get it straight an' don't make any mistakes. How many telephones you got in this apartment?"

"Two," she says. "There's one in my room and one in the library."

"O.K.," I say. "Right now you go inta your room. You get long-distance on the telephone. You tell 'em to get you through as quick as they can to the de Elvira stage door in Mexico City. When you got the stage door you ask to be put through to Zellara's dressin' room. Tell 'em they got to get her quick, that it's a matter of life an' death.

"Right. When you get Zellara on the line you gotta be all steamed up, see. You gotta act that you was half nuts.. Here's what you tell her:

"You say that hell's bust here. That Caution has been around bustin' everythin' wide open. You tell her that an hour ago Caution an' the cops have pinched your husband Jake Istria an' framed him on a false charge. Say Caution's told him that he's goin' to get twenty years in a Federal prison.

"Tell her that you've seen Jake for a minute down at Police Headquarters. Say that Jake has told you to get through at once to Zellara an' tell her that he wants to send the Jamieson half of the formula to the Yatlin mob in Paris. Say that you've got the formula an' a plane waitin' in the airfield here, that you're takin' the plane for New York with Tony Scalla an' the formula an' catchin' the New York boat to Paris.

"Say that Jake says he'll play ball with Yatlin. That once Yatlin's got both halves of the formula safe in Paris he's to let the Federal Government know that unless they release Jake right away Yatlin will sell both halves of the formula to some foreign government.

"Say that Yatlin knows that the Federal Government will do anythin' to keep that formula safe, that they'll offer Jake an' Yatlin a free pardon an' a million to get it back.

"An' when you've told her all that, ask her where you're to go in Paris. Ask her where you can contact the Yatlin mob there. You got all that?"

I make her repeat it all. She gets it all right.

I take her inta the bedroom an' grab off the telephone. I get the chief operator at the Chicago main exchange an' tell him that Mr. Zetland V. Kingarry wants every line on the Mexican switch closed down except one an' that one is to plug in right away for the de Elvira in Mexico City, that when they get it they get the stage door an' say that Mrs. Georgette Istria is makin' a personal an' urgent call to Zellara. I tell this guy to move like he had the devil on his tail.

He says give him five minutes.

I leave Georgette by the telephone an' I scram inta the library. I find the bell-push, move the shelves an' there is the wall safe.

I stick the key inta the safe an' turn it. I am runnin' with sweat. I reckon I ain't ever been so steamed up in my life.

The door swings back. Inside the safe is a big leather case closed with a locked zipper. It is covered with Government oilskin an' my heart gives a bump when I see that at both ends the Federal seals are intact I reckon Jake knew his chemistry wasn't good enough to make him curious to look at the Jamieson half of the formula!

I stick it under my arm an' listen. Through the open door of the bedroom I can hear Georgette speakin'. After a bit she starts in again.

She has got Zellara!

There is a lot more talk. Georgette is doin' fine. She is puttin' on an act like she was plenty scared. She is cryin' inta that phone an' goin' on like she was nuts. I hear her tellin' Zellara about the plane an' all that stuff, an' then I hear her say . . .

"Yes . . . yes, I understand. I am to go to the Armine Lodge at Neuilly, near Paris. To ask for the resident doctor. . . ."

I flop in a chair. Me, I could cheer. We got the contact an' with a bitta luck I'm goin' to get that Yatlin rat where it's goin' to hurt him plenty.

I grab off the library telephone. I get through to the office of the Agent-in-Charge of the Federal Bureau in Chicago. I stick around while they get him.

After a bit he comes through. I tell him who I am.

"Look," I tell him. "I gotta leather wallet here, Federally sealed. It's plenty important. This wallet can start about fifteen wars an' a coupla revolutions. You get around here an' take it off me because I'm scrammin' for New York in a quick plane. You get yourself another plane an' you get over to Washington. When you get there you're goin' to hand that wallet to J. Edgar Hoover an' nobody else. You got all that?"

He says he's got it an' he's comin' right over.

I go over an' give myself a little drink. Georgette comes inta the room an' stands lookin' at me.

"Georgette," I tell her. "It looks like we pulled it off. You go pack your grip, baby. I'm takin' you places. I'm gettin' a plane fixed up pronto an' we're scrammin' for the New York boat right away."

She looks sorta washed up. I reckon she is feelin' all in.

"I'm glad, Lemmy," she says.

She comes over an' puts her hand in mine.

Then she flops.

I catch her as she falls. I'm tellin' you this Georgette is the berries. She even looks good when she faints.

I HAVE already told you guys that I am a mug who likes to lie around on his back an' do a spot of thinkin'. Well, believe it or not, I have had plenty time on this boat for doin' just nothin' else but.

Don't you get any ideas in your head that I reckoned that this trip was goin' to be just another sweet joy ride all one hundred per cent Georgette, deck tennis, drinks in the smokin' room bar an' walks around the boat deck in the moonlight, with all the stuff that is thrown in with them moonlight walks.

Me, I am supposed to be Tony Scalla an' I am not such a sap as to show myself around this boat with Georgette, just in case there is some fly baby aboard who has got an idea as to who I really am.

So what!

I been stickin' around this cabin for five days, goin' for a walk around the boat deck by myself late at night when I ain't likely to be seen, an' amusin' myself by wonderin' just what guys are makin' a big play for Georgette an' just how that momma is reactin' when she ain't got my eye on her an' she knows that her husband is nice an' dead an' no trouble to anybody. I get to thinkin' that it is just my luck that I should be the bozo who irons out Jake an' then has to stick around a state-room all the time pickin' my teeth an' singin' "*I Wonder Who's Got My Girl.*"

I've had plenty of time for wonderin' I'm tellin' you.

It's a sweet night. I go over an' open the porthole an' look out. The sea looks pretty good to me, an' somewhere the ship's band is playin' a swell number. The tune sorta brings me back to thinkin' of Georgette. Maybe you guys will think I am a bit nutty about this dame an' maybe you are right. She's got plenty. She's got looks an' brains an' plenty of guts an' I reckon that she is the sorta dame that I could settle down with an' run a chicken farm with some time, that bein' a profession that I think I could go for any time I was not chasin' thugs around the world.

I get the idea back of my head that one of these fine days—when I got all this bezusus cleared up—I will proposition Georgette in a very big way even if I only get a first-class smack on the beezer.

Just what the hell I am goin' to do when I get to Paris is another thing that is givin' me plenty to think about.

Figure it out for yourselves. I gotta keep durn quiet about what the job is. I gotta keep my nose clean an' look after Georgette an' I gotta get my hooks on that Grearson half of the formula.

Yatlin will surely be around in Paris an' if he or any of the mugs he has got workin' for him there—an' I reckon they will be a sweet bunch of babies—so much as get a smell of the fact that I am kickin' around they would fill me so full of holes that I would look like Aunt Mabel's antimacassar.

But the main thing that is worryin' me is Georgette. This dame has got to play a lone hand when we get to Paris. She is the one who has gotta contact this Armine Lodge place that the Yatlin crowd is usin'. Maybe they are there an' maybe Zellara told Georgette to go there just as a sorta contact place where she could meet up with somebody in the mob who would put her on to the main joint where they are operatin'.

An' Georgette has gotta do her stuff on her own because the Yatlin mob will expect her to turn up with the real Tony Scalla. It would be a sweet set-up if I went along an' one of these thugs knew who I was.

So whatever play I fix for us to use when we get there has gotta be worked by Georgette on her own until such time as she can tip me off as to where the end of this job is to be pulled, after which I reckon I can take care of things myself.

I give myself a shot of rye an' turn on the gramophone. I am consolin' myself that I am goin' to get some sorta action pretty soon, because the steward tells me that we shall hit Le Havre, France, to-morrow evenin' some time.

Me, I am sorta worried an' I don't know why, because it is not like me to get that way unless somethin' screwy is goin' on.

There is a knock on the door an' the steward comes in an' says the chief radio guy wants a word with me. He scrams an' the officer comes in.

"I've got a radio for you, Mr. Scalla," he says. "An' I'm asked to deliver it to you personally. I'm sorry we've not seen more of you this trip. But perhaps you don't like the sea."

I tell him that I am not a very good sailor an' that the sea always makes me see double an' a few other things. He has a drink an' scrams.

I open the radio. It is addressed to Tony Scalla, S.S. *Paris,* French Line. It says:

"Advise immediate contact Corporation Office Paris stop Market falling stop Father."

an' it means:

"Instruction contact U.S. Embassy Paris immediately on arrival stop Watch your step stop Director Federal Bureau of Investigation."

What the hell!

I burn the radio message an' I sit down an' smoke some cigarettes an' wonder what has broke. I reckon that if Washington Headquarters have been cablin' the U.S. Embassy in Paris with information for me, somethin' has broke loose since we left New York. But what I don't like is that "Watch your step"—this is an expression that is only used when there is plenty trouble stickin' around an' any time that I am runnin' into trouble I always like to know just what it is an' where it's comin' from.

An' right now I don't know anythin' very much. Most of the time I been guessin'.

Well, I gotta do somethin'. I look at my watch. It is eleven o'clock. I sit down at the writin' desk an' I write a note to Georgette:

"Dear Georgette,

We shall be pullin' in at Le Havre some time to-morrow afternoon or evening. Here's what you do. Directly the Paris *docks you get through the Customs and take the tie-up train for Paris. When you get there you go straight to the Hotel Grande-Claremont and check in as Mrs. Georgette Istria.*

Tell the clerk at the reception that you want a suite with telephone in the sitting and bedrooms. Mention sort of casually that you are expecting a visit some time from your friend Mr. Scalla and that any time he comes around or calls through he is to be put right on to you. This will make it easy for me to get you directly I want to.

If you see me when the boat docks don't take any notice of me.

I shall be in Paris before you. I shall take a plane from Le Havre and get there good and quick because maybe something has broke that I ought to know about.

When you pull in at the Grande-Claremont go to bed and get all the sleep you can. I don't reckon to have to contact you until some time the day after to-morrow.

So long, soldier,

Tony."

I seal this note up, an' ring for the steward. I give him ten bucks and tell him to leave the note with Mrs. Georgette Istria's stewardess so she'll get it directly she goes to her cabin.

I have a final cigarette an' I turn in. Because I have always found that bed is a sweet place especially if you ain't quite certain of anythin', an' I have always found it to be a very good thing to be certain of nothin' at all.

When we dock at Le Havre I don't waste any time. I am lucky with Customs an' get through quick. I grab a car, get over to the airfield, an' I am lucky enough to find a taxi-plans that has just pulled in to meet the boat, an' the pilot is just ridin' back to Paris. This must be my lucky day.

While we are doin' this hop I just sit back an' relax. It is a quarter to eleven when we get inta the airfield at Le Bourget. I grab off a cab an' tell the driver to step on it. We go straight to the Hotel Welling-ton, which is a nice quiet sorta place, where I check in as Tony Scalla an' get myself a room with a telephone.

I go up to my room, wait till my bags are brought up an' get straight on to the U.S. Embassy. I say I wanta talk to the Senior Embassy Officer who is on duty, an' that my name is Tony Scalla. After a bit he comes on the line.

"Good-evening, Mr. Scalla," he says. "By the way," he goes on, "is there any other name, probably the name of a friend of yours, that you'd like to mention to us?"

"Yeah," I tell him. "I got a great friend. His name is Zetland V. T. Kingarry."

"That's all right, Mr. Scalla," he says. "We have a communication for you here. It arrived two days ago—a cable letter. Will you tell me where it can be sent?"

I tell this guy that I am at the Hotel Wellington, an' I tell him not to send the communication, whatever it may be, round by one of the Embassy messengers, but to send it around by the local messenger agency.

He says O.K. He also says that his name is Varney, an' that he has instructions to stick around the Embassy so as to be there any time I want him. I tell him thanks a lot an' hang up.

I walk up an' down my sittin' room wonderin' about this communication. I reckon this is a cable letter from the Director an' I reckon he must have sent it within about ten or twelve hours after the *Paris* left New York. Anyhow I am soon goin' to know.

In the meantime I think I will get a little action. I get hold of the phone book an' I look up the number of Hinks Agency. This agency is an American private detective agency run by Cy Hinks, a right guy who used to be in the New York State Police one time, an' who now makes some sweet dough runnin' a swell private dick's business in Paris, an' gettin' the big American play-boys outa jams when they get sucked in by the pretty ladies an' suchlike. Cy is a nice bozo an' a straight shooter.

When I get through to the office they tell me that Cy has gone home, but after a lotta palava, during which I tell 'em that I am practically his long lost brother, I get the number outa these guys. Five minutes afterwards I get him on the telephone.

"Look, Cy," I tell him. "I don't wanta give you a name because sometimes phones can be dangerous, but if you don't recognise my voice maybe you will remember the little stick-up job at the Ivy road house near Albany in 1934. If you do you'll remember the guy who was with you."

"I get it," he says. "I guess I know who I'm talking to."

"O.K.," I tell him. "Here's what I want you to do. There is a dame pullin' in at the Grande-Claremont Hotel some time to-night. She got off the *Paris* that docked at Le Havre. She'll be comin' inta town by train. I'm stayin' at the Wellington, an' callin' myself Tony Scalla.

"Now this dame is a sweet piece of work, an' also she is mighty important at the present moment. I got the sorta idea in my head that there might be one or two not-so-good boys stickin' around waitin' for her to check in, an' takin' an interest in this dame's movements. They mighta guessed that she was comin' in on the *Paris*. You got that?"

He says he's got it.

"Well," I tell him, "you stick a coupla good boys around there, really intelligent guys who don't look like dicks. Put 'em up at the hotel. You want fellers who look good an' can behave themselves, an' tell 'em to stick a rod under their arms. But they're not to use it unless they've absolutely gotta. I don't want any shootin', but if it looks really tough an' as if this dame is really in a jam, they can get busy an' shoot their heads off, because it'll be O.K. You follow me?"

He says he's ahead of me an' will take care of it right away. I say I will contact him somehow during the next two three days an' maybe have a talk.

I hang up an' order myself a bottle of Cognac. I'm feelin' pretty tired. Stickin' around in that steamship cabin for days on end don't sorta suit my temperament. Just when I have nicely negotiated the drink, the messenger from the theatre ticket service comes round an' gives me a letter. I give this guy a dollar an' after he has scrammed outa the room I lock the door an' go sit under the electric light in front of my dressin' table an' decode an' read it, an' believe it or not it gives me heart disease.

"Federal Government Secret.
Headquarters F.B.I. Washington Identification 472/B
To S.A. Lemuel H. Caution for transmission by cable via U.S.
Embassy Paris in code.

Reference Jamieson-Grearson stop Director F.B.I. informs Special Agent L. H. Caution of the following events which have transpired since Special Agent Caution left New York stop.

1. The Jamieson formula handed by Caution to the Agent-in-Charge Chicago F.B.I. has been examined and found to be a fake stop Whilst the formula is written in the same scientific form, numerals, code signs, quantities and names of chemicals have been altered. The leather wallet containing this fake formula is without doubt the original wallet used to enclose the true formula. The oilskin covering is also the same and the Federal seals which were unbroken were obviously removed by an expert and replaced after the fake had been put in the wallet. It would seem therefore that this change must have been effected shortly before the arrival in Chicago of Special Agent Caution. The transposition of the fake formula into the

*original sealed case was no doubt effected for the purpose of gain-
ing time. The situation is made more difficult owing to the fact that
on receipt of the information from the Agent-in-Charge of Chicago
Field Office that the Jamieson formula had been handed to him the
very close watch on all U.S. ports and frontier lines was relaxed.*

*2. Reference Pinny Yatlin. Information has been received by the
Director F.B.I. Washington that Pinny Yatlin was last night shot
dead outside an apartment house in Mexico City. Killer is unknown.
Further information is being sought by the Director and if secured
will be transmitted in due course to the U.S. Embassy Paris.*

*3. Reference Zellara. With reference to the information requested
by Special Agent Caution in regard to any police record on file
against this woman, it is now established that she has served terms
of imprisonment in a women's reform home and two State peniten-
tiaries. Complete record of her fingerprints and handwriting are
on file in the Oklahoma women's penitentiary.*

*4. A photograph of this woman, whose full name is Zellara Magda-
lena Riozos, together with some associates has been secured and
has been transmitted over the wire to the Editor of the Paris New
York Times. This gentleman has received an instruction to transmit
a print of this photograph immediately he receives an application
from Tony Scalla and will treat this matter as confidential. Director F.B.I. Washington wishes to advise Special Agent Caution,
having regard to the importance of the investigation on which he
is engaged, and that such investigation is now taking place in a
foreign country, that he should proceed with the utmost care. Good
luck. Read learn destroy."*

I read this stuff through again an' I burn it. Then I sit down in
a chair an' give myself a cigarette. I will not try to tell you guys the
names I start callin' myself, because I have gotta idea back of my head
that I am the king-pin sucker of the whole wide world, that I have
laid myself wide open an' been taken for the sweetest ride that ever a
bonehead who called himself a Federal Investigator has ever been on.

Boy, am I a sap or am I?

I grab off the telephone an' I ring down to the desk. I tell 'em to
send a messenger round to the office of the Paris *New York Times* to

see the night editor in charge an' ask for the picture he has got for Mr. Tony Scalla. They say O.K.

I walk up an' down the room an' I do a little bit of heavy thinkin'. So Pinny Yatlin has been shot in Mexico City. That means to say he never come over to France, that he was just stickin' around there, an' you'll agree that this seems a very funny thing. Of course maybe he's got somebody lookin' after the job this end, somebody he can trust, but you woulda thought that Yatlin woulda got over here good an' quick. He'd have been a durned sight safer in France than he would be in Mexico City. Another interestin' thing is the fact that he's shot outside an apartment house. I reckon I'm prepared to lay a shade of odds that he was shot outside Zellara's place, in that sorta passageway leadin' out to the street; the passage they took me through the night Yatlin an' his two boys tried to bump me.

Well, you're goin' to agree that it is an extraordinary thing that Yatlin, who is the wise guy an' very clever, should get himself shot just at this time, *after* Istria had agreed to play ball with him an' to hand over the Jamieson half of the formula.

Which I reckon is what he had done. Istria had sent off that half of the formula either just before I get inta Chicago or just afterwards, an' all that stuff that was played on me, all that stuff that Tony Scalla put up to me, all the bunk that the little Georgette has been pullin' on me with her swell figure an' them hot blue eyes of hers, was just to keep me blowin' around like a two by four sucker sufficiently long to give Istria time to make his deal with Yatlin, to send off the *bona fide* Jamieson half of the formula an' to replace it in the Federal cover with a fake one. An' is this clever?

Because if the guy who is carryin' the formula hangs around for a bit, then he is goin' to get away with it easy because just about the same time I hand over the phony formula to Washington an' they take the heavy watch off all ports an' passengers. Now you tell me if I'm a mug.

I can't work this business out at all. Something is sorta missin'. I walk up an' down the room thinkin' of half a dozen schemes that I can pull. But what the hell can I do? I've gotta stick around an' take a chance of gettin' a line on what is really goin' on around here.

After a bit there is a knock on the door. It is the bell-hop an' he's got the picture from the *New York Times* place. I give him a dollar bill, then I bust the cover off the picture an' take it under the light.

An' when I look at it I let go a wail that you coulda heard in China.

The picture is one of two women an' two men. *The two women are Zellara an' Fernanda!* I don't know who the two guys are. I turn the picture over an' on the back I read this caption:

"Señora Fernanda Martinas succeeds in obtaining release on parole of her sister Zellara Riozos from the Oklahoma Women's Penitentiary."

Sufferin' Hell-cats! So Fernanda is Zellara's sister and all these goddam dames have made me look like somethin' that the cat found under a stick in the garden an' wouldn't eat.

I chuck the picture down an' I flop in a chair. I got it all right. That little wise-guy Caution has got things worked out at last just at the time when it's too late an' not likely to be any durn good to anybody.

I sit there lookin' in the glass in front of me an' realise that I am lookin' at the biggest sap that ever carried a "G" badge.

I reckon I got the whole sweet set-up because it looks to me that the brains in this business is not Jake Istria or Pinny Yatlin. It is stickin' out like the New Connecticut jetty that the ace brains in this job belong to the dames, and outa the lot of 'em I am rewardin' the prize to my little friend Fernanda Martinas.

Do you remember what I told you guys when I got back from the *hacienda* to Fernanda's *casa* in Mexico the night I found Pedro shot? Do you remember me reconstructin' that business an' tellin' you that I thought the reconstruction was lousy? Well, I was right.

I reckon I know why Fernanda shot Pedro an' it wasn't to save my life either.

I sit there feelin' sorta cold an' a little bit desperate, a way I don't often feel. Me, I reckon I am in a jam, an' if I am goin' to do any good for myself an' anybody else, I gotta take it easy an' use my headpiece.

Right then for no reason at all there flashes through my mind that remark of Ma Caution's, the time when she told me that maybe I would get some place some time if some dame didn't tear me in pieces first. Well, was she right or was she? Because I reckon I have been torn in pieces by three dames, not one, an' those dames are Fernanda Martinas, Zellara Riozos an' Georgette Istria.

I get some action. I grab off the telephone an' get through to Cy Hinks again. After a bit this guy gets outa bed an' talks to me.

"Listen, Cy," I tell him. "I'm in a spot. I gotta get some quick movement outa you. You tell me something, have you got those two boys on the Grande-Claremont Hotel?"

He says he ain't got two, he's got three. One of 'em is in there as a waiter an' two as guests. He says that Mrs. Istria blew in there on time an' she's got a suite on the first floor, that she's gone to bed.

"O.K.," I tell him. "I tell you what I want you to do, Cy. Don't make any mistakes. You get outa bed an' do this job yourself, an' the bill don't matter. Whatever it costs is O.K. Get yourself a car, get out to Neuilly. Out there is some place called Armine Lodge. You gotta find out all about the guy or guys who own that place, where they come from, what they're doin' there. Get a plan of the house even if you have to bribe somebody in the local surveyor's office with a thousand dollars to get it. I want to know every goddam thing you can find out about Armine Lodge an' everybody who's been connected with it for the last year.

"Now don't start shootin' off your mouth about what time of night it is. Get action. Wake 'em all up. Tell 'em somebody has left somebody else a million dollars an' you wants to find 'em quick, but get me information an' get it good.

"If there is people livin' there, find out where they get their provisions from, find out what time the delivery boys come, find out what letters go there, how many telephones they got. Just play around an' find out everything you can about this place. When you've done that you report personally to me, an' remember this, Cy, you're workin' for Uncle Sam this time."

"O.K.," he says. "I get it. I'll get action. But I do wish to God I could get one night in bed."

I hang up. I put the telephone down, take off my coat, undo my shirt collar an' go an' lie on the bed. I reckon that the news I have just got about Yatlin bein' bumped an' the picture that I have just looked at, the picture that shows me that Fernanda an' Zellara are sisters, have just about filled in the missin' blanks in the true set-up in this bezusus.

Work it out for yourself. Fernanda an' Zellara are sisters. Zellara was Pedro Dominguez's common-law wife. Afterwards Pedro gets around with Fernanda an' Zellara gets around with Yatlin.

O.K. So what? So this. Dominguez gets himself shot by Fernanda, an' Yatlin gets himself shot by Zellara.

Now have you got it or have you got it?

I grab a cigarette outa the box by the side of the bed an' light it. When I look at it I see the words "Lucky Strike." I grin. I remember when I saw those words before, when I was talkin' to Georgette, when I thought she was a lucky strike. She was, *like hell she was!*

Looking up at the ceilin' through the smoke, I see the whole goddam story. Here it is:

Pinny Yatlin is down in Mexico City because Chicago was a bit too hot for him. Somehow or other he gets to hear about these two chemists an' the gas formula, an' the *hacienda* in the desert. He gets through to Jake Istria an' says here's where they pull off a big job. Istria says yes get busy, so Yatlin starts organisin' it.

The first thing he wants is some Mexican guy who is good to do the killin' at the *hacienda*, so Zellara tells him that she knows the very guy; Pedro Dominguez is the man he wants. So they get Pedro in on this job. Pedro is to fix himself the job as guard at the *hacienda* an' to bump the chemists when the time comes.

O.K. About this time Pepper gets a line on this business. He don't know what it is all about, but he thinks he oughta investigate. He tried to get information outa Zellara because he thought he'd got somethin' on her because he knew her U.S. prison record. Zellara tells Yatlin an' Yatlin knows that Pepper has gotta be taken care of.

So Zellara puts Pepper on to Pedro who has got instructions to bump him off when he gets the chance. Right now Pedro is gettin' around with Fernanda Martinas. Pedro can't keep his mouth shut. He blows the whole works to Fernanda. I reckon it was Fernanda who tipped off Pinny Yatlin that it would be a great idea to double-cross Istria, to get both chemists down at the *hacienda*, grab off both halves of the formula an' then stand Istria up for eighty per cent of the dough. What could Istria say anyway?

An' I reckon it was Fernanda's idea, when she thought Istria was gettin' suspicious, to kidnap Grearson on the border before he got to the *hacienda*. Yatlin agrees an' they play it that way. But they didn't think that Istria would send one of his thugs with a moll inta Mexico, probably posin' as a coupla desert tourists, to blow inta the *hacienda* an' keep an eye on things.

An' these two get plenty suspicious an' start somethin'.

All right, there is a show-down. In that show-down Pepper who is stickin' around gets shot. It looks like Jamieson got killed, although there wasn't any trace of his body, but there was an explosion, an' when you come to remember that Istria's mobsters used to do some very heavy bombin' in the old days, blastin' in shop fronts an' blowin' up the places of people who wouldn't pay for protection, you don't have to think twice about that explosion. I reckon that the guy that Istria sent down there hadda coupla pineapple bombs in his suitcase just for luck, an' when Pedro Dominguez started a little gunplay this bozo started to chuck bombs, which would account for the funny sorta way that the *hacienda* looked with only two walls of that room blown out.

I reckon Pedro don't like this bomb stuff very much. He ain't used to it, so he scrams outa the *hacienda* good an' quick an' while he is out the Istria thug an' his girlie get their hooks on the Jamieson half of the formula, an' scram like they had a coupla rattle-snakes after them. They scram back to Chicago an' they hand it over to Jake. So now Jake *knows* that Yatlin is aimin' to pull a fast one.

So there is the set-up when I arrive on the scene. Fernanda is in on the job workin' with Zellara an' Yatlin. Didn't that wire say that she had a quarrel with her husband about dough? Well, Fernanda is a clever dame an' she knows that there is all the dough in the world in this job if it is pulled properly.

The next thing she hears is that I'm blowin' around Mexico lookin' for Pepper, so it is left to Pedro to get rid of me. Fernanda knows that I am lookin' for Pedro so she takes good care that I find him. He knows I will fall for that gettin' stuck in the jail stuff so as to be able to get his story from him nice an' quietly an' they both aim to get me bumped off—"shot while attempting to escape." This keeps their noses clean about me an' any trouble about my death is goin' to lie between the U.S. an' the Mexican Governments.

You will realise that this dame Fernanda has surely got brains. But I bust outa that jail an' I do the thing that Fernanda don't expect. I turn up at her *casa* an' I tell her the truth. If you ask me why she didn't bump me off then, when she had the chance, the reason is because I told her a bitta hooey about havin' been on the telephone to our police across the border. She just daren't do it at that moment.

So she gets rid of me. She gets me off to the *hacienda* pretendin' to help me, to give time for Pedro to come back so they can have a meetin'.

Pedro comes back. Now I have told you guys before that I have always considered Pedro to be a small time bandit. I reckon when he heard that the U.S. Government was takin' a heavy interest in this business he didn't feel quite so good. Maybe he wanted to throw his hand in. If anybody was goin' to get scared he would, not Fernanda. So he gets tough. Maybe he wants payin' off an' to get outa the business.

So Fernanda does a little quick thinkin'. She knows durn well that Grearson has been snatched an' is on the boat on his way to France. She knows that Pedro has served his turn an' is anyway liable to talk when he's, drunk too much *tequila*.

So she grabs up my gun an' she shoots him, an' then she sticks him up in that chair an' leaves the light on so that when I come back I will see him, an' I will know that the dear little Fernanda has been nice an' brave an' has shot this wicked bandit just so he shouldn't lay for Lemmy Caution.

So much for Fernanda.

I swing myself off the bed an' I bring my mind to bear on this second hell-cat—this Georgette, this dame who I thought was the one super lovely of the whole wide world, and who has played me along so sweetly that I reckon if the Director of the F.B.I. knew just what a sap I was he'd give me the air an' suggest that I oughta get a job croonin' or in some other sweet profession like that.

O.K. Well, I reckon I am goin' to have a little talk with this Georgette. An' here we go!

CHAPTER ELEVEN
EXIT GEORGETTE

CAN life be lousy, but maybe you heard that one before.

Sittin' back in the cab that is takin' me around to the Grande-Claremont, puttin' two an' two together an' tryin' hard not to make six of it, I start wonderin' what in the name of everything that opens an' shuts am I goin' to do with this hell-cat dame Georgette when I get my hooks on her.

Two seconds' quiet thought an' any guy who is not absolutely eligible for election to the local nut-house will see that I am in a tough spot and that the Fernanda Martinas momma is holdin' all the cards. By now, the mobster whose job it was to bring over the Jamieson formula has got here. I reckon he started one or one an' a half days ahead of us an' if I am right about this it means that Fernanda and the Yatlin boys that she has got workin' with her over here are sittin' in right on top of the game an' have got me beat all ends up—that is unless I can pull something very good out of the bag right away.

I come back to Georgette. This baby has got me properly steamed up, an' when I say steamed up I don't mean perhaps. I woulda put my shirt on this dame bein' on the up-an'-up and the double-cross that she has pulled on me just goes to show you that you don't ever know where you are with a doll.

An' the more a guy thinks that he knows about dames, an' the more experience he has stuffed inta his lifetime only goes to make him a worse sucker who falls hardest when some lovely with burnin' eyes gets up close to him an' gives him one of them "I-won't-say-yes-but-I-also-won't-holler" look that mean so much to a bozo who is right then tryin' to win the wide world cuddlin' handicap.

Me, I oughta have known better. I been over enough ground to know that when some wide-eyed blonde honeypot who has got a shape that would make the Queen of Sheba look like a stand-in for a ring-tailed baboon starts handin' out a line that begins with that old-time refrain "I can refuse you nothin'," it is time for a wise guy to pull out so fast that he will burn up the ground under him.

But he don't. He just thinks that it is all goin' to be different this time an' plays around tryin' to see how many times he can get his big strong arm around the baby's waist an' just how true it is that her lipstick is really waterproof an' won't come off all over his silly pan.

Maybe you heard of this great lover Casanova. Well, I reckon that if somebody come across with the truth this guy is just another big punk who is just beefin' about what he thought happened with all the dames that he got around with.

Because it is the inexperienced sap who has just come down off the farm, the guy who is so pop-eyed an' innocent that he thinks a *brassière* is a place in France where they go for a drink, that wins out with the clever babies. Why? Because he *is* so durned nutty that every hot momma who streaks across the horizon is tryin' to set the mug on his feet an' teach him all the things a young man should know before some other doll gets her hooks inta him.

Because she has always got a swell alibi. She can always say that she is tryin' to mother the big sap—which is an alibi that was used by that dame Cleopatra when she was tryin' to get a strangle-hold on Mark Antony who was supposed to conquer Egypt but who got so steamed up about this baby an' her takin' ways that he woulda hocked the Roman Empire anytime she wanted somethin' new in step-ins.

I do not wanta get historical but I am tellin' you guys that Henry the Eighth was the first right royal palooka to find out that the only way you can stop a dame rushin' about the place an' wailin' that she has surrendered everythin' an' got nothin' for *it* but a succession of bilious attacks, an' shootin' off her mouth mornin' noon an' night about the way she has been let down, is by doin' what he usta do, an' that is sendin' an urgent an' confidential note around to the executioner tellin' him to sharpen up the old battleaxe an' slice the dame's pineapple in one try on the battlements at dawn prompt.

You're tellin' me!

But the question that is troublin' me right now is what I am goin' to do with this little double-crossin' sweetheart Georgette.

I get an idea. I stop the cab at the next telephone kiosk an' get out. I call through to this guy Varney at the U.S. Embassy an' am very glad to find that he is stickin' around. I have a little conversation with him an' he says that he reckons it will be O.K. to do what I want him to. After this I feel a bit better an' go on to the Grande-Claremont.

When I get there I have a word with the night reception guy an' tell him that Mr. Scalla wants to see Mrs. Georgette Istria rather urgent an' after a coupla minutes' wait she phones down to the desk will Mr. Scalla please go up.

Goin' up in the elevator I light myself a cigarette an' say that piece outa the Child's First Primer about keepin' cool, because the way I am feelin' at the moment I would like to take hold of this Georgette an' smack fourteen different kinds of sparks outa her. An' how would you feel?

I knock on the door an' she says come in. I go in.

She is standin' by the table smilin', with her hand sorta held out ready for me to take. She is wearin' some soft, blue sorta wrap thing that goes with her eyes an' if I did not know that she was one of Satan's own sisters-in-law an' a pretty fly one at that I would think that a large lump of butter wouldn't melt in her mouth. She has got that innocent sorta pan that makes you wanta think that it musta been the other guy's fault all the time an' that she couldn't blot her copy-book even if she tried.

I reckon I will play this baby along for a bit.

"Sit down, Georgette," I tell her. "I wanta talk to you an' it's important. Just sorta relax an' let's concentrate on what we gotta do."

"All right, Lemmy," she says.

She sends me over a smile guaranteed to knock the stuffin' out of a brass monkey. Then she goes over to the big chair an' sits down. I'm tellin' you she is just too cute for words. Before she fixes her wrap I get a quick look at a piece of leg an' I'm tellin' you that whoever it was designed this dame oughta get a prize even if she is coloured dark black inside.

"O.K.," I tell her. "Well, here is the position. We're over here an' I'm supposed to be Tony Scalla. Well, it's stickin' out a foot that whoever you are supposed to contact when you go to the Armine Lodge to-morrow might be one of Yatlin's boys who knew Scalla in the old days. That bein' so he'd know I *wasn't* Scalla an' he'd start smellin' a rat."

She nods.

"You mustn't go there, Lemmy," she says. "I must go alone. You ought to keep in the background until I find out who *is* there."

"That's very nice of you, Georgette," I say, tryin' hard to stop myself vaultin' across the room an' smackin' her a king smack where it would hurt her most. "I reckon that's very sweet an' brave of you. O.K. Well, how do you suggest you play this thing?"

She thinks for a minute. Then:

"I think I ought to go out to Neuilly to-morrow morning," she says. "When I get there I go straight to the Armine Lodge and tell whoever is there that I am Mrs. Istria and that I have come there at the request of Zellara.

"I don't suppose there will be anybody very important there," she goes on. "I expect they will have somebody there who doesn't matter very much and who knows very little of what is going on. But I expect there will be a telephone and when I arrive some one will telephone through and give some further instructions. They will tell me to go on to some other place and take the Jamieson formula. Directly I get this instruction I return here and report to you."

I look at her an' I grin.

"An' so you think they'll do that, do you?" I tell her. I give an imitation of the way she talks. "You think they'll tell you to take the Jamieson formula to some other place, an' you're goin' to come back here an' tell me where."

I chuck my hat in the corner. I go over an' I stand lookin' down at her.

"You think I'm the world's best sap, don't you, Mrs. Double-Cross?" I tell her. "You think I'm still fallin' for all this punk that you've pulled on me. Well, if I was to tell you what I think about you an' your lousy supposed brother Tony Scalla, and your lousy husband that you was so keen on gettin' away from, I reckon it would take me about fourteen years an' I would only stop then because I couldn't think up any new words."

She goes as white as a sheet. She looks at me like she has seen a coupla ghosts.

"I don't understand," she says. . . . "Tony Scalla . . . my brother. . . . Why that's ridiculous."

"You bet it's ridiculous, Gorgeous," I say. "I reckon if the truth was told Tony Scalla has been your boy friend for years an' probably sharin' you with the late Jake an' anybody else who likes the looks of you. Now shut up an' get this, because I'm tired of lookin' at that sweet an' beautiful an' pure face of yours an' because it's about time that you an' me understood one another.

"I've heard from Washington. The formula that I took outa Jake Istria's wall safe in the library at the Depeene Hotel was a fake, an' you knew it. Pinny Yatlin never left Mexico City. He was shot there a coupla days ago. I reckon I knew who fixed for him to get shot an' that was your friend Fernanda Martinas an' the one who did it was her sister Zellara an' you knew she was goin' to do it.

"When Jake Istria got the wire that I made Zellara send him he thought up a sweet one—or maybe you thought it up for him. The scheme was one hundred per cent water-tight. Tony Scalla meets me an' tells me a helluva story about bein' your brother an' that you an' he are scared stiff an' wanta get right out of this business. I fall for that one. He tells me that you hate your husband who has given you a lousy deal an' that you'd do anything to get away from him an' get a clean slate by helpin' the law. I fall for that one too. I am a little prize sap, ain't I? I fall for everything!

"All Jake an' you an' Scalla want is to get time so that Jake can hand over the real Jamieson formula to Scalla who will hang around New York until I get the fake one an' send it to Washington. You know that the watch will be taken off the ports then an' Tony can get a boat a day or two days ahead of me. Then he joins up here in France with Fernanda who is already over here, an' then she has got *both* halves of the formula. She has got somethin' she can trade with.

"She has got somethin' that is goin' to stop the whole durn lot of us dead in our tracks, an' I reckon that all she is doin' now is sittin' down with a pencil an' paper and workin' out just how much dough she wants from the U.S. Government before she returns the Jamieson an' Grearson formulas or else . . .

"You put the big scheme up to me about you an' me pretendin' to come over here with the formula. You knew that I'd ask you to ring through to Zellara to find out where you was to make your contact. The very fact that you rang through to her is goin' to tell her that the time has come to bump Yatlin so that, with Yatlin out of the way an' Istria in jail or dead, you an' Fernanda can run the whole goddam business the way you want it run an' take all the dough.

"O.K. An' you also know that when you get here I've got to let you go to the Armine Lodge on your own in case I get recognised by somebody as *not* bein' Tony Scalla, an' you reckon to take that opportunity of takin' a run-out powder on me an' joinin' up with the rest of the mob an' blowin' me sweet raspberries from afar.

"Well . . . it was a swell scheme an' most of it's come off. Fernanda's got both halves of the formula. I reckon we got to do a deal with her on her terms to get 'em back an' I reckon she's goin' to charge plenty for the privilege.

"But I'll tell you one thing that certainly is *not* goin' to happen. You're not makin' a getaway. I'm goin' to make a certainty of one pinch in this case an' that pinch is goin' to be Mrs. Georgette Istria.

"An' that sorta surprises you, don't it? Because you thought that I couldn't do that there in France. You thought that you'd be safe here anyhow. Well, you're not. You forgot one thing.

"There is a bit of the United States right here in Paris. An' that is the U.S. Embassy. Once I got you there I've got you on United States territory.

"I'm goin' to take you around there now. I'm goin' to stick you in there an' they're goin' to keep you nice an' safe until I've fixed with Washington to frame some sweet charges against you, after which you'll be extradited back to the United States, and by the time I'm through you're goin' to get such a helluva sentence that it woulda been cheaper for you not to have been born at all.

"An' how do you like that, you beautiful gorgeous creature? Also," I go on, "you can shut up an' say nothin' because there is nothin' that you could think up that I wanta listen to".

She gives a long sorta shudderin' gasp. Her eyes look like purple coals. I reckon that if she coulda got away with it she'd have torn me in little pieces with her fingernails.

I take a look around the room. Her baggage is not unpacked except one case an' through the open door leadin' to the bedroom I can see her frock lyin' over the back of a chair.

She is still sittin' in the chair lookin' at me with them big eyes, strugglin' to tell me what she thinks about me.

"Just scram inside the bedroom an' put your frock on," I tell her. "An' keep your mouth shut because anything you say would only make me feel ill. An' while you are puttin' on your frock you can leave the door open because I am not takin' any more chances on you. After which you can come back here an' we'll scram. You can take one suitcase with you—the little one. Get goin', sister!"

She gets up an' goes inta the bedroom. She takes off her wrap an' slips inta her frock, puts on a fur coat an' a little hat an' comes back.

I stand there watchin' her while she is puttin' the bottles she has brought from the dressin' table into the suitcase.

She don't look in my direction at all. When she closes down the lid of the suitcase she has got her back to me. As the lid shuts she snaps around an' I see that I am lookin' inta the business end of a baby automatic. It must have been in the suitcase.

"Don't move," she says. "If you do I shall kill you. Just stand where you are and put your hands up. And keep quiet please. You've made quite enough noise for one session."

She is smilin' now. I reckon she thinks this is a swell joke.

I stand there an' watch her. I reckon that I have got so used to bein' taken for a ride by dames over this case that nothin' at all would surprise me. If this baby was just to disappear in a flash of blue flame you wouldn't hear a crack outa me. I guess I am so washed up that I wouldn't even recognise myself in a shavin' mirror.

She walks across to the telephone. Even though I am hatin' this dame's guts more than I care to say I still gotta admire the way she walks an' holds that gun on me as if she'd been used to doin' it all her sweet young life.

"This is Mrs. Istria speaking," she coos inta the telephone. "Will you please call a taxicab for me?"

She hangs up. Then she walks over to the wall connection to both the telephones and rips the cord out. She goes over to the bedroom door, locks it an' puts the key in her pocket. She walks over to the main door that leads to the corridor an' takes the key out of it.

She stands there by the door, lookin' at me.

"Good-night, Mr. Caution," she says.

She steps out inta the corridor, shuts the door an' I hear her lock it. I give a big sigh an' take my coat off.

I reckon it will take me three or four minutes to bust open that door.

It is nearly two o'clock when I get back to the Wellington. When I get inside the door the night porter informs me that some guy has called in durin' the evenin' an' asked if Mr. Scalla has checked in—the Mr. Scalla who arrived at Le Havre on the *Paris* this evenin'. They tell this bozo yes an' ask if he wants to leave any message an' he says no that it is quite all right thank you an' scrams.

So there you are. This tells me all I wanta know an' you guys know it too. There was only one guy could know that I would come over here with Georgette as Tony Scalla and that was Tony himself.

He's sent guys all around the hotels findin' out if I have checked in usin' that name.

An' it tells me that my guess that Scalla has brought over the Jamieson formula is right.

An' the reason he is interested in my whereabouts is because he knows that if I'm here Georgette is here, that pretty soon she will be goin' to the Armine Lodge at Neuilly an' he is probably makin' arrangements to pick her up some place.

Well, he needn't have worried because if I know anythin' about Georgette she has gone streakin' out to Neuilly, laughin' all over her face an' all ready to fall inta Tony's arms an' have a big horse laugh at little Lemmy, Public Sap No. 1, the little old guy who is gettin' a bit slow above the ears an' bein' taken for sweet rides all the time by pretty ladies.

An' if they are laughin', well they are dead right. Me . . . I would be laughin' too if I was them.

I go up to my room an' give myself a short shot of rye just for luck. Then I get through to Varney at the U.S. Embassy an' tell him that I have changed my mind an' that I shall not be bringin' Mrs. Istria along like I thought I was goin' to.

He says O.K. an' if it is all the same to me he will go to bed. I tell him that everything is all the same to me an' that so far as I am concerned everybody can go to hell an' play skittles for all I care.

He says quite so, sorta old-fashioned, an' hangs up.

I take off my coat an' lie down on the bed an' wonder what the next move in the game is goin' to be. So far as I am concerned I reckon it consists of my sittin' here in this hotel waitin' until this Fernanda-Georgette combination starts sendin' in the ransom notes tellin' me just how much dough they want to return the formulas an' knowin' that I can't do a durn thing because I don't even know where they're workin' from an' because I daren't ask anybody official here in this country to help me to find 'em.

Well, if they send in a note to me tryin' to deal they gotta put some address on it, haven't they? They gotta ask for the dough to be delivered some place?

But even if I do know where they are what can I do? I cannot go bustin' around shootin' the place up an' raisin' hell and skittles without lettin' these French guys know about the poison gas formula, which is the thing I am not supposed to let people know.

There's no two ways about it these two dames Fernanda an' Georgette are right on top of the job. They are holdin' all the aces all right. They know durn well that if I go chasin' after 'em or raisin' any sorta trouble all they gotta do is to shoot the works about the formulas an' they know durn well that I know it.

I get to feelin' that if somebody would give me a tip what to do I would give 'em a diamond medal.

I stand myself another shot of rye an' try to give up thinkin'. I have nearly succeeded when the telephone goes. It is Cy Hinks.

"Hey, playboy," he says. "You wanted me to keep an eye on your pal Mrs. Georgette Istria, an' this is to tell you that we are doing same with our usual efficiency. An hour ago this dame leaves the Grande-Claremont an' takes a cab. She drives out to Neuilly.

"Well, I already had four guys operatin' around in Neuilly tryin' to get a line on some of that information you wanted about the Armine Lodge people. About half an hour before this dame arrives out there in the cab some guy drives up in a big Canadian Buick an' goes into the Lodge. He parks the car in front of the door. He opens the front door with a key he's got. My fella is standin' in the shrubbery an' says that he reckons there wasn't anybody at all in the place before this Buick guy arrives. You got that?

"Well, about thirty minutes afterwards Mrs. Istria pulls in inside a Paris taxicab. She pays the driver off outside the main gates of the Lodge an' my man who has chased out after her from the Grande-Claremont pulls his cab up an' gets out an' eases along to see if he can hear anythin'.

"He hears this dame havin' a few words in French with the driver because she has only got American money, but after a bit they get this business straightened out an' she goes in an' starts walkin' up the drive. When she gets three-quarters of the way along, my bozo slips through the gates an' goes after her.

"But it's no good. She gets to the front door an' rings the bell an' the door opens an' she goes in. There wasn't any light on inside the hall so he can't say who let her in or what happened.

"Presently the first guy an' the Istria dame come out an' get in the car. Then the Buick drives off around the carriage drive that runs away back of the house. An' that's all I can tell you right now. Maybe I'll have something else in the morning."

"You can skip it," I tell him. "I don't want any more information about this Armine Lodge dump because I reckon I know plenty now. Where are you talkin' from?"

He says he is talkin' from his own place, an' I tell him to hang up an' stick around for a bit an' maybe I will ring him back, because I got a faint an' funny sorta idea knockin' about at the back of my brain-box.

I light myself a cigarette an' lie down some more. I reckon that I've been one hundred per cent right in my last guesses. The guy who went out to the Armine Lodge was Tony Scalla an' he went out there to pick up Georgette. An' maybe that's the last thing I'm goin' to see of that baby.

An' I am plenty sorry for this. Because I would give a year's pay to stick that good-lookin' starry eyed, swell-figured hellcat of a so-an'-so behind some steel bars.

Because that little sweetheart has worked on me like a striptease baby does on the boy who has come down from the farm.

Only maybe the boy from the farm gets *something* outa the game.

It is nearly four o'clock in the mornin' an' I am still lyin' there ponderin'.

Because it looks to me that all there is left for me to do is to send an Embassy cable through to the Director at Headquarters an' tell him that I am all washed up, a total an' complete loss to one an' all, an' ask for instructions.

An' I reckon that his instructions will be that I am to stick around until this Fernanda-Georgette combination indicates just how much dough it wants to return the Jamieson-Grearson formulas, and whether it wants the dough paid in China or Siam.

I also realise that as these babies will want the dough paid over first we got no guarantee at all that they will hand over the formulas when they have got the jack which is another sweet proposition which don't please me any.

I reckon these babies will have one swell time on that jack too. All they gotta do once they've got it is to keep out of England an' the U.S. for a coupla years until the whole bezusus has blown over, after which they can run around an' do some really heavy spendin'.

I reckon that Georgette an' Fernanda will have enough fur coats an' swell frocks to set up a coupla dozen stores.

Boy, what would I like to do to those two honey-belles! I swing my legs down to the floor an' give myself another cigarette. Usually my motto is "when in doubt don't," but I reckon that when it comes to cases like this I'm gonna change it to "when in doubt *do.*"

I go over to the telephone an' ring Cy Hinks.

"Look, Cy," I tell him. "Maybe you know a lot of shady guys around this city. You know American boys who for some reasons best known to themselves don't ever consider goin' back to the States. I reckon you know all sorts of cusses like that, hey?"

"An' how," he says. "There are a few guys here who have beat murder raps by scrammin' out of the States quick an' one or two bank robbers an' a few phoney marriage guys an' bigamists, an' half a dozen sweet counterfeiters an' forgers an' a few million honest-to-goodness fellas who would just take the last pumpernickel out of a blind guy's dinner pail."

"Swell," I tell him. "Well, Cy, I reckon you are a good boy an' can keep your trap shut if you wanta."

"Sure," he says. "I'm like a graveyard. Boy, if you knew some of the things I know an' don't even mention in my sleep. . . ."

"O.K.," I tell him. "Well, you put your hat on an' come around here. I reckon you an' me is goin' to do a little very heavy business together."

He says all right an' that maybe he will get some sleep sometime next year.

I go across to the table an' pour myself out another short one. I start thinkin' about Georgette again an' that sweet smile on her pan when she pulled the gun on me.

"O.K., baby girlie," I say to myself. "Maybe I ain't through with you yet!"

CHAPTER TWELVE
FUNNY BUSINESS

IT IS seven o'clock in the mornin' when Cy Hinks scrams. We have had a swell talk an' I have told him just as much as it is good for him to know, havin' regard to the scheme I have got in my mind.

Because I reckon that things have got to such a helluva pass with everybody pullin' funny stuff all over the place that there is not any reason why we shouldn't try a bit. There ain't anything else we can lose anyway.

I give myself a hot shower an' turn in. I am so durn tired that I reckon I could sleep for a coupla years but I get up at ten o'clock an' doll up a bit an' take myself around to the U.S. Embassy an' tell 'em that Mr. Zetland V. T. Kingarry would like to have a few words with the Ambassador.

I don't have to wait long. An' after I have took one peek at our U.S. representative in France I feel a little bit better, because this guy has got the sorta pan that an Ambassador oughta have. A good big forehead, a square jaw an' a coupla steady eyes that look as if they knew something.

I say my piece. He knows all about it because Headquarters advised him when I left New York, an' he don't seem particularly surprised when I tell him the way things are breakin'. But when I wise him up to the idea that I have got in my head an' the job that I have sent Cy Hinks out on I gotta admit that he shoots his eyebrows a bit.

He looks at the blotter an' then he says:

"Mr. Caution, you have got a reputation for achieving results. I have heard it said that your methods are sometimes somewhat irregular. Whilst I am not giving any official approval to the steps you have taken, yet at the same time, I do not feel inclined to officially forbid them."

He looks up at me an' smiles.

"In other words," he says, "if you pull it off, Caution, I imagine it will be all right. If you don't . . ."

He shrugs his shoulders.

"That's O.K. by me, Sir," I tell him. "I don't think I'll be worryin' you any more. I'll just go right ahead, an' if you don't hear anything from me that'll be just too bad."

"Good luck to you," he says. "I can only tell you what I feel about this business myself. It is this. I believe that the Jamieson-Grearson formulas in the hands of our own and the British governments will be instruments of peace which will never be used for aggressive purposes. But you can imagine what would happen if they were to fall into the hands of an ambitious nation. The very possession of the formulas, the knowledge of the potential results of the Jamies-on-Grearson gases, the ease with which they may be manufactured and transported and the fact that the No. 2 gas is probably the only truly effective lighter-than-air poison gas in the world to-day, would place a weapon in the hands of an aggressor which would bring the rest of the world to its knees in a month.

"Once again the best of good luck to you. If you want anything from us besides the letter which I am about to write you have only to contact Varney. He will be standing by here all the time until we hear something definite from you one way or the other."

He writes the letter, signs it, puts the official Embassy seal on it, sticks it in an envelope an' hands it to me.

I scram. In the cab on my way back to the Wellington I take it out an' read it. It says:

> "*Embassy of the United States of America,*
> *Paris, France.*
>
> *To Whom It May Concern:*
>
> *Under the authority vested in me as Ambassador of The United States of America to the President of the French Republic I hereby authorise Mr. Lemuel H. Caution, a Special Agent of the Federal Bureau of Investigation of the Department of Justice of the United States of America, to receive from me and pay to any person or persons at his sole discretion any sum or sums up to Two Million Dollars without demanding or accepting a receipt for any such payment.*
>
> *Signed: Rodwill H. Gleason,*
>
> > *Seal.*
> >
> > *U.S. Ambassador.*"

Sweet work an' very nice dough, hey?

When I get back to the Wellington it is eleven o'clock, an' there is a message waitin' for me that one of Hinks's boys will be expectin' me at the Armine Lodge at Neuilly, an' that he will hang around in the shrubbery until I get there.

I grab another cab an' I get out there, but although I am tryin' to kid myself along I am still feelin' not so hot about this business. If Hinks don't get away with the job that he is on, an' if everything gets gummed up, then I reckon the only thing we can do is to stick around until we hear something from the Fernanda-Georgette set-up, pay 'em the dough an' trust to luck that we get a square deal—which is something that I believe in anything else but, because the idea of these two mommas givin' anybody a square deal just makes me split my lip laughin'.

I pay off the cab just by the Armine Lodge gates an' go in. The house is a big place, standin' back well off the road in a big shrubbery with a wide carriage drive runnin' through up to the clear space in front of the lodge, an' then runnin' around each side.

I walk along the drive an' after a bit some guy comes out an' says good mornin'. I tell him that Cy Hinks is a pal of mine an' he says O.K. an' starts talkin'.

"The Armine Lodge was taken three months ago," he says. "It was booked already furnished through a New York agency. Three months' rent was paid in advance and an insurance policy taken out to satisfy the owners that the furnishings and effects would be safe. People have visited the place, but seldom stayed for more than a few hours. Residents in the neighbourhood and the tradespeople are definite that no one has actually stayed in the place. No provisions or stores or deliveries of any sort have been made by the local tradesmen and . . ."

"O.K., buddy," I tell him. "You've told me all I wanta know. Have you got that key of the front door made yet?"

He says yes an' brings it out. I take it off him.

"Now scram," I tell him. "I justa wanta meander around here on my own."

"Very well, sir," he says.

He looks a bit disappointed. Maybe he thought he was goin' to see a coupla murders.

I ease along the carriage drive to the front of the house. When I get there I start steppin' about so as not to disturb any marks on the gravel. It was sorta damp the night before an' I can see easy as easy the tyre marks of the Buick where it drove up to the front porch an' stopped.

Startin' at the bottom of the porch steps an' goin' towards the place where the car was parked, I can see two sets of heel-marks, one belonging to a guy an' another set made by high heels—Georgette's I guess.

I walk along the carriage drive that runs around the side of the Lodge to the back, following the tyre marks. They go right around the back an' I can see where the car stopped just outside the back entrance. From this door to the car there is another set of prints—a man's—but different to the first lot.

So it looks easy. When Georgette arrived there last night there were two guys waitin' for her. One of 'em went out with her to the car an' they drove around to the back an' picked up the other guy who had come out by the back way. Then they drove off by way of the iron gate at the bottom of the drive at the back of the Lodge.

I go around to the front an' open the door an' go in. Inside the hall is dark an' smells sorta stale. I light my cigarette lighter an' find the switch just inside the hall an' I look around.

The place is big an' oak lined, an' there are suits of armour an' stuff stuck all around. I reckon this is a classy sort of place except that it smells of onions.

I go through the rooms on the ground floor. They are all big an' the furniture is covered over with dust-sheets. Beyond the fact that there is an empty brandy bottle on a sideboard in one of the rooms I can't see anythin' that looks interestin'.

I come back to the hall an' go up the wide oak staircase. On the first floor there is another hallway an' the door of one of the rooms on the right is open. I go in an' switch the light on.

The window blinds are all pulled down an' the furniture is covered over, all except one table an' some chairs, an' I can see where the dust sheets have been thrown down by the door. On the edge of the table is a plate with a bit of sandwich left on it, an' there is an empty bottle of Connecticut Bourbon an' a coupla used glasses. On the window ledge on the right of the room is a pile of magazines. I go over an' look at 'em. There are two or three American magazines, a copy of the *Strand Magazine*—an English one this—an' half a dozen French periodicals. I can see the top French one is a thing called *Le Magazine des Arts* with a swell cover with a dame on it who looks as if she had got what it takes.

I go over to the door. I am just goin' out when my foot touches somethin' hard under one of the dust-sheets that is lyin' on the floor. I pull the edge up an' look under it. There is an automatic, a .22 lyin' there. I pick it up an' look at it. It is a nice little ten shot gun, an' when I pull the clip out I can see that it is fully loaded.

I put the gun in my pocket an' I ease around this place from top to bottom, but there ain't a thing that tells me anything at all. The Armine Lodge is just another house an' that's all there is to it.

I go out an' walk down the drive an' hang around until I pick up a cab that is crawlin' around. I drive back to the Wellington an' I buy myself a first-class lunch an' a bottle of wine.

I reckon I need buildin' up anyway.

I sleep all afternoon. I get up at eight o'clock an' take a hot an' cold shower an' get myself inta my tuxedo which the hotel valet has pressed up an' scram down into the bar. I have one shot of rye to keep the influenza germs away, after which I grab myself a cab an' drive along to Charlie's Bar. I sit there thinkin' deeply about nothin' at all an' eyein' some dame who is sittin' on a high stool along at the other end of the bar. This doll is a sweet looker. She is wearin' a blue suit that fits her so snug that it looks as if it had been pasted onto her, a double fox fur, white kid gauntlets an' a little black osprey toque with a diamond question mark. Her heels are so high that I reckon her theme song must be "Tiptoe Through the Tulips." She has got such a sweet sorta innocent an' sad smile playin' around her pretty mouth that if she was not drinkin' down double highballs like it was her last night on earth I would think that she was the parson's daughter who had just dropped in to see what the time was.

Anyway she is an easy looker an' very sweet an' I reckon that if she had to choose between givin' in to the wicked squire or havin' the mortgage foreclosed on the old home farm, well I reckon the farm would be one hundred per cent safe for ever.

I have just finished these deep thoughts about this dame when the bar guy informs me that my friend Mr. Hinks is on the telephone in the little room behind the bar. I ease along there.

"Look," says Cy, "I have had one hell of a time trying to get sense inta the heads of these boys. I have got seven of 'em here at Le Quantro. I have been trying to sell 'em this proposition for an hour and they're still cold. They think that there has gotta be something phoney about it which, when you come to think of their own peculiar temperaments, is not so strange."

"So what?" I tell him. "An' what comes next?"

"Only this," he says. "I have got here with me Charles and Antonio Grazzi—remember that bank job in Oklahoma City in '34?—Willie Geel an' his cousin Martellini—these two boys pulled that bill bond job in New York in '37—Arthur (Wooly) Jugenheimer, John Pansinelli—he come out of Auburn two months ago—and, last but not least, Larvey Rillwater, that clever boy who sucked in the Associated Western Bankers in 1932, and who has been living like a duke on the proceeds ever since. I always had a sorta idea that you handled that Associated Western Bankers job."

"You're dead right," I tell him. "An' where do we go from there?"

"They don't like it," he says. "Larvey Rillwater is the big noise with these fellas an' he can't sorta believe that the proposition is a true one. He says it smells just a little bit."

"Can I persuade 'em?" I ask him.

"No," he says. "But Larvey Rillwater's wife Juanella is sitting along at the end of Charlie's Bar right now sorta examining you and I reckon that if you can sell it to her then they're all in on the job. Rillwater says she never makes a mistake about any cuss that ever wore pants and he says that if you can get by her you're sold with the rest of the boys."

"O.K.," I tell him. "Me, I am a guy who has always believed that the difference between the guy who tries to kiss a girl and gets a smack in the beezer an' the guy who gets almost continual neckin' is merely salesmanship. So I will get busy on this proposition. That is if I can reach up as high as this dame is, havin' regard to the heels she is wearin'."

"I wish you luck," he says. "If you make it, come along to the Quantro and bring her along. I'll feed this crowd liquor on the expense account until you get here with or without Larvey's sweet momma."

I say so long an' hang up. When I look through the glass door inta the bar I see my girl friend switchin' to a double martini an' a cigarette.

I ease along an' tip my hat.

"Mrs. Rillwater," I tell her. "I am so pleased to see you that you just wouldn't know. When I heard you was you I was very glad because I have been lampin' your ankles for the last five minutes an' nearly gettin' myself an overdeveloped blood-pressure in the process. Can I buy you a little drink?"

She looks me over.

"So this is Mr. Caution," she says. "Well, I've always wanted to have a look at you. I've always had a yen to meet the guy who was supposed to be a menace to any really respectable mobster. In U.S., I mean," she goes on, sorta sweetly cynical. "Of course you're not really dangerous in *this* country without an extradition warrant."

"Forget it, honey," I tell her. "I am not dangerous at all where guys like your friends are concerned, an' I would only be dangerous where you are concerned if Larvey was tied up in a dungeon in China an' could not get at me if I tried to make his wife, who is a honey that I would give two years' pay, the big toe off my left foot an' an old gramophone that belonged to Robert E. Lee to make."

I drop my voice sorta serious.

"Babe," I tell her, "I been lookin' at the dames over here an' I think they're swell, but when I come inta this dump tonight an' saw you I reckon my heart skipped two beats an' then stopped for a minute. Has anybody ever told you how you look when you're sittin' on a high stool?"

Her eyes twinkle. I guess this line is goin' with her.

"No, cowboy," she says. "Nobody ever has. You tell me."

I tell her. When she has finished laughin' I pick up the drinks an' we go to a little table in the corner where it is nice an' quiet.

"Look, lovely," I tell her. "We don't want to waste any time flirtin' around with this proposition. Let's get down to cases."

I light a cigarette for her.

"Charlie an' Antonio Grazzi pulled that Oklahoma bank job in '34," I tell her. "They done well. They got over here with twenty grand an' there wasn't any evidence left behind 'em. They're as safe as houses whiles they stay here. If they go back they'll be pinched on some alternative charge. Willie Geel an' his cousin are in the same boat. Jugenheimer's wanted now but is not worth applyin' for extradition for, but he can't go back home. Pansinelli is the only one with a clean slate."

I stop for a minute. I can see her eyelids flicker. She is waitin' for me to start talkin' about Larvey.

"Larvey is in a spot," I tell her. "I handled the Associated Western Bankers job. It was a Federal job. At the time we hadn't got anything to make it stick onto him."

I wait for a minute an' then start tellin' a sweet story I have just made up.

"Three weeks ago," I continue, "Salen Jakes—who was with him in that business—gets himself pinched under the Baumes Act an' they try to hang the Associated Bankers job onto him as well. He gets good an' scared because it looks like twenty years, an' so he starts squealin'. He comes across with enough evidence to get Larvey a sweet fifty years' sentence on four different counts in Alcatraz."

I wait an' light a cigarette slowly to let all this stuff sink in.

"I reckon Larvey can sway the rest of these boys," I tell her, "an' I reckon you can sway Larvey. I'm talkin' propositions now an' I'm talkin' the truth. If you don't believe me look inta my pretty blue eyes.

"Larvey an' his pals are a hot lot," I tell her. "But the whole darned gang of 'em are permanent expatriates. There's not one of 'em can go back home without wonderin' when some copper is goin' to spring outa the undergrowth an' grab 'em. Sooner or later though they're goin' to get homesick. They're goin' to take a chance an' go back an' they're goin' to get pinched. You know I'm right, honey—they always do —they can't win.

"O.K. You get these boys to play ball with me an' I'm goin' to promise you that I'm goin' to get a permanent postponement of any sentence against 'em on the grounds that they've rendered effective service to the Federal Government. That's what happens if they play ball. If they don't I'm not goin' to worry about the other guys but I'm goin' to get extradition against Larvey, an', with the new evidence we got, he'll be in Alcatraz when you're playin' skittles with your great-grandchildren. You got that?"

"I got it," she says.

She looks at me hard.

"Look," she says, "I heard once that you were a straight guy even if you are a Federal dick. All right. Well, I'm goin' to get Larvey an' the boys to play in on this job although how it's goin' to be fixed is just nobody's business. I'll get 'em to try it an' I hope it'll come off."

She pulls her furs around her an' gets up.

"But if you cross Larvey up on this," she goes on, smilin' sorta pretty. "If he comes in with you on this an' you pull a fast one on him afterwards, I'm goin' to shoot your insides out as sure as my name's Juanella even if they fry me for it. An' have you got that?"

I grin at her, an' put my hand out.

"I got it," I tell her.

"I'll take one martini for the road," she says, "an' then we'll get along to the Quantro."

We go back to the bar an' I order the martinis.

She looks at me very old-fashioned.

"An' don't get fresh in the cab," she says. "Because even if I have got faults, I am very faithful to Larvey—well, most of the time, although I've often wondered what it would be liked to be necked by a 'G' man in a taxi. An' they tell me you have got a sweet technique with dames."

"Take no notice of 'em, honey," I tell her. "They're lyin'. Me, I'm a guy who is always very respectful to women an' I owe my success in life to readin' a correspondence course entitled 'How to Read Your Sweetheart's Mind,' an' because I never eat onions in my hamburgers. Also when I am with a wonderful lookin' baby like you I get sorta nervous."

"Yeah?" she says. "I noticed that. I can see you tremblin'. Only I'm a bit stuck on gettin' back to New York some time an' I wanta get Larvey to play along with you so I do not wish to arrive at the Quantro lookin' like I have been havin' a free-for-all with a steam roller. He might think things."

"Don't worry, Juanella," I tell her. "Nothin' like that has ever sorta crossed my mind. You have got my assurance that when I am in a cab in Paris at night with a swell woman like you I just keep my fingers crossed an' keep on bein' very good."

"I know," she says with a sorta far-away look in her eyes. "That's what I was afraid of."

We get back to the Wellington at a quarter to twelve. Cy Hinks is very pleased with himself at havin' fixed for these boys to play ball an' help me along in my scheme, but he is now crackin' his brains as to how he's goin' to organise things. I tell him to get along an' see Varney at the Embassy in the mornin' an' that Varney will probably have a suggestion or two as to ways an' means.

We are just passin' the reception desk when the night clerk starts wavin' to me, an' when I go over he tells me a long spiel that makes my ears open a bit.

"This evening, m'sieu," he says, "a man comes here and asks for Monsieur Tony Scalla. He says he 'as got somezing ver' interesting for heem. We tell 'im that you are out and we do not know when you return. We suggest 'e leave a message for you. He say no. He say that 'e come back 'ere again after midnight to spik to you."

I ask him who this guy is. He says he don't know but that he is a truck driver—a fruit an' vegetable truck driver, that he drives a truck in every night from Corneilles to the markets here, returning early in the morning. This guy says he will come back to the Wellington for me after he has delivered his onions an' stuff.

I say O.K. send him up when he comes back.

I take Cy up to my sittin' room for a short one an' we are there for an hour talkin' about the Larvey Rillwater set-up an' wonderin' whether these boys can work fast enough. We are in the middle of an argument about this when the night clerk comes up with the vegetable guy.

I send the clerk off an' we give this onions merchant a drink. He is a rough, peasant sorta cuss, with a nice smile. He is about thirty-five years of age an' he drinks bourbon neat like it was water.

After he has finished his drink he starts fumblin' with his cap an' after a lot of playin' around he pulls outa the linin' a bit of blue paper. He hands this to me with a big grin an' starts talkin' so fast that anybody would think he was nuts.

I look at the bit of paper. It is the corner torn off some sort of fancy paper. Maybe a magazine or paper-backed book. One side is a nice sorta blue colour an' the other—the inside—white. Written on the white side, in a scrawly handwriting that looks as if the guy who wrote it had got the jitters, I see something in French, an' I recognise the words "Monsieur Tony Scalla" an' "Wellington Hotel, Paris." I sling it across to Cy an' tell the Frenchman to shut up.

"What's it say?" I ask Cy.

He looks at it.

"Here's a funny one," he says. "It's written in soft-leaded pencil and it says that 'if the finder of this will take it to Monsieur Tony Scalla at the Wellington Hotel, Paris, he will be given two hundred and fifty francs.'"

I tell Cy to ask the onions guy about it. Where he got it from an' anything else he knows.

Cy starts talkin' French at forty miles an hour an' the French guy weighs in an' after a minute it sounds like an all-in wrestlin' competition with nothin' barred but double consonants.

After a few minutes they both shut up.

"Here's what he says," Cy tells me. "He says that to-night about ten o'clock he starts from Corneilles and his first stop is Brionne where he has to pick up some potatoes. Just after he leaves Brionne which would be about a quarter to eleven—about ten miles down the Louviers road—that's the main road to Paris—he passes a big car. This auto is eatin' up the road like hell was after it and he just manages to swing his truck right into the side of the road otherwise they would have hit him.

"He pulls up and looks back out of his cab, sayin' a few words about these tourist guys, when he sees this bit of paper dropped outa the car window onto the road.

"He thinks that maybe these guys have dropped a ten franc note for him because they gave him a scare. He goes back and finds this message. So he thinks as he's this way he'll look in and ask if there is a Mr. Scalla here. He comes here and they say yes and he thinks that maybe there's a chance for him to collect a few francs. He says he don't expect two hundred and fifty because maybe the whole thing is a joke. What do I tell him?"

I turn the piece of paper over in my hands. I am lookin' at the blue side—it is a funny sorta blue—an' I am wonderin' where I've seen this colour blue before.

Then I get it. It hits me like a brick dropped off the roof. I get out my billfold.

"Look, Cy," I tell him. "You give this guy the two hundred an' fifty francs. Tell him I think he's a smart fellow and then get him outa here."

He does it. I sit there lookin' at the bit of paper.

"That's big dough to pay for that bit of stuff," he says when the guy has gone.

I grin.

"Listen, Cy," I tell him. "Use your nut. This handwritin' is all scrawly, ain't it? It's not like that because it was written in a car that was goin' fast—it's even too bad for that. It's written as bad as it is because whoever wrote that on the inside of that cover was writin' it under a car rug, see? They had their hands under a rug an' was tryin' to write a note so that the other guys in the car shouldn't see.

"Well, this isn't *all* the note. The dame who wrote this note was goin' to continue writin', but she hadn't got the chance. All she could say was 'If the finder of this will take it to Tony Scalla at the Wellington Hotel, Paris, they will get two hundred an' fifty francs.' Then she was goin' on to say something else but she never got the chance. I reckon that when they nearly hit the vegetable guy's truck the rug got pulled aside or something—they got a shake-up, see, an' all she could do was to tear the corner off an' get rid of it out of the car window before the other guys got wise."

"That sounds all right," he says. "But how do you know the writer was a dame? You seem to have a lot of ideas about this stunt."

"You're dead right, baby," I tell him. "You get your car around here. I'm goin' to show you somethin' funny."

We drive out to the Armine Lodge. When we get there we park the car an' go up to the door. The place is dark an' quiet. I open the front door with the key I got off Hinks's man in the mornin' an' we go in. Cy has got a gun in his fist in case there is anybody around. But there ain't, the place is empty.

We go up to the room on the first floor, the room where I saw the sandwich on the table an' the empty glasses; where I found the gun.

I switch on the light. I go over to the window ledge and grab the pile of magazines. I take the French one—the one with the dame on the front—the *Magazine des Arts*.

"Look at this," I tell Cy. "See—it's the same colour. That bit was torn off the corner of another of these magazines. One they had in the car.

"Now you tell me something, Cy," I go on. "You take a look at these magazines. They're all American, ain't they, except the *Strand*—an English one. This *Magazine des Arts* is the only French one here. So it looks as if the guy who was stickin' around here was a guy who couldn't read French. He usta go for English readin'. O.K. Then why does he have *this* magazine here an' why do they have another one like it in the car?"

"I don't know, Sherlock," he says. "You tell me."

I start turnin' over the pages of this *Magazine des Arts*. It's stickin' out a foot that whoever has been readin' this thing has not been very interested in the front part because some of the pages aren't even cut. I flip the pages over towards the back of the magazine an' there it is!

One page has the corner turned up. It is an advertisement page. An' there is a little tiny pencil tick against one of the small ads.

"What's that ad. say?" I ask Cy.

"It's an advertisement for an expert photographer, Lemmy," he says. "A guy called Raphallo Pierrin. This guy advertises expert photography of all sorts, sizes and conditions. He says he's practically the world's best—in fact he hates himself."

"Where does he live?" I ask.

"He's at Dives—on the coast," says Cy. "That's a little place not far from Deauville."

I start grinnin'. Boy, am I beginnin' to feel good!

"Look, Lemmy," says Cy. "What's all this mysterious stuff? How did you know that a dame had written that note? What's goin' on around here?"

"Listen, bozo," I tell him. "Last night Georgette Istria pulls a gun on me an' gets away from the Grande-Claremont. She locks me in her room. I reckoned that she had a date here with the real Tony Scalla. I was right. He was waitin' for her.

"O.K. She comes around here an' she's got a gun. She's not feelin' so good because I've told her half an hour before that somebody has bumped off Pinny Yatlin, the one time boss, in Mexico City. Georgette wonders if they are goin' to try somethin' funny with her too—after *she's* served *her* turn, see?

"She comes around here an' she rings the bell, an' she's got her gun in her hand. She's goin' to look after herself, she thinks.

"Tony Scalla opens the door. He starts handin' her a lot of smooth stuff, but she still keeps the gun on him. He brings her up to this room an' he comes inside. She stands in the doorway hold-in' the gun waitin' to ask questions.

"But what she don't know is that there is another guy in the house with Tony. I saw his footmarks around the back of the house this mornin'. I saw where Tony drove around there to pick him up.

"While she is standin' in the doorway this second guy gumshoes up behind her an' knocks the gun out of her hand. I found it this mornin' under those furniture covers.

"O.K. Tony takes her downstairs an' sticks her in the car. The other guy follows 'em down, switches off the lights, shuts the front door after 'em an' then goes through to the back. He locks the door from the outside there an' waits for Tony to drive around an' pick him up.

"O.K. Well, Tony has joined up with the rest of the mob. Georgette is scared stiff. She thinks they're goin' to bump her like they bumped Yatlin an' Pedro Dominguez, so she starts writin' this note to me on the inside of the cover, but she can't finish it an' she chucks the bit she's written outa the car window so's they shan't get wise. You got that?"

"I got it," he says. "But what about the photographer's ad.? Where does that come in?"

I get up.

"Cy," I tell him. "I'm gettin' a line on this mob. I got hope. Maybe I'm goin' to ditch 'em yet. These guys have been lookin' for a photographer. An' I reckon the one they picked is this Pierrin guy—just because he lives in the place they wanted a photographer to live in."

I light a cigarette an' give him one.

"Now, you big palooka," I tell him. "You're really goin' to get to work. You're goin' to work so fast that you'll wonder what's happenin' to you."

"It's O.K. by me," he says. "Maybe in 1946 I'm goin' to get some sleep."

"Let's get goin'," I tell him. "Stop at the first call box. I wanta call the Embassy. We gotta get that Varney guy out of bed. We're goin' to have one big, very swell meetin' an' then, boy, are we goin' to town or are we?"

CHAPTER THIRTEEN
DYNAMITE

IT IS twelve o'clock when I wake up and a sweet mornin'. There is a cold winter sun an' outa the window I can see dames walkin' up the boulevards with that sorta swing that a pretty woman always puts on when she knows that her make-up is lookin' dead right against a silver fox.

I ring for some coffee an' get back inta bed. I start thinkin' about things in general an' wonderin' just how they are goin' to break.

Some lovely momma with turquoise eyes that I met up with in Tulsa one time told me that just when the whole world looked as if it was goin' to fall in on a guy's dome somethin' would always happen to set the guy on his feet. She said that life had always proved this to her an' that she had always banked on somethin' turnin' up at the right moment.

After which she gives me a hot, lingerin' look an' proceeds to sling her arms around my neck an' show me how Katherine of Russia usta slip a half-nelson on the young lieutenant of the guard who was hangin' around tryin' to get himself made a General without knowin' anything at all, just by bein' helpful to his Empress at any given moment.

An' the thing that turned up at the right moment then was some guy who said that he was her husband an' who proceeds to unlimber a gun an' shoot up the place like it was *fiesta* night in San Antonio.

All of which brings me to Georgette. I sit there thinkin' about this baby an' wonderin' just how she is likin' what has turned up so far as she is concerned. I reckon she is plenty surprised.

I guess she was good an' surprised in the first place when I told her about Yatlin bein' shot. But right then she was only thinkin 'about one thing. She was thinkin' about ditchin' me, gettin' away an' joinin' up with the rest of the mob.

But when she was in the cab an' on her way out to the Armine Lodge to meet up with Scalla that was the time when she began to cool off a bit an' look at things from a strictly logical point of view.

It must have hit her right then that this mob are not the sorta boys who are goin' to carry deadweight—even if the deadweight is a lovely like she is. She musta got the idea inta her head that if they was prepared to bump Pedro Dominguez an' Yatlin there wasn't any reason why they shouldn't bump her too—or get rid of her in one of the not-so-nice ways that gangsters have of ditchin' dames when nobody sorta wants 'em any more.

Or maybe Scalla had his eye on her. I remember how she looked when I said that he had told me that he was her brother. . . . I reckon that Georgette was wise to Scalla. Maybe she knew that he was thinkin' that with Jake Istria—who gets himself conveniently shot by me—out of the way, an' Pinny Yatlin—who I reckon was bumped by Zellara on her sister Fernanda's instructions—little Tony was sittin' right on top of the game an' goin' to be good an' rich by cuttin' the dough they make outa this job only two ways—himself an' Fernanda—because I reckon the other mugs in the game are not goin' to get a lot.

Maybe the only thing that Scalla wanted to meet up with Georgette for again, was that he was out to make her, an' I can understand that because, without fear of contradiction, I am saying that she is the sweetest looker that I have taken a quick look at.

I reckon she come to this conclusion too while she was goin' out to Neuilly in that cab an' I bet she was talkin' very cold turkey to Scalla when the other guy gumshoed up behind her an' knocked that gun out of her hand.

An' I bet she ain't feelin' quite so good now. I start wonderin' what she woulda said in that note that she started writin' if she'd been able to finish it. It might have been very interestin'!

It just shows you that some of these smart dames can sometimes be just a little bit too smart. But at the same time I feel sorta sorry for Georgette because I reckon she is in a bad spot however much she is a double-crosser.

After a bit Cy Hinks comes around. We have lunch an' Cy tells me that he is gettin' one hundred per cent support from Varney who has fixed up an appointment to see Juanella Rillwater about gettin' organised. Cy says that he has taken a short lease on some basements in the Quartier an' that Larvey Rillwater an' the boys are gettin' the machinery an' stuff put in there right now.

So it looks as if that part of the job is goin' on all right. Cy says that he never reckoned to live an' see a member of a U.S. Embassy staff playin' around an' doin' business with a mobster's baby like Juanella, but that you never know what can happen these days. He don't know how right he is. Anyhow I reckon that maybe Varney an' Juanella can both teach each other something, that is if she don't try to make Varney just to sorta keep her in hand.

After lunch Cy gets the car around an' we scram. I am lookin' forward to meetin' this photographer guy in Dives because I have got an idea way back of my head that if what I think is happenin' then maybe I can still pull a very fast one an' get my little girl friend

Fernanda Martinas an' her bunch of thugs just where it's goin' to hurt 'em most.

It is five o'clock when we pull inta Dives. This is a pretty sorta place with a funny little quay an' some odd houses. It looks like one of them week-end spots that you read about in books where everybody is human an' there ain't any house-detectives.

We get around to the address of this Raphallo Pierrin as per the advertisement in the *Magazine des Arts*. The guy is in. He is an old bozo with white hair an' big blue eyes an' a blue beret. He also looks as if he has got some brains an' he talks English better than Cy talks French.

I give him the works. I tell him that I reckon that he is a guy who is not in business for his health, an' that whatever dough he was goin' to make outa the job that I think somebody has asked him to do, is nothin' to what I am prepared to pay him if he plays along with me. I flash a coupla thousand franc notes an' I watch his eyes glisten.

"M'sieu," he says, "I am very much at your disposal. I am a photographer and an artist, but I am also, I hope, a good business man."

I say O.K. an' that just for that I am slippin' him five hundred francs. I give him the note an' I tell him to get busy an' tell me the whole goddam bag of tricks from the start an' not to leave anythin' out. He lights himself a Caporal cigarette an' gets goin'.

He says that he has had that advertisement in the *Magazine des Arts* for one week out of every four for the last two years. Four days before he gets a letter from some guy in Trouville. The guy signs the letter in the name of Anselmo Dalada an' he says that he wants Pierrin to do some very special photography for him—photostats an' stuff like that—an' that he will pay plenty if the work is done properly. He says that it will be necessary for Pierrin to take the plates, develop an' print the photostats an' finish off all in one go, that he must be prepared to stay right on the job an' not leave until it is done. He also says that if Pierrin is willin' to do it he must be ready to get his cameras an' apparatus packed up in one hour from the time he gets notice an' leave Dives for the place where the job has got to be done. If Pierrin is agreeable to all this he can name his own price an' write to this Anselmo Dalada at the *poste restante* Trouville, which is the next place along the coast.

Pierrin says that it looks good business to him, so he writes an' says that is O.K. an' that he is prepared to do the job, but that his cameras an' equipment are pretty big an' heavy an' that some sorta transport will have to be arranged. He says he wants one thousand francs for the job an' another hundred for each photostat he makes.

Pierrin posts this letter, an' it is stickin' out a foot that the Dalada baby is waitin' right on the doorstep of the post office at Trouville for it, because within a coupla hours after it reaches there this guy Dalada turns up at Pierrin's studio in Dives an' introduces himself.

He tells Pierrin that everythin' is O.K., that he is willin' to pay the price asked an' that if Pierrin makes a good job of the photography then he will add on an extra thousand francs for luck. He also says that Pierrin needn't worry his head about transport because he will send a car along for him an' a coupla men to handle the cameras an' stuff. Pierrin then starts askin' a lotta questions about lightin' an' electric current at the place where the photographs are to be taken and the Dalada guy says that he needn't bother his head about details like that because they will all be taken care of an' that when Pierrin gets there he will find there is plenty of electric lights an' what-nots for him to do his work.

The Dalada guy then gives Pierrin two hundred francs as a deposit an' tells him to stand by an' that he will be telephoned when he is wanted. He takes Pierrin's number.

O.K. Pierrin says that about ten o'clock this mornin' the Dalada baby comes through on the telephone an' tells Pierrin that he is to be ready to-morrow night at eleven-thirty o'clock. That some guys will call in a car with a trailer-truck for the equipment an' that they will pick up Pierrin an' take him off to do the work. Dalada says that there will be plenty of photographin' to be done an' that he reckons that Pierrin will be workin' all night an' that he will be back in his place at Dives by eleven o'clock next day. Pierrin says O.K. that will suit him fine.

So there you are. It was like I thought, an' I am gettin' one helluva kick outa this business because with a bit of luck I reckon I am still goin' to up-end these mugs properly. I will bet my bottom dollar this Dalada baby is nobody else but Tony Scalla an' they are goin' to play it just like I thought they would.

I get to work on this Pierrin. I tell him a helluva tale that I make up as I go along that sorta fits in with the situation as he sees it, an' I give him another five hundred francs an' tell him that if he does just what I want in the way I want it I will slip him another two thousand francs in two days' time.

He says that he is goin' to play ball. By the way his eyes shine when he gets his hooks on the dough I reckon he woulda photographed the devil himself if the dough was O.K.

I tell him just what he has gotta do an' just how he is to do it an' I make him repeat it over an' over again until I see that I have got it right into his head.

After which I get him to show me around his studio. I make a coupla mental notes about one or two things an' then I get back inta the car with Cy an' scram.

Paris is callin' me.

When we get back to the Wellington I go inta a long session with Cy Hinks. I have already told you guys that Cy is an intelligent sorta cuss but I make certain that he knows what he is goin' after because any slip-ups from now on are not goin' to be so good for me.

I work on Cy until it looks like he knows his end of the game an' then I telephone through to Varney at the Embassy an' tell him that Cy is comin' round an' that Varney has got to rustle up twenty thousand francs for him an' that I want him to get the Naval Attaché around at the Embassy so as to give Cy some information about one or two things.

He says O.K. he will do anythin' I want.

After Cy has gone I go downstairs an' give myself a very nice dinner with a small bottle of champagne an' I drink my own health because I reckon that pretty soon I am goin' to need all the health I got.

I then ease inta a phone booth an' call up Juanella Rillwater. I tell her that I wanta have a little talk with her an' that I shall be stickin' around at Charlie's Bar in half an hour. She says it's O.K. an' that as Larvey is workin' down in the basement like he was already servin' in a chain gang that she reckons he won't even miss her.

Juanella is sittin' on the high stool along at the end of the bar when I get there.

On my way, smokin' a cigarette in the car I been wonderin' just how far I can trust this Juanella dame. Because you gotta realise that crooks are funny guys an' their dolls are even funnier.

I have always found that a really high-class an' expert crook, whether he is in the safe-blowin' or counterfeitin' or forgery rackets, is always sorta inclined to look down on the crook who is just a common or garden mobster who don't specialise. I have known guys who specialised in big safe-cracking jobs who wouldn't even talk to a stick-up man.

An' another thing is that a crook is very often a patriotic sorta guy in a quiet way. He don't mind pinchin' an' stealin' from his countrymen, an' he don't mind gettin' outa payin' income tax or anything else like that, but in nine cases outa ten, when there is some sorta national trouble brewin', you will find the guy is roarin' to join the Marines an' blast somebody down just because he is American.

An' if you don't believe me you get somebody to tell you the story of the formation of the Apache Battalions in the French Army at the beginnin' of the World War, when every goddam crook in Paris who was worth a cuss went along an' joined 'em singin' the Marseillaise an' wavin' a flag with one hand an' grabbin' off anybody's pocket book that was handy with the other.

But did those boys fight or did they?

Juanella hands me a sweet smile.

"Hey, soldier," she says. "So you're back again. An' what is it this time? Ain't you pleased with the way things are goin' or is it that you can't keep away from my beautiful figure? Also I would like to drink a double Vermouth-Cassis followed by a little chaser made outa Canadian bourbon with a cherry on a stick."

I take a look at her while I am orderin' the drinks. She is wearin' a black close-fittin' frock with a three-quarter coat an' a black an' white tailor-made hat. She has got on white doeskin gloves with a black motif on the cuff an' her eyes are shinin' like they was stars.

I reckon that if this dame would only take a pull at herself, reduce the height of her heels to about three inches an' get Larvey to go straight, she would get herself—an' him—some place in practically no time.

"How's it goin'?" I ask her.

"Fine," she says. "That Embassy guy Varney is a scream. I reckon he's been thwarted in youth because every time he got the chance he was lookin' at my legs like he'd never seen any before."

"An' he ain't the only one, Juanella," I tell her. "Me, I have seen a lotta legs in my time but I reckon that your legs are sorta special an' if I hadda lot of time I would tell you just what I think about you in general an' it would make you feel *very* good. Maybe you sorta realised why I put you next to Varney, hey?"

"Yeah," she says. "I reckoned that you wanted us to know that you were on the up-an'-up on this job, that we're really, for once in our lives, workin' for Uncle Sam."

She grins at me sorta friendly.

"It was certainly a sweet gesture," she says.

She drinks the Vermouth-Cassis an' starts in on the bourbon. She pulls the cherry out an' looks at it, holdin' it just a few inches from her mouth. I get to thinkin' that her lips are just about the same colour as the cherry.

"The boys are workin' like they was nuts," she says. "An' with the machinery that Varney has got in I reckon they're goin' to be through by about seven o'clock this evenin'. It was a swell idea of Varney's to give us a real set of steel plates to work from."

She looks at me very old-fashioned.

"An' is that all you wanted to know?" she says.

"Nope," I tell her. "I wanta ask you to do somethin' for me. Some-thin' sorta personal."

She drops her eyes an' wriggles a bit.

"Well . . ." she says. "I shall have to sorta think it over, because I have already told you that Larvey is a very jealous guy. But maybe when we got this business . . ."

"Just a minute," I interrupt her. "You're gettin' me wrong. This business is personal all right, but not as personal as anything that would get Larvey all steamed up—see?"

"Yeah," she says. "Oh well, I knew I was goin' to get a big disappointment to-day. I saw it in the bottom of the teacup this mornin'. O.K. Go ahead, Lemmy. What's eatin' you?"

"Look, Juanella," I tell her. "You remember way back in 1932 somebody blew the time-lock off the vault in the Third Associated Farmers Bank in White River. It was a swell job. Whoever done it had planted some sorta' time-bomb in the outer casin' of the vault, an' this bomb was fixed to blow the lock off at exactly five o'clock next day.

"At a quarter to five next mornin' there is a county fire an' police call put through to all fire an' police stations, an' this call concentrates every fireman an' copper at some place about thirty miles away. While they are all there wonderin' who the hell has pulled this trick on them the bomb in the bank vault goes off, blows in the vault lock an' the crooks walked inta the bank an' got away with the County an' Borough pay rolls—one hundred an' fifty thousand dollars. You remember about that?"

"Yeah," she says. "I heard about it."

"O.K.," I tell her. "Well, although they was never able to hang that job onto Larvey, everybody had the sorta idea that he was the guy who pulled it. Me, I was interested in it because although I knew that Larvey was one of the finest counterfeiters in the U.S. I never knew that he was an expert at fixin' time-bombs. I was sorta interested, see?

"Well, I go easin' around tryin' to get an angle on this, an' what do I find? I find that about three months before Larvey's charmin' an' delightful wife—a honey by the name of Juanella Rillwater, to whom I have the pleasure of talkin' at this moment—had got herself a job in the office of the Oklahoma Minin' an' General Corporation as stenographer to the Chief Engineer in charge of the blastin' works. She worked there for six weeks as Jane Lowkell, an' after six weeks she resigned.

"I reckoned she took that job to learn how to make that time-bomb."

"Very interesting," she says. "An' where do we go from there?"

"Look, Juanella," I tell her. "I reckon I am goin' to be in a spot pretty soon, an' I guess that there is only one thing that is goin' to give me a chance of gettin' out of it an' that is a really swell time-bomb. But I gotta have it right away. I gotta have it in about three hours' time."

She looks at me an' she smiles.

"I reckon I'm plenty important to you," she says. "I don't know what you'd do without Juanella. O.K. big boy, it's easy. You get me the makin's an' I'll fix you up a time-bomb so mild that it'll just wake you up in the mornin' or so goddam hot that it'll blow the whole street up."

"Sweet sister," I tell her. "What would I do without you? Now you tell me what you want."

"It's as easy as makin' a strawberry shortcake," she says. "An' I'm good at that too. All you gotta get me is a first class electric chronometer. I want a really swell electric alarm clock that I can take outa its case an' mount on a wooden platform. O.K. Well, I wire this clock up to a small battery an' I bore holes through the wooden platform which is about ten inches square an' run three or four leads from the clock alarm system through the holes, an' on the other end of the leads I fix little tiny fulminate of mercury caps to act as detonators.

"O.K. Well, I take another little wooden platform an' I drill holes in it an' in each hole I put a stick of dynamite accordin' to the amount of explosion I want.

"Then I fix on the leads with the detonators so that each stick of dynamite has got its detonator cap. See?

"All I've got to do then is to fix a trigger wired on to the battery one side an' connected with the clock alarm on the other. If I set the clock alarm for three o'clock then, just at the moment that the alarm goes off the trigger is released an' it bangs down the fulminate of mercury caps, the dynamite sticks are detonated an' the balloon goes up.

"I guess," she goes on, sorta reminiscent, "that was the way those guys blew that time-lock off the White River vault right at the very minute they wanted to."

"Juanella," I tell her, "you're a honey, an' one day I'm gonna give you a big hug. In the meantime you get back to the factory an' get the boys movin' hard. I'll be with you in an hour an' I'm sending you the best chronometer we can get an' the other fixin's. Varney'll get 'em for me. Then you can get busy an' I'll tell you just the sorta explosion I want."

"O.K.," she says. "Well right now I'll take a double martini."

I order the drink. When she has finished it she gets up.

"I'm always bein' very friendly to some guy," she says. "But I never thought it would be a 'G' man. I suppose it's the mother in me!"

I go back to the Wellington an' lie down on the bed. I smoke a cigarette an' just think around everything.

Lookin' back I can see where I was the big mug. The idea that Fernanda an' the mob would be livin' somewhere in France was wrong from the start. I mighta known that they would never have taken a chance of bein' anywhere where anybody coulda got at them.

The Armine Lodge was just a set-up; a place where they could pick up information, where they could work from an' where Georgette could cash in when the time was right.

But if I'd used my headpiece I mighta known that there was one place where they would be as safe as a bank, where nobody could get at 'em an' where they reckoned they would be protected under international law.

An' that place is on a boat outside the three-mile limit where nobody can touch 'em an' where they can negotiate with anybody they like without bein' afraid of coppers of any sort, shape or nationality.

An' I never even thought of this until I saw Cy Hinks read that photographer's advertisement outa the *Magazine des Arts*. Then I knew why they had picked a photographer who lived on the coast.

An' it is stickin' out a foot that the boat they are usin' is the boat that Yatlin had got to bring the chemist guy Grearson over here on. That brainy dame Fernanda was pretty quick to see that the job ought to be played from that boat an' that's what she's doin'.

Then she reckoned it was easy for them to get inta touch with the photographer Pierrin without givin' themselves away, by givin' him a *poste restante* address in Trouville, an' havin' found out that he was willin' to do the job, Tony Scalla, callin' himself Dalada, comes around an' fixes everything up.

She's got brains all right.

I get through to Varney at the Embassy an' tell him about the things I want for Juanella to get to work on. By now we have got this guy so well-trained that I reckon that if I rang him up an' asked him to send a coupla elephants around he would just sigh an' say O.K.

He says he will get 'em within an hour somehow an' send 'em around to Juanella at the dump where the boys are workin'. I tell him that I hope he won't blow himself up by mistake while he is fixin' this business an' he says he hopes I am right.

I give myself a hot shower an' am about to turn in when Cy Hinks comes through. This boy has been doin' some sweet work with the naval attaché at the Embassy.

"You're dead right about the boat," he says. "She's a fair-sized tramp steamer *Madrilena Santaval,* registered as a Spanish boat and flyin' the Spanish flag. She's lyin' three and a half miles out— half a mile outside the three-mile limit between Courseuilles and Deauville. The Captain and crew are Spanish and Mexicans. They've been cleared for quarantine from Courseuilles. The medical officer's been aboard and they're allowed to land. They've got a motor launch.

The Customs' guys at Deauville say that nobody of the crew has landed—only the Captain and one or two other guys who are supposed to be passengers. These guys say that the *Madrilena Santaval* is a private charter job with the charter owner aboard. The ship's papers are in order an' they are not landin' any cargo. There isn't any doubt that you're dead right. This is the boat."

"Nice work, Cy," I tell him. "Have you got that other job fixed?"

"Pretty well," he says. "The naval guy at the Embassy has done most of it. I'm leavin' at five o'clock to-morrow morning to fix everything. We reckon we ought to pick the job up around the mouth of the Seine."

"O.K.," I tell him. "Well, when you go you better take Larvey Rillwater, the Grazzi boys an' Martinelli with you. All those boys can scrap if they haveta. They ought to be through with their job by then. An' I want you to take the other stuff with you too."

I fix to meet him around at the dump where the boys are workin' at five o'clock. He says O.K. an' that maybe I'll leave him alone for an hour or so until then so's he can get some sleep.

I hang up an' look at my watch. It is one o'clock in the mornin'. I ring the desk downstairs an' tell 'em to call me in three hours' time— at four o'clock. Then I turn in.

Just before I doze off I wonder just where I will be sleepin' to-morrow night—if I am interested in sleepin', that is!

I get up at four o'clock an' at half past Cy Hinks comes around in his car. We have some coffee an' we get around to the basement where the boys are workin'.

An' it looks as if they have done a swell job. Away in the corner, by herself, workin' under an electric light an' wearin' an old overall with the sleeves turned up, Juanella is gettin' ready to screw down the case over the time-bomb.

"What time do you want this bit of business to perform?" she says.

I tell her. I tell her to set it so that it goes off at twelve midnight to-night.

She says O.K. and she fixes it.

Then we get busy. We get the stuff packed up and put in the big leather cases like the ones I saw in Pierrin's studio. We pack up Juanella's time-bomb in another leather case that looks like a big plate holder.

Outside the dawn is just comin' along. When we get the stuff into the car I say so-long to Cy.

"You know your stuff," I tell him. "You get the cases delivered to Pierrin an' give him another talk about what he's got to do an' for the love of mike don't make any mistakes."

He says he won't. He gets inta the car an' Larvey Rillwater an' the other three boys that I have assigned on the job get in with him.

They are just goin' off when I feel somebody touch my arm. It is Juanella. She has got outa the overall an' she is wearin' a mink coat an' looks like a million dollars.

"Say, listen, sweetheart," she says. "I been a lotta things bat I ain't ever been a sailor. What about me goin' along on this job? I can use a rod as good as any guy here?"

"Skip it, honey," says Larvey. "This is not a game for dolls. I don't wanta see you spilled all over the floor some place. Stick around here an' buy yourself some clothes an' a few thousand new hats."

"That sounds all right to me," she says. "But I got a sorta idea in my head that it might be less dangerous to come along with you boys."

Larvey looks at her for a minute sorta ponderin'. Then he takes a peek at me. He gets it.

"Yeah," he says, "you might be right at that. Because," he goes on, "it wouldn't be so hot if just when I have got myself a nice free pardon an' wanta settle down to bein' legitimate you took it inta your head to fall for some copper."

"Why worry, Larvey," I tell him. "You don't haveta worry about Juanella. She'd be O.K."

He grins.

"I wasn't worryin' about her," he says. "I was worryin' about you. You don't know Juanella."

I watch the car drive off. Believe it or not I feel sorta lonely.

I go back to the Wellington an' I go to bed.

CHAPTER FOURTEEN
CONFERENCE FOR MUGS

I LOOK at my watch an' I see it is nearly ten o'clock, an' I reckon that the hired car is goin' to be O.K. where I've left it. Anyway if somebody pinches it, it's just too bad.

I start walkin' down to the quay.

It's a dark sorta night, an' there is a little drizzle of rain. The guy who laid out this Dives place oughta have done something about the cobblestones—they're not so hot either.

I stop for a minute an' light myself a cigarette. Away out to sea I can see a light blinkin'. I wonder if that is the *Madrilena Santaval*. I also wonder just what sort of luck I'm goin' to have when I get aboard this pirate junk an' whether they're goin' to be really nice or just slip me a coupla lead slugs below the belt to help my indigestion along.

I ease along the quay. After a bit I see a white speed-boat with a light in the stern an' some guy sittin' there smokin' a cigarette. He is a thin-faced palooka in a striped jersey an' a beret.

I call across to this guy. He starts up the motor an' brings the boat alongside the quay. He hands me up a piece of paper. It says: "*This is the guy. He seems O.K. an' he knows where the boat is.*" It is signed by Cy Hinks.

"Listen, pal," I tell this bozo. "You know where the *Madrilena* Santaval is lyin'?"

He nods.

"Yes, M'sieu," he says. "Eet is all arrange. I take you. Pleez get in."

I step down inta the boat an' he gives it the gun. Outside the quay the sea is choppy an' by what I can see of it, it looks damn depressin'.

I light myself another cigarette. I sit there with my head down, drawin' the smoke inta my lungs an' thinkin' about nothin' at all. Next thing I know we are there.

The guy cuts out his motor. He stands up an' lets go a hail.

"*Madrilena Santaval!*" he goes on bawlin' in French.

Away on our right—we are driftin' towards her with the current—is a big tramp. She looks a good seaboat. Some guy comes to the stern with a lantern. He starts bawlin' back to my guy in French. It sounds like a dogfight to me.

I prod the boy.

"You tell 'em that Mr. Lemmy Caution would like to have a coupla words with the Señora Fernanda Martinas, an' that he's left his visitin' cards behind."

He starts yellin' some more. After a bit somebody flashes a light in the stern of the tramp. I can see a guy hangin' over an' a dame—Fernanda!

I stand up.

"Hey, Fernanda," I yell. "How's it comin'. Mr. Caution is comin' aboard, so you better get the guard of honour ready!"

The man in the stern bawls to my guy an' we sneak under the stern an' along the starboard side. There is a gangway down from the ship all ready. We pull up there.

I step onto the gangway.

"You can scram," I tell the guy in the motor-boat. "You got your dough from Hinks, didn't you?"

He says yes. He swings the motor-boat around an' goes back.

I start walkin' up the gangway. When I get to the top I stop. Facin' me are two guys an' a dame. They are Tony Scalla, who is holdin' a .44 automatic, Fernanda in a chinchilla wrap that musta cost some mug some real jack, an' some other guy. The third guy looks to me like the captain.

"So what?" says Tony. He is snarlin' like a dog.

Fernanda puts her hand on his arm.

"Quietly, my friend," she says to him. "Just see that Mr. Caution—my dear Lemmy—is not also carrying a weapon."

"Don't you worry, honeypot," I tell her. "I ain't even got a fountain pen. I left it behind because I reckoned that some of your lousy heels would probably pinch it off me. But go ahead an' search—it might make you feel happier. Besides there's only about twenty-five of you guys aboard an' I might fall on you an' bite you."

Tony comes over an' frisks me. He steps away. He looks as if he has been hittin' the hooch for plenty. He is as near drunk as they come.

"I'd like to give it to you, you goddam copper," he says. "Me . . . I would like to shoot your insides out an' throw you in the drink while you are still livin'. I would . . ."

"Like hell you would, you cheap double-crossin' crocodile spawn," I crack back at him. "You'd like to do all sorts of things, wouldn'tya?

But you won't. An' you won't just because your lady boss here is already worryin' that pretty little head of hers as to how I knew where to find you mugs, an' why I've got the nerve to come aboard this crooks' hang-out without even a gun."

I step over towards him sorta easy an' placid.

"I don't like you, Tony," I tell him. "I wouldn't like you even if you was sober and didn't smell of garlic an' soused hamburger."

I do a quick side step an' bust him a mean Japanese slash on the neck with the side of my hand, twist the gun outa his hand an' throw it overboard. Then, before he's got over that I give him my left knee in the stomach—hard. It's all over so quick that he don't even know what's hit him. He goes down on the deck squirmin'. Maybe I caught him a bit low.

"That's that," I tell him. "If you think I've come aboard here to listen to a lotta cheap heroics from punk mobsters you can think some more."

He gets up. He is plenty hurt. He stands against the rail holdin' his stomach.

I look at Fernanda. Boy, she looks good to me. She is wearing a lacey sorta evenin' frock, long at the back an' short in front, an' I can see her little feet peepin' out. Fernanda is surely a dame to look at.

She is smilin'. The same slow soft sorta smile that she handed me out in the *casa* that night in Mexico when she was tryin' to give me Lesson One from the Young Man's Guide to Neckin'.

"Lemmy," she says in that soft voice that makes Spanish sound like it was treacle bein' poured over a satin quilt. "You are still as delightful, as foolhardy, as ever. You are quite charming. How nice to talk to you again. There are so many things for us to discuss. And, my friend, now that you are here you can save us a great deal of trouble."

She takes out a gold cigarette case an' takes out a cigarette. She looks at me over the flame of her lighter.

"Tony is inclined to be ridiculous, sometimes," she says. "Either he does not think at all or he thinks too much. But you must come below. You must have a drink."

She slips me a big smile. Then she says the same thing that she said when I was at the *casa,* when she was wonderin' just how she could double-cross me easiest.

"My house and everything that is in it is yours," she says.

She gives me a little curtsey.

Me . . . I wanta be sick. This dame gives me the creeps. I reckon she would sing you a lullaby an' cut your throat at the same time.

"O.K., Fernanda," I tell her. "I wanta do a little talkin' myself, but if I have a drink somebody else has gotta sample it first. I been poisoned before."

This is a proper mugs' conference. We are sittin' around in the Captain's saloon—a pretty big cabin, lookin' at each other. Some guy in a dirty steward's jacket with a nasty grin on his pan that I would pay ten dollars to smack off right now brings in some liquor.

What a sweet set-up. I get to thinkin'—in the way a guy does think at times like this—about all the tough spots I been in before, an' wonderin' whether this business is goin' to pan out. I reckon the chances are about six to four against it. Because, as you guys have probably worked out for yourselves right now, *if they knew it* this bunch of so-an'-so's are holdin' every card in the deck.

Me, I am just bankin' on one thing an' that is that the crook is always a bit scared in one little spot right back of his mind. He works out a scheme an' he plays it along an' all the time he is wonderin' if there ain't just one spot that he has left himself open.

I take a look around. I reckon that this bunch would win the first prize any time somebody liked to start a world contest for skulduggery, murder, mayhem an' what-have-you-got.

Fernanda, who ain't drinkin', is sittin' on the other side of the table with her fur thrown back showin' a sweet slice of neck. Tony Scalla, still feelin' his stomach an' fifty per cent more sober than he was, is loungin' alongside her.

The Captain, who has got a pan like a contour map of the Sierras, is standin' up against the wall smokin' a stogie that smells like a bad onion, an' draped around the place are three other guys. Two of 'em I know; they are Willy (Swede) Munskill, who beat a State policeman, who was already wounded, to death with a chair leg one time, an' a Mexican called Mesa Parallio who is also an expert in causin' guys a lotta pain. I don't know the other boy but he is young an' has got a cruel mouth an' twitchin' hands. He looks like a dope to me.

I take a drink of rye. They are all watchin' me like cats lookin' at a mouse. Fernanda is still smilin'.

"Dear Lemmy," she says. "I am so glad to see you here."

She sends a sweet smile flashin' around the saloon.

"Now," she goes on, "will you talk or shall I? But first of all, will some one go along to the main saloon and ask our friends not to make quite such a noise because we are talking very important business."

The dope guy goes off. Somewhere in the ship I can hear a bunch of guys singin' an' shoutin' an' playin' a gramophone.

"Look, Fernanda," I tell her. "We're all friends here, an' I've come along to talk business to you. If you wanta know how I knew you was here, well that's easy. I reckoned that you would play this thing out somewhere where you'd be safe—such as on this boat. I knew that you was all concentratin' in France. So I put two an' two together an' looked around for a Spanish boat that had been stickin' around for some time, an' that's that.

"You see I ain't concealin' anything up my sleeve," I go on. "I'm puttin' all my cards on the table because I gotta. It's the only way I can fix this job."

"Like hell it is," says Scalla. "You been outsmarted for once—you big flatfoot. An' how do you like it? We got you an' the Government just where we want 'em. We . . ."

Fernanda puts her hand on his arm. He closes down. It looks like she is the boss all right.

"Look, Fernanda," I tell her nice an' easy, "you tell me something. What happened to that guy Grearson—the American chemist guy? You got him around any place?"

She looks sad.

"I am very, very sorry for the unfortunate Mr. Grearson," she says. "He was so very valuable and kind to us. After a certain amount of persuasion he consented to supply us with all the information we required in order to dovetail the two formulas. It was terrible that after being so good he should have the misfortune to fall overboard. A horrible accident but, I am afraid, his own fault. All the details are to be found in the Captain's log-book."

I nod.

"Yeah," I say, "I suppose it was just one of those accidents that happen at sea. O.K. an' what happened to my other little sweetheart?"

Fernanda laughs.

"You mean Georgette Istria?" she says.

She looks at Tony Scalla. He starts grinnin'.

"That, Lemmy," Fernanda goes on, "is really the cream of the whole jest. I really must congratulate Tony on the way he played that. You see Georgette was always trying quite honestly, to help you. She had nothing whatever to do with our little plan. She was absolutely and entirely innocent. She just happened to fit into the scheme."

I look at her with my mouth open an' my eyes poppin'!

"She is quite safe," says Fernanda, "except that she is petulant about the rather intimate suggestions that Tony makes to her from time to time. You see he has a ridiculous passion for Georgette and he believes that she should be considered part of his share in this business—and why not?"

Scalla lights himself a cigarette. He is grinnin' across at me like a hyena. This boy is pleased with himself. He is doin' fine!

I put up a weak sorta grin.

"So I was a sap, hey?" I say. "Me an' Georgette Istria, we was both the big suckers."

Fernanda laughs—a little soft laugh.

"Work it out for yourself, Lemmy," she says. "After I found it necessary to shoot my unfortunate Pedro, I contacted the bright Tony who had been sent down to Mexico by Jake Istria to find out exactly what was happening. I explained the whole position to Tony and he agreed that we might work together.

"He returned to Chicago and told Istria exactly what the position was. He told him that his only chance was to get the Jamieson half of the formula to Yatlin whose headquarters were in France and that being done he would be safe and Yatlin would share fifty-fifty with him.

"Tony did not, of course, explain to him that we had already arranged between ourselves to dispose of Yatlin when the time came.

"Just at this time Istria received the wire from Zellara—the one you made her send from Mexico City. He was rather scared but Tony had a brilliant idea. He suggested to Jake Istria that it was certain that you would be following that wire; he suggested that he talk secretly with Georgette, point out to her that here was her chance to escape from Istria and the mob, and that the way for her to do it was to contact you and show you a way in which you could get the Jamieson half of the formula and in the process find out just where the Yatlin headquarters were in France.

"He knew that once you believed you had the formula, the watch on American ports would be relaxed. If you could be palmed off with a fake, Tony could get over here with the real one.

"Istria thought this an excellent plan. He knew Georgette loathed him and the idea of making her an accessory to our little plot amused him immensely.

"Tony then approached Georgette with his great idea. He told her that he had seen me, that I was a very nice woman who feared that she had embroiled herself in something illegal and that I had given him the fullest information which I had secured from Pedro. He told her that he had not reported to Jake Istria; that he had told him practically nothing, that he, Tony, was scared stiff and that here was the chance for both he and Georgette to escape from the mob, to help the course of justice and generally to behave like two dear little angels.

"Poor Georgette jumped at the chance. Tony told her that he would wait for you at the airport and bring you to her. I think you know the rest."

She lights herself a cigarette an' looks at me sorta sarcastic.

"Then the supreme thing happens. *You* shoot Jake Istria. When we heard of this we were really amused because we had agreed—Tony and I and our friends—that when the time was ripe we should deal with Jake. However, you saved us the trouble."

She flicks the ash off her cigarette.

"There remained only one person to be dealt with—and that was Yatlin. Yatlin thought that he would be coming over here to take charge of things. We thought differently and so Yatlin was taken care of."

"An' your little sister Zellara was the dame who took care of him," I say. "Well, Fernanda, you are all brains. I gotta hand it to you. Here you are sittin' right on top of the game with all your old partners nice an' dead so that you haven't got to cut the dough with anybody except Scalla here."

I grin at him.

"Don't you ever get a bit scared?" I ask him. "Don't it ever occur to you that maybe the little lady here is goin' to come to the conclusion that she don't wanta split with anybody an' one day you might easy wake up an' find yourself dead?"

He gives me a scowl. Then he thinks of something an' grins.

"O.K., copper," he says. "Maybe you think your cracks are smart, but they ain't goin' to help you. In fact," he goes on, "I'm a bit pleased with you. First of all you fell like a heap of coke for that phoney story that I pulled on you in Chicago—when I told you that Georgette was my sister an' didn't even know it!"

He looks around for applause for this an' he gets it; everybody is laughin' like hell.

"And in the second place," he goes on, "if it hadn't been for you jumpin' to the wrong conclusion about Georgette an' shoutin' your mouth off at her I wouldn't have got my hooks on her again."

I nod.

"I suppose you grabbed her when she came out to the Armine Lodge?" I ask him.

"Yeah," he says. "I knew she'd be goin' out there anyway, either to hold up the front that you was trying to pull on us originally or else—an' this was the way it happened—to find out just why I'd double-crossed her."

He looks around again.

"Was it funny or was it?" he says. "Georgette comin' out to the Lodge with a gun an' tellin' me that she was goin' to take me back an' hand me over to Caution an' prove that she was the little innocent." He laughs. "She mighta got away with it too," he goes on, "only she didn't know that Parallio was hangin' about downstairs an' when he heard her shootin' off her mouth he come up an' knocked the gun outa her mitt. Was she surprised!"

I don't say nothin'. I am just registerin' a quiet sorta oath with myself that one of these fine days I am goin' to take this Scalla guy an' tear him inta little pieces. He makes my stomach turn over.

Fernanda chimes in.

"All this is very interesting and exciting," she says, "but at the same time I am perfectly certain that my dear Lemmy has not come aboard the *Madrilena Santaval* just for the purpose of having a discussion of things which have happened in the past. The future is so much more interesting. Possibly he has some sort of proposition for us."

She smiles across at me.

"Have you, Lemmy?" she asks.

"Sure," I tell her, "I've got a proposition an' it's a good one for you. It makes you guys millionaires."

I get up an' take outa my pocket the Ambassador's letter to me. I throw it across to Fernanda.

"You'll see that that letter says I can pay Two Million Dollars to anybody I wanta without takin' a receipt," I tell her. "O.K. Well, here is the offer. You hand me over the complete Jamieson an' Grearson formulas an' I'm goin' to pay you Two Million Dollars, an' that's all there is to be said."

She reads the letter. The little half-smile is still playin' about her mouth. I get to thinkin' just how good this dame would look danglin' on the end of a rope.

"There's just one string to that offer," I go on. "One condition—an' it's me that's makin' it. If an' when I go off this boat to-night I'm takin' Georgette Istria with me an' I'm tellin' you that that's definite and final."

Scalla jumps up.

"Yeah?" he says. "Like hell you will. She stays here an' likes it!"

I shrug my shoulders.

"O.K.," I say, "I ain't worryin'. You have it your own way."

Fernanda butts in.

"We shall have to consider the offer, Lemmy," she says. "We are all partners in this deal, including the captain and crew of this ship. The matter must be discussed and in any event we shall not be able to give you a reply to-night. We shall be able to give you our reply in the morning."

She walks over to me. When she gets near I can sniff the perfume she wears. I'm tellin' you it's swell stuff. She puts her fingers on my arm.

"To-night you shall be our guest, Lemmy," she says. "We shall have a little *fiesta* in the main saloon and you shall join us."

She shoots a wicked smile at me.

"Come, Lemmy," she says. "We welcome you not only because we like you but because you are the bringer of good tidings."

She leads the way outa the saloon. Away down in the main saloon they have started up the music again.

I do some quick thinkin'. So they ain't goin' to do a deal until to-morrow mornin'. I reckon I know why! I grin to myself.

Walkin' along the deck I take a quick look at my watch.

There are about twenty people in the main saloon. Some of 'em are the crew of this tramp an' some of 'em are friends of Fernanda's an' Scalla's. About half are American an' the other half are Spanish, Mexican an' latins generally. A sweet crowd.

Down at the end of the saloon, sittin' by herself, is Georgette. She is wearin' the same clothes as when she walked outa the Grande-Claremont. She looks sorta tired, an' I don't wonder.

I ease over to her an' sit down beside her. Nobody takes much notice. The Captain an' Fernanda an' one or two of the heads of this mob are on the other side of the saloon. Some guy starts doin' tap-dancin'. Everybody is drinkin' like blazes. I get to thinkin' that if the *Madrilena Santaval* ain't the original hell-ship I would like to take a quick look at the one that is.

Georgette looks at me. There is a little smile in her eyes.

"Well, honeypot," I tell her. "It looks as if they tried to take us both for a ride an' maybe they've got away with it an' maybe not. You don't have to explain anythin' at all, I reckon I know the story an' if you'd tried to tell me anythin' else when I was bawlin' you out at the Grande-Claremont I wouldn'ta believed you. Fernanda's given me the whole works. You an' me was the suckers."

"It's all right, Lemmy," she says. "I know. There was no reason why you should think anything but what you did. I realised it wasn't any good trying to explain."

I drop my voice an' put on a big grin as if I was tellin' her sweet nothin's.

"I found this boat through the corner of that magazine you wrote the note on an' dropped outa the car window," I tell her. "Nice work, baby. Just stick around an' whatever happens don't get excited. Everything is goin' to be all right—at least I hope so."

The steward guy with the funny grin comes over an' says do I wanta drink. I say yes we want some brandy. He goes off an' gets it. When he comes back with the liquor I make Georgette have a stiff one. Away on the other side of the saloon I can see Tony watchin' us.

I get up an' stand with my back to him so that he can't get any big ideas about what I am sayin'.

"When the time comes, Georgette, you do what I tell you an' do it quick," I tell her. "I'll be, seein' you."

As I turn around three guys come inta the saloon, two Americans an' a Latin. They go over to where Fernanda is sittin'. I ease over sorta casually, lightin' a cigarette an' takin' everything very easy.

"Well," says Fernanda to these guys, "is he here?"

"Nope," says the big one. "His mother died this afternoon an' he had to go over to her place to fix things. He left a message that we was to go back at a quarter to one an' that he would be waitin' for us. An' he said that we was to get all his stuff aboard—it was all ready an' packed up, an' there's a helluva lot of it. He's goin' to be waitin' on the quay at a quarter to one."

Fernanda nods.

"That is excellent," she says. "Where have you put his equipment?"

"We took it down to the engine room—where the other stuff is. We got the lights an' everything all ready," says the guy.

Fernanda nods. She gets up. She is holdin' a little glass of champagne in her hand.

"My friends," she says. "Please be quiet while I talk business."

Everybody closes down. Some guy turns off the gramophone. One guy is roarin' drunk an' wants to talk so somebody busts him one an' throws him in the corner.

Then they're all quiet. You coulda heard a pin drop.

"I think that I can say that our hard work and energy have borne fruit," says Fernanda smilin' around like the President of the Fork Plains Women's Literary Club. "Mr. Caution has brought us an offer of two million dollars from the U.S. Government. I think we shall accept it.

"But there is one point which I must make quite clear to him. We shall not hand over the formulas until the money is paid, and until we have some definite guarantee that we shall not be molested in the future.

"As you all know I have considered this point. Much as I like Mr. Caution—my dear Lemmy—I am afraid that, in a matter of such importance as this is, I could not accept anyone's word. So I have taken these precautions.

"A photographer is coming aboard shortly. He will make photostat copies of the formulas. We shall retain these. Tomorrow morning I propose to hand to Mr. Caution the original Jamieson-Grearson formulas. He can take them away with him and he can arrange to pay us the two million dollars aboard this ship.

"That is our bargain. We shall retain the photostat copies of the formulas in order to ensure the payment and our safety in the future."

She raises her glass.

"Gentlemen," she says, "let us drink to the brilliancy of three brilliant people—Mr. Jamieson and Mr. Grearson, who were probably the greatest chemists in history, coupled with the name of our dear Lemmy Caution who has been very successful in the past even if not in the present!"

She raises her glass. Everybody is laughin' their heads off. Everybody drinks.

I look at my watch. It is six minutes to twelve. I take a coupla quick steps an' get my back against the end wall of the saloon. I turn around an' look at 'em.

"O.K., mugs," I tell 'em. "You're doin' fine. Well, take a tip from me an' keep quiet an' listen to what I'm sayin' an' listen good. If you don't you'll be sorry."

"I ain't the sucker. You are—the whole damn lot of you. You think that a photographer is comin' aboard this boat. He ain't. We got at him first. But he's sent his cameras an' stuff aboard. It's been taken down to the engine room, the place you got fixed up to take the photographs.

"There ain't any cameras or plates or what-nots in that stuff. There's just two sweet little infernal machines. Just in case you bozos don't believe what I'm tellin' you, stick around an' listen."

I look around at 'em. They are all starin' at me. Each an' every one of these guys is wonderin' whether I am tryin' to pull a fast one or whether I have got the goods on 'em.

Scalla makes as if he's goin' to move, but Fernanda clutches his arm. I can see her long white fingers grippin' him. Her eyes are starin' straight at me. I know what she is thinkin'. She is wonderin' whether she's made the one slip that the crook always makes; she is wonderin' what I'm goin' to do. I can see she don't like it.

I look at my watch. I go on talkin' fast.

"The first time-bomb goes off at twelve o'clock. It's just a little one. It's just big enough to blow a bit outa the engine room an' show you lousy heels that I mean business.

"Four an' a half minutes after that bomb goes off the second one goes. The second one is in the big camera case. There are forty twelve-inch dynamite plugs in it. It's so damn big that when it goes this goddam ship an' everybody on it, includin' me, go to blazes with it.

"So you can bite on that, you lousy heels. You thought you was sittin' pretty. You thought you was goin' to get away with kidnap, torture an' murder an' hold up two Governments for big dough. Well, you'll get the dough, but you'll get it my way or else this is goin' to be my last case. We'll all go together.

"O.K. Well, don't get excited. I'm still gonna play ball. *I can turn that second bomb off. I got the key of the case in my pocket. I can turn off the chronometer switch but I am the only guy aboard who can, an' there ain't even time to get that heavy case upstairs an' dump it overboard!*"

I look at my watch. It is twelve o'clock.

"Stick around, mugs," I tell 'em, "an' listen. I'll turn that second bomb off if somebody hands me the formulas right now!"

Fernanda opens her mouth to speak, an' the first time-bomb goes off. There is a hell of a rumble an' an explosion that knocks the glasses an' bottles all over the place.

They are all lookin' at me with their mouths open. Fernanda snaps out of it.

"Parallio," she says, an' her voice is shrill. *"Take him down to the engine room. Give him the formulas. Nobody else is to move."*

Parallio streaks for the door. I go after him. He goes like a rabbit for the companion way. He is takin' four-five steps at a time. I go after him.

The engine room is a blaze of light on one side an' the lamps are all smashed on the other through the explosion, which hasn't done anything else much except make a big noise. I can see where they've run arc lamps from the electric batteries to give old Pierrin plenty of light. Parallio slams over to a big steel box, opens it, shows me the stuff inside. He is sweatin'. His eyes are poppin'.

"Señor," he says, "here are the formulas. Turn off that thing! *Por Madre de Dios!*"

I step back an' I hit him under the jaw. He flops. I feel in his hip an' grab his gun. I put it in my coat pocket.

I look at the formulas. I go through 'em. I reckon I got the real thing this time.

I stick 'em back in the leather wallets. I put the wallets under my arm an' ease back to the saloon. When I go in I can hear a big sorta sigh go around. These boys were scared all right but now they're gettin' over it. They're beginnin' to look nasty. Fernanda is standin' up there lookin' at me with snakes' eyes.

"Well, Mr. Caution," she says, "so you have disposed of your second bomb."

She begins to smile again.

"An' what now?" she says.

Chapter Fifteen
THIS WAY OUT

I DON'T say a word. I just grin at Fernanda sorta placid an' grab a loose cigarette outa my pocket. I light it nice an' easy an' go over an' lean up against the saloon wall—where I was before.

This is what the dramatic playwright would call a tense moment. I reckon that right now any of these guys is liable to pull a gun an' give me the works—that is if they don't do somethin' worse than that—just outa sheer bad temper. They sorta got the idea that I've fooled them.

Fernanda is still standin' there lookin' at me like a snake. The other guys have formed a sorta half-circle across the saloon facin' me.

I get to thinkin' about Daniel in the lions' den, an' I reckon that Daniel was on the best end of the stick compared with me right now.

I throw a quick look over to the left at Georgette. She is still sittin' there. She throws me a quick smile. That baby has got her nerve all right. I grin back.

Fernanda is standin' as still as a statue. She is waitin' for the next move in the game.

"O.K., you mugs," I tell 'em—tryin' to make my voice sound sorta casual—"So I've got the formulas an' my girl friend Fernanda is keen to know what the next move is."

I look at my watch. It is just after ten minutes past twelve. Inside my heart I am hopin' like a fool that the end of this job is goin' to break.

"First of all, sweetheart," I tell Fernanda, "you tell that wall-eyed Captain of yours that if he ain't got a good look-out on the bridge he oughta have, because maybe somethin' is goin' to happen in a minute from a quarter where he ain't expectin' it."

Nobody moves. They all stand there lookin' at me an' not sayin' anythin'. I reckon they look like a lotta mad dogs an' how would you look if you thought you'd got your hooks on two million dollars with no strings to the take an' then some lone guy starts a four-flushin' act like I have?

"Well, you bums," I tell 'em. "The point is this. I've got the formulas but I ain't such a sap as to think for one minute that you guys are goin' to let the matter rest there an' not do anything about it. I reckon you are all feelin' a bit desperate like a dog who thinks that he's pinched a joint of beef an' ain't quite certain as to whether some other guy ain't goin' to grab it off him.

"O.K. Well, you mugs have made one very bad mistake, an' if you'll give me a coupla minutes I'll point it out to you.

"You guys thought that the U.S. Government wouldn't let anybody in on this job. You thought they'd keep it as quiet as a coffin just because they didn't even want anybody to know that the Jamieson-Grearson formulas were in existence. Well, you was right.

"But when I found out that you was aimin' to get the stuff photographed I thought it about time that I let somebody inta this job besides myself, because you gotta realise that I'm pretty good an' tired of carryin' this business on my own shoulders. Besides which lookin' at you guys makes me feel ill."

Fernanda starts talkin'. Her voice is low an' as cool as an iceberg.

"Come to the point, Lemmy," she says. "And if I were you I should be quick. My friends here are inclined to be a little impatient."

"Sure I'll come to the point, Fernanda," I tell her. "Well, here's the point. You guys have been pretty well organised right through this job. You've worked it swell an' your information's been good an' things have broke for you."

I throw my cigarette end away after I have banged out the butt-end on the wall. I am wastin' as much time as I can.

"It was a bit tough on you boys," I go on, "that nobody aboard this boat took the trouble to find out that there was a U.S. torpedo boat on a friendly visit around here, lyin' off Havre. O.K. Well, I took the trouble of lettin' the Commander know that a U.S. Federal Officer was visitin' aboard the *Madrilena Santaval* to-night, that he was goin' aboard to investigate a suspected piracy charge made against this ship by the Mexican coast authorities a coupla months ago. I sorta suggested to the Commander that somebody around here might like to get tough. You got that?

"Right. Well, I've got these formulas an' I'm takin' 'em off this ship, an' . . ."

A guy busts inta the saloon. He is sweatin' an' his eyes are poppin' outa his head.

"Hey, listen," he says to the Captain. "There's a ship just made a signal. It's the U.S. torpedo boat *Tucson*. She's lyin' about a half a mile away. She says she's waitin' to take off a U.S. Federal Officer an' that if we don't make an O.K. signal she's goin' to arrest this boat on a piracy charge!"

I grin.

"Well, you mugs, what did I tellya?" I say.

There is a sorta low growl goes around the saloon. Now is the time. If it's comin' I gotta take it. My mouth is sorta dry. I know durn well that every one of these guys knows that if he gets pinched he's for a life sentence or the hot seat.

Fernanda puts up her hand. The noise dies away.

She takes a step forward an' I'm tellin' you guys that just at that minute she looks swell. Her eyes are blazin' an' her breast heavin' like it was bein' worked by a pneumatic pump. She looks like Boadicea leadin' the Britons against whoever it was, Queen Elizabeth orderin' Drake to take a quick smack at the Spanish Armada an' a meetin' of Apache Indian chiefs workin' out whether they shall boil, fry or slow roast the original settlers.

"You poor fool," she blazes. "Do you think that we're going to let you get off this boat with those formulas? Do you think that after all my planning and scheming you're going to get away with this?"

She turns around to the mob.

"It's a bluff," she says. "That torpedo boat would never dare arrest this ship!"

I take a quick look at 'em. I can see the doubt in their ugly pans. They just don't know what to do, but the odds are they are goin' to do me!

"Listen, you two-cent saps," I holler. "Listen to some sense for once in your lousy lives. That boat out there don't wanta arrest anybody. Fernanda says the U.S. Government want this job kept quiet. She's dead right. That torpedo boat is aimin' to take two people off this ship, that is Georgette Istria, myself an' the formulas. Once we're aboard that torpedo boat everything is O.K.

"All right, well what are you goin' to have? Are you goin' to have the two million dollars an' let us scram with these goddam papers or are you goin' to get the electric chair—the whole damn lot of you—for nothin'?

Some big guy jumps forward.

"How the hell do we know we're goin' to get the two million?" he says. "Once you're gone we shan't see a goddam nickel!"

He turns around to Fernanda.

"What the hell is all this?" he yells. "You said that we was on a sweet thing here. You told us that the U.S. Government daren't make a stink about this an' now here's a goddam torpedo boat playin' around that will probably blow us outa the water if we don't let this heel go off like he says. There won't be any talk if they sink this ship an' leave the whole damn lot of us in the drink."

There is a sorta murmur of applause. I put up my hand.

"Listen, you lunatic palookas," I holler. "What are you worryin' about the dough for? I tell you you got it aboard here. There's two million dollars in high denomination U.S. currency in the big camera case—the one I told you was the second time-bomb. Parallio's lyin' across it where I left him with a bust jawbone!"

Somebody gasps. Fernanda looks at Tony. She nods. In two minutes a dozen of these guys are stampedin' outa the saloon like hell was after 'em.

Fernanda starts smilin' again. She looks at me sorta mischievous. She has got back her nerve.

"Lemmy," she says, "I believe you have more brains than I thought. You have certainly a superb sense of the dramatic. I think you are doing very well. I hope that we shall meet again one day under more pleasant circumstances."

"Me too," I tell her, but I am thinkin' that I would rather run a mile through a bush fire an' then swim six miles through seven feet of snow rather than meet up with this female gorilla except the way *I* wanta.

Scalla busts in. He is sweatin' with excitement.

"Jeez," he says. "He was talkin' truth. The dough's there. Two million in big notes!"

I walk across the saloon. I take Georgette's hand an' pull her onto her feet. I turn around an' face 'em.

"All right," I say. "I'm goin' an' I wish you a very good night. You got your two million an' I'm bettin' each one of you ten dollars that it won't do you any good. You'll die of liquor in six months.

"An' here's somethin' else," I crack at 'em. "Take a tip from me an' stay clear of the United States, because if I see any of you mugs around I'm goin' to frame you on any charge that I can think of quick."

There is a roar of laughter. Somebody says:

"Scram, copper!"

They make a way for us. At the doorway I turn my head.

Fernanda is grinnin' like a cat with two tails.

We stick around an' wait at the top of the gangway. Behind us are Fernanda an' Tony an' half a dozen of the others. Downstairs I can hear the mob yellin' an' chuckin' glasses about. I reckon they think it's a holiday.

Georgette points her finger. Churnin' towards us is a grey launch. She has gotta searchlight on us. She does a sweet turn an' slides up to the bottom of the gangway. Standin' at the wheel is a naval officer wearin' a gun.

I hear Georgette sigh.

"Inta the boat, sweet," I tell her, "an' be quick!"

I turn around.

"*Adios,* Fernanda," I crack, "an' you too, Tony. Maybe one day I'll be seein' you!"

Fernanda puts up her hand.

"Go with God, *cara*," she says.

Maybe she's feelin' religious now she's got the dough.

I go down the gangway. When I step inta the boat I haveta take a quick pull at myself because the naval guy is Cy Hinks. His coat is two sizes too small for him an' his uniform cap has slipped over one eye.

He looks like the guy outside the cinema.

"Get outa here an' get out quick," I mutter at him.

I am thankin' my stars it is a dark night because I reckon if any of the mob hadda taken one good look at Cy it woulda been all over bar the funeral.

He gives the launch the gun an' we shoot off.

As the *Madrilena Santaval* fades outa sight Larvey Rillwater with a tommy gun under his arm, an' the other boys lookin' like the U.S. Armoury at Washington, come outa the cabin.

"What the hell," says Larvey. "An' me, always wantin' to be a gunman an' I ain't even hadda shot at a fish!"

Behind him is Juanella. She is holdin' a magazine rifle an' I bet she was achin' to use it.

"Me too," she says. "But there, I never get any fun."

She gives Georgette the once-over.

"It's always the way," she says. "It's always some other dame stars in a big rescue act. All I get is the sea-air an' my complexion ruined by shell-fish. What the hell!"

We pull up to the boat. She is a big sea-goin' French tug that Cy has chartered like we arranged. I take a look at her. She looks good to me.

Up on the deck Georgette gives my hand a helluva squeeze.

"There isn't much I can say to you, Lemmy," she says, "except that I think you're wonderful!"

I grin at her.

"Don't tell anybody, honey," I tell her, "but so do I. Me, I was so scared that I was prayin' in Chinese."

"Everything's O.K., Lemmy," says Cy, takin' off the uniform jacket an' lookin' more human every minute. "I got it all fixed up with the captain. He's got an unofficial diplomatic guarantee from the Naval Attaché guy at the Embassy. Everything's okey doke."

"Right," I tell him.

I turn around to Georgette.

"Honey," I tell her. "You get below with Juanella. She'll take care of you. I gotta lot to do. I'll be seein' you."

When they have scrammed I go inta a huddle with Cy an' the French tug captain. Some guy brings me a drink an' it tastes like nectar.

I give myself a cigarette an' take the formulas below an' lock 'em in the Captain's safe.

So far so good!

A bit of a mist has come up.

The Captain has swung the tug around an' is goin' easy. I lean over the side an' take a look at her. She is broad in the beam, big an' heavy. A nice job.

I look up to the bridge. The Captain is standin' strainin' his eyes. Now an' again we sound a siren.

Cy Hinks comes up an' says hello.

"A sweet job, Lemmy," he says, "and plenty expensive."

I give him a cigarette.

"How much?" I ask him.

"We paid twenty thousand francs," he says. "And we're paying another twenty thousand to-morrow."

"Chicken-feed," I say. "For this job, that's cheap!"

Away ahead somethin' looms up. We let go some sharp blasts on the siren. I hear the Captain bawlin' through a megaphone.

"That's her," says Cy, sorta excited. "That's the *Madrilena Santaval!*"

Our siren starts goin' again.

Cy grips my arm.

"That means we're going to turn about," he says.

Guys are tearin' about the boat. Up in the bows I can see some deck hands gettin' collision mats over the side.

I hear Larvey and the other boys come up behind us. They stand there watchin'. I can hear 'em breathin'.

Our siren goes again. As the last blast finishes a shape comes up on our left. I can see the lights in the saloon an' I can hear some guy bawlin' on the bridge.

Behind me Larvey draws his breath through his teeth.

"Jeez!" he says.

We smash clean inta the starboard bows of the *Madrilena Santaval*. The bump knocks me off my feet. As I get up I can hear our Captain yellin' to lower away the boats.

I light a cigarette.

I ain't ever seen an accident at sea before. But I think this one is swell.

Our boat starts backin' away from the *Madrilena Santaval*. After a minute we get a searchlight on her and was the deck of that boat like a first-class movie or was it? I can see guys rushin' about the place—most of 'em drunk—tryin' to get the boats away. After a bit they get two boats away from the port side an' one of our boats—with a tommy gun in the bows—goes after her.

Presently the *Madrilena* begins to settle down by the bows, the water is lappin' over her side. I can make out two or three figures on the bridge—one of 'em is Fernanda. I start grinnin' because I reckon this dame is goin' to get her feet wet.

The boats from our ship are hangin' around, waitin' to pick up people outa the water.

I rush up onto the bridge and grab the megaphone off the Captain.

"Pick 'em up, boys," I howl. "An' whatever you do get that little lady in the fur coat an' the guy who's with her. I wouldn't like 'em to drown . . . they both got a date with the electric chair!"

Fernanda is standin' on the deck lookin' like a cat that's been dipped in a bucket of water. Somebody has put a blanket around her shoulders.

Tony Scalla is lyin' on the deck cryin'. Maybe he is havin' a premonition of what's comin' to him.

"Well, Fernanda," I tell her. "So we played it out, sweetheart, an' you lost. Ain't you sorry you didn't give me the works when you had the chance?"

She calls me a rude name. She calls me a whole lotta rude names. She is *very* burned up.

"I thought maybe you'd like to know about them friends of yours," I tell her. "I reckon we saved most of 'em for Uncle Sam. One or two of 'em have got themselves drowned. We couldn't find 'em an' I don't suppose that anybody's goin' to miss 'em much."

She pulls herself together.

"I congratulate you, Lemmy," she says. She is fightin' to keep her voice cool. "But you will realise that I cost you two million dollars. You didn't save them, did you?"

Just behind me I can hear Larvey laughin'.

"Two million nothin's," I tell her. "All that dough was phoney." I grin at her.

"Let me present to you the guy who made it," I crack at her. "This is Mr. Larvey Rillwater, one-time biggest an' best counterfeiter in the U.S. an' when I tell you that Larvey an' five boys workin' with him made it in two days an' nights I think he deserves a hand!"

Fernanda looks at Larvey. Then she takes a step toward him an' smacks him across the pan.

"O.K., lady," says Larvey. "Just for that I'll come an' see you fried!"

Cy pulls Tony Scalla onto his feet. He is a sweet sight. I look at him an' Fernanda.

"Fernanda Martinas an' Tony Scalla," I tell 'em, "I am an officer of the United States Department of Justice, an' I am arrestin' you on this ship, chartered by me, for the murder of John Ernest Jamieson, a citizen of Great Britain, the murder of Arthur Villby Grearson, a citizen of the United States, an' for conspirin' to steal documents, the property of the Governments of the United States an' Great Britain. I am takin' you to England where I shall apply for your extradition to the United States."

Tony goes on cryin'. Fernanda spits in my face.

"Take 'em away, boys," I say. "Stick 'em in the brig with the other heels, an' shoot 'em if you get a good excuse. They make me sick."

I grab a rug an' go along to the bows. Georgette is standin' there lookin' over the sea. I wrap the rug around her.

"Is this swell, honey," I say, "or is it? Don't you think that when all the trouble an' turmoil an' shoutin' is over a little quiet on the rollin' sea is what the doctor ordered?"

She looks around at me. The sea-mist is fadin' an' away over the clouds the moon is comin' up.

I look at Georgette. Her eyes are sorta purple like I told you, an' they are swimmin' in tears. Me, I start feelin' poetic which is a thing that happens to me on a nice night at sea.

She puts her hand in mine.

"Lemmy," she says, "are you *ever* serious?"

I look at her sorta surprised an' hurt.

"Gorgeous," I tell her. "I am always serious." I make my voice sorta tense. "I wanta tell you, Georgette, that I am nuts about you. I am entirely bughouse any time you are around, but I know that I am not fit to kiss the deck you are standin' on."

"Oh, Lemmy," she says. "Do you really mean that?"

"Nope," I tell her. "But I read it in a book an' I wanted to see what it sounded like. Besides, I hate kissin' decks anyway!"

She don't say nothin'. She just looks out to sea. I step up beside her an' before I know what is happenin' she is in my arms an' her mouth is on mine an' I am feelin' so goddam poetic that I woulda made Lord Byron look like a stale hamburger.

There is a cough behind me. I let go of Georgette an' turn around. It is Juanella Rillwater.

"O.K.," she says, "I got it. The woman always pays. I suppose it's only the mother in me that appeals to men. But," she goes on, "after all I done for you, Lemmy, makin' your lousy bombs an' generally nursin' you around I *do* think that you mighta given me a tumble instead of importin' this dame. Me . . . I'm *hurt*!"

"Look, Honey," I tell her. "Why don't you give Larvey a break? After all the guy's your husband, ain't he?"

"Yeah," she says. "I suppose so."

She gives me a big grin.

"An' after the deal I got from you, I reckon I better stick to home-made pastry," she says. "Well, copper, I'll be seein' you."

She scrams.

Georgette has gone over to the rail. She is leanin' over watchin' the sea.

Standin' there I get to thinkin' that my old mother usta tell me that I was always lookin' so far ahead that I never took notice of what was right under my nose.

Well, Ma Caution was wrong because lookin' at this dame I get to thinkin' that when I got all this business fixed up I am goin' to do somethin' very serious about this baby. Because, when I am not workin' I am a very poetic guy an' a poetic guy must always be tryin' to understand what everything is all about.

An' if you m

ugs have ever kissed a dame like Georgette you will be wise to what I mean. . . .

But don't get me wrong!

THE END

Printed in Great Britain
by Amazon

34040956R00108